Undead and Unstable

Anthologies

CRAVINGS
(with Laurell K. Hamilton, Rebecca York, Eileen Wilks)

BITE
*(with Laurell K. Hamilton, Charlaine Harris,
Angela Knight, Vickie Taylor)*

KICK ASS
(with Maggie Shayne, Angela Knight, Jacey Ford)

MEN AT WORK
(with Janelle Denison, Nina Bangs)

DEAD AND LOVING IT

SURF'S UP
(with Janelle Denison, Nina Bangs)

MYSTERIA
(with P. C. Cast, Gena Showalter, Susan Grant)

OVER THE MOON
(with Angela Knight, Virginia Kantra, Sunny)

DEMON'S DELIGHT
(with Emma Holly, Vickie Taylor, Catherine Spangler)

DEAD OVER HEELS

MYSTERIA LANE
(with P. C. Cast, Gena Showalter, Susan Grant)

MYSTERIA NIGHTS
*(includes Mysteria and Mysteria Lane, with P. C. Cast, Susan Grant,
Gena Showalter)*

UNDERWATER LOVE
*(includes Sleeping with the Fishes, Swimming Without a Net,
and Fish out of Water)*

UNDEAD AND UNSTABLE

MaryJanice Davidson

BERKLEY SENSATION, NEW YORK

THE BERKLEY PUBLISHING GROUP
Published by the Penguin Group
Penguin Group (USA) Inc.
375 Hudson Street, New York, New York 10014, USA

Penguin Group (Canada), 90 Eglinton Avenue East, Suite 700, Toronto, Ontario M4P 2Y3, Canada (a division of Pearson Penguin Canada Inc.) • Penguin Books Ltd., 80 Strand, London WC2R 0RL, England • Penguin Group Ireland, 25 St. Stephen's Green, Dublin 2, Ireland (a division of Penguin Books Ltd.) • Penguin Group (Australia), 250 Camberwell Road, Camberwell, Victoria 3124, Australia (a division of Pearson Australia Group Pty. Ltd.) • Penguin Books India Pvt. Ltd., 11 Community Centre, Panchsheel Park, New Delhi—110 017, India • Penguin Group (NZ), 67 Apollo Drive, Rosedale, Auckland 0632, New Zealand (a division of Pearson New Zealand Ltd.) • Penguin Books (South Africa) (Pty.) Ltd., 24 Sturdee Avenue, Rosebank, Johannesburg 2196, South Africa

Penguin Books Ltd., Registered Offices: 80 Strand, London WC2R 0RL, England

This book is an original publication of The Berkley Publishing Group.

Copyright © 2012 by MaryJanice Alongi.
Cover illustration by Don Sipley.
Cover design by Lesley Worrell.
Interior text design by Kristin del Rosario.

FIRST EDITION: June 2012

Library of Congress Cataloging-in-Publication Data

Davidson, MaryJanice.
Undead and unstable / MaryJanice Davidson.—1st ed.
p. cm.
ISBN 978-0-425-24757-0 (pbk.)
1. Vampires—Fiction.   2. Taylor, Betsy (Fictitious character)—Fiction.
3. Paranormal romance stories.   I. Title.
PS3604.A949U527 2012
813'.6—dc23
2012005332

PRINTED IN THE UNITED STATES OF AMERICA

10   9   8   7   6   5   4   3   2   1

For women in their ninth month of pregnancy:
my sympathy.
Nothing against the miracle of life,
but being a fetal slumlord is no job for the cowardly.

Author's Note

The events of this book take place just before the events of *Wolf at the Door* (Fall 2011). You don't have to read *WatD* to follow *Unstable*, but it might be amusing. And not just for me.

Also, I'm a dog person. No, really (though after reading this, you may have your doubts). Betsy and I have many things in common: the vanity thing, the not-learning-from-mistakes thing, the bitchy thing, the self-absorption thing, the shrill when freaked thing, the—you know what? I don't have all day here, people. My point: of our many commonalities, her loathing of canines is not one of them. Dogs rule. Everybody knows.

The Story So Far

Betsy ("Please don't call me Elizabeth") Taylor was run
over by a Pontiac Aztek about three years ago. Because
she'd been attacked by several feral vampires days
before, she didn't die from their attack, but later at the
hands of the Pontiac corporation. This was unprecedented in all things vampire, and she woke up their
foretold queen and, in dazzling succession (but no real
order), bit her friend Detective Nick Berry, moved from
a Minnesota suburb to a mansion in St. Paul, solved
various murders, attended the funerals of her father and
stepmother, became her half brother's guardian, avoids
the room housing the Book of the Dead (*Book of the
Dead*, noun: the vampire bible written by an insane
vampire on human flesh, which causes madness if read
too long in one sitting), cured her best friend's cancer,
visited her alcoholic grandfather (twice), solved a number of kidnappings, realized her husband/king, Eric
Sinclair, could read her thoughts (she could always read

his), and found out the Fiends had been up to no good (*Fiend*, noun: a vampire given only animal [dead] blood; a vampire who quickly goes feral).

Also, roommate Antonia, a werewolf from Cape Cod, took a bullet in the brain for Betsy, saving her life. The stories about bullets not hurting vampires are not true; plug enough lead into brain matter and that particular denizen of the undead will never get up again. Garrett, Antonia's lover, killed himself the instant he realized she was dead forever.

As if this wasn't enough of a buzzkill, Betsy soon found herself summoned to Cape Cod, Massachusetts, where Antonia's Pack leaders lived. Though they were indifferent to the caustic werewolf in life, now that she was dead in service to a vampire, several thousand pissed-off werewolves had a few questions. ("What, now? You care, *now*?")

While Betsy, Sinclair, BabyJon, and Jessica were on the Cape answering well-it's-a-little-late-*now* questions, Tina, Marc, and Laura remained in Minnesota (Tina to help run things while her monarchs were away, Marc because he couldn't get the vacation time, and Laura because she was quietly cracking up).

They hadn't been gone long before Tina disappeared and Marc noticed that devil worshipers kept showing up in praise of Laura, the Antichrist.

In a muddled, misguided attempt to help (possibly brought on by the stress of his piss-poor love life . . . an

ER doc, Marc worked hours that would make a union-less sweatshop manager cringe), he suggested to Laura that she put her "minions" to work helping in soup kitchens and such.

As sometimes happens, Laura embraced the suggestion with zeal. Then she took it even further, eventually deciding her deluded worshipers could help get rid of all sorts of bad elements: loan officers, bail jumpers, contractors who overcharge, and . . . vampires.

Meanwhile, on the Cape, Betsy spent time fencing with Michael Wyndham, the Pack leader responsible for 300,000 werewolves worldwide, and baby-sitting Lara Wyndham, future Pack leader and current first grader.

With Sinclair's help (and Jessica's cheerful-yet-grudging baby-sitting of BabyJon), Betsy eventually convinced the werewolves she'd meant Antonia no harm, that she, in fact, had liked and respected the woman, that she was sorry Antonia was dead and would try to help Michael in the future . . . not exactly a debt, more an acknowledgment that because she valued Antonia and mourned her loss, she stood ready to assist Antonia's Pack.

Also, Betsy discovered that her half brother/ward was impervious to paranormal or magical interference. This was revealed when a juvenile werewolf Changed for the first time and attacked the baby, who found the entire experience amusing, after which he spit up milk and took a nap.

Though the infant could be hurt, he could *not* be hurt by a werewolf's bite, a vampire's sarcasm, a witch's spell, a fairy's curse, a leprechaun's dandruff . . . like that. Betsy was amazed—she suspected there was something off about the baby, but had no idea what it could be.

Sinclair, who until now had merely tolerated the infant, instantly becomes besotted ("That's *my* son, you know.") and begins plotting—uh, thinking about the child's education and other necessities.

Back at the ranch (technically the mansion on Summit Avenue in St. Paul), Laura has more or less cracked up. She's fixed it so Marc can't call for help (when he discovers their cells no longer work, he sneaks off to find another line, only to be relentlessly followed by devil worshipers who politely but firmly prevent this), and she and her followers are hunting vampires.

Betsy finally realizes something's wrong (a badly garbled text secretly sent by a hysterical Marc), and they return to the mansion in time to be in the middle of a Vampires vs. Satanists Smackdown.

Betsy wins, but only because Laura pulled the killing blow at the last moment.

People went their separate ways, for a while. And nobody felt like talking.

Three months later, Betsy decided to take the Antichrist by the, uh, horns, and invited her to go shoe shopping at the Mall of America. It was at this time she learned the Antichrist was fluent in every language on earth, and had little or no working knowledge of big-screen devils. Thus, Betsy hauls her sis home for a devil-a-thon (starting with *The Omen* and including Al Pacino's Satan, Elizabeth Hurley's sexy devil, and the baby in *Rosemary's Baby*). It's at this time Laura confesses that she feels guilty whenever she's interested in finding out more about herself, her capabilities, or her mom, Satan. ("It's like I'm slapping my adopted mom and dad in the face by wondering about her.") It's also at this time that Betsy realizes she's sick of having a never-fail resource in her own home, the Book of the Dead, which she doesn't dare use because anyone who reads it for longer than twenty minutes or so goes insane.

So she and Satan strike a deal, which actually makes sense at the time: Betsy will help Laura embrace and use her supernatural powers, and in return the devil will fix it so Betsy can read the Book without the accompanying nut-jobbery.

In addition to Laura's weapons (stabbing weapons and a crossbow, which normally stay in hell unless she calls them up), she learns she can teleport almost anywhere. Cool, right? Yeah, not so much. In fact, that turns out to be a huge problem, as any*where* encompasses any*when*. In rapid, annoying succession, Betsy and Laura find themselves in Salem, Massachusetts, during the witch hunts of the 1600s; Hastings, Minnesota, before the spiral bridge was replaced (so, anywhere between 1895 and 1951); and the future.

The Story So Far

A thousand years in the future. Also, the future? Sucks. There was some sort of cataclysmic global thing-gummy, and Minnesota in the future has winters even worse than the ones it has now. Nobody wants to worry about heat exhaustion on the Fourth of July, but frostbite and hypothermia are just as bad . . . and since the average temperature in the year July 3015 is thirty below, nobody's getting rich off selling sunscreen.

In fact, nobody—except Future Betsy—is getting rich, period. They're mostly hanging out in below-ground enclaves and focusing on not dying.

To make matters even yuckier, Future Marc is a vampire. And not just any vampire . . . after hundreds of years of being Betsy's personal whipping vampire, he's dangerously insane. So much so that Laura and Betsy can feel how *wrong* he is after a glance. In fact, neither of them can bear to look him in the eyes, or even be around him.

BabyJon is there, too, and he's as charismatic and charming as Marc is creepy and nutso. He won't tell Betsy how he can be walking around one thousand years in the future and not be a vampire, though she tries and tries to wheedle it out of him.

In the forty-five minutes or so they're in the future, they discover Future Betsy has taken over (most of) the country, can raise and control zombies, and has a crippling lack of empathy for anyone. More troubling, Sinclair and Tina are *nowhere* to be found. Worse, no one will even talk about them . . . except Undead Marc, until Ancient Betsy shuts him up and sends him away. And BabyJon is wildly uncomfortable about the subject.

They return vowing to figure out a way to save the future. Or undo it. Laura teleports Betsy back to the mansion and goes on her merry, hell-bound way.

Betsy has returned to find out Tina and Sinclair remember meeting her in the past. They explain that they've always known Betsy would be headed on a time-travel romp, and the only way to help her was to stay out of the way.

To Betsy's amazement, Jessica is heavily pregnant by Nick Berry. And Nick is happy to see her, thoughtful and warm; since Betsy prevented her younger self from feeding on him, he didn't experience any vamp trauma this time around. Also, in this timeline, he insists he goes by Dick. Which Betsy just can't wrap her mind around.

Now Betsy has to explain to her loved ones about the future, about the fact that they're living in a tampered timeline, and figure out a way to, as Betsy would put it, "Get bad shit done."

Unfortunately, Betsy's plan to get bad shit done involves fighting with the Antichrist and waking up in a Chicago morgue, realizing the Marc Thing *followed her back* from the future and told Human Marc enough dreadful things about what was in store for him that

Marc killed himself. After which, Betsy killed the Marc Thing. But not before going back to hell (again) and persuading the devil to let Antonia live again, on earth, in the mansion. The devil also tries to tell Betsy that the Book of the Dead is Sinclair, but Betsy flat-out doesn't believe the Lady of Lies, to the devil's great delight. Laura then steals the Book of the Dead so Betsy can't read it and find out what happens to Sinclair.

Undermined ends with Betsy seeing that for something wonderful to happen in her life, something dreadful must also happen. She's determined that it *will not be like this*, and decides to find a way to bring Marc back to life while *not* becoming the icy monster from the future, Ancient Betsy.

Unstable opens not even a week after she comes to this conclusion . . .

Pray . . . you never have to call us.

—THE FROG BROTHERS, *THE LOST BOYS*

Behold, I shew you a mystery; we shall not all sleep, but we shall all be changed.

—1 CORINTHIANS 15:51

You know what else the Bible asks for death as a punishment? For adultery, prostitution, homosexuality, trespass upon sacred grounds, profanity on a Sabbath and contempt to parents.

—SISTER HELEN PREJEAN, *DEAD MAN WALKING*

I'm gonna kill 'em. Anyone that was involved. Anyone who profited from it. Anybody who opens their eyes at me.

—JOHN CREASY, *MAN ON FIRE*

The world will not be this way within the reach of my arm.

—THOMAS HARRIS, *HANNIBAL*

[Christian] Louboutin helped bring stilettos back into fashion in the 1990s and 2000s, designing dozens of styles . . . the designer's professed goal is to "make a woman look sexy, beautiful, to make her legs look as long as they can" . . . Louboutin is generally associated with his dressier evening-wear designs incorporating jeweled straps, bows, feathers, patent leather and other similar decorative touches.

—WIKIPEDIA

A clear and innocent conscience fears nothing.

—ELIZABETH TUDOR, HUMAN QUEEN

I don't have one of those.

—ELIZABETH TAYLOR, VAMPIRE QUEEN

Undead and Unstable

PROLOGUE

Dear Betsy,

I'm gone now, but not forever. Couldn't leave without giving you the scoop, though, so listen up.

First, although you will, don't blame yourself. Even as I'm writing this, I get that it's a waste of time, but I'm jumping in and trying, anyway. Again: don't blame yourself, dumbass.

I wanted to do this. Frankly, I have inclinations like this all the time. It even runs in my family (along with alcoholism and the ability to make hospital corners). Shit, remember the night we met? I was about to do a swan dive off the hospital roof and you wouldn't let me. You saved me . . . for a while.

Now I'm saving you.

It's only fair.

It's also only fair to tell you that you shouldn't blame the others, either. In hindsight, letting me spend time alone talking with the dead me seems careless and risky, right? Sure . . . in hindsight.

But it's not their fault. I only told them the stuff they'd find most helpful, the bare minimum. The stuff that would make them feel okay about me going back into that room. And back. And back. They're as invested in saving you as I am. And they don't know a fifth of what I know.

Listening to yourself tell yourself about the awful things you'll do someday is an experience, I won't deny it. But before you break off a chair leg or something and march into the basement to kill the other me like John Wayne with fangs, please believe that the other Marc DID NOT MOJO ME INTO DOING THIS.

He just told me what would happen to me if I didn't.

So I've saved myself. And I've saved you. And I was glad of the chance. Do you know why?

Because I love you, dumbass. From the moment we met. You've been like the little sister I never wanted. (That's a joke. Not a very good one, I agree.) And right now you're thinking dark thoughts about how you can't protect your friends and being the vamp queen has ruined your life and no job in the world is worth this and how could you not see what I was going to do, blah-blah-blah.

But here's the thing, and it's the stone truth: knowing you has only ever made me feel one way. Not scared, not horny, not crazed, not pissed, not despairing, not thwarted. Lucky.

Knowing you has made me feel lucky. Even now, prepping this little cocktail, I feel lucky. I'm controlling how I leave this world, something that poor bastard down in the basement couldn't do. And look at the price he paid!

By doing this to myself, I'm undoing some seriously bad shit.

But don't take my word for it.

Go to the basement, and ask me. Ask me for yourself. You won't like what I say, but you'll see the truth behind his awful smile.

I love you.

I will see you again. Believe it.

Your friend,
Marc

CHAPTER
ONE

I used to be one of those weirdos who liked funerals; you
believe that? People always wear their best shoes to funerals.
Not weddings. They'll scope their closet, they'll think
about the bride or the groom, and they'll go, "Yeah, I can
wear these, I don't need to go to the mall," and they think
nothing of wearing last season's pumps.

But if it's a funeral, they'll think, "Aw, jeez, I was so
mean to Aunt Ginny that time and now she's dead," and
out come the new Guccis.

Me, I was so lucky. *So* lucky. I was so lucky I didn't know
how lucky I was; I'd think, "Jeez, Aunt Ginny was such a
jerk to Cousin Brian, I wonder what he's gonna wear to
her funeral?" I never had to go to the funeral of anybody I
really, really loved. Well, except for my dad's. But I spent

most of *that* funeral in a state of high pissed-off, so my focus was elsewhere. (It turned out an evil librarian was out to get me, and not—for a change—owed from all the overdue charges from late returns. And there was a cursed engagement ring involved. Nightmare. The whole thing. Just awful.)

My focus was often elsewhere, and too often, my focus was often in the exact place it *should not be*. Case in point: my dead friend Marc. (Also: the future, but I can't think about that right now. One soul-shriveling crisis at a time, please.)

Once, a long time ago (in my head, I mean . . . in real life, it hasn't even been five years), I talked a man out of committing suicide. Two weeks ago, he killed himself. I'm ashamed because I didn't see it coming. How's *that* for the Lex Luthor level of lame? Who doesn't see someone they know to have suicidal tendencies committing suicide? He practically wrote it on his forehead in red Sharpie.

I wasn't at his funeral, by the way. Nobody was. He'd strictly forbidden one in a number of letters he'd left for me; he also left his diary. Words, words, they were all over the place. He was nagging me more in death than he had in life, which was a pretty good trick given that, nag-wise, he trailed only behind my friend Jessica. Okay, and maybe my mom.

I couldn't stand to read too much of his stuff at a time. I'd cry, and then look ugly, and cry harder, and make my husband sad, and then we'd sad-fuck. Which was great, but sad. (Thus the name.)

Still.

The stuff I've read. It's like he knew he was going to die within a few years of meeting me. But he doesn't say how he knew. It's all over his diary, it's all over his suicide letters. Who writes suicide letters? He wrote me a suicide *manuscript*, the heartless bastard . . . he knows if it's not *Gone with the Wind* or Pat Conroy, I've got zero interest. He knew he was doomed, he had a plan, but what he never said was why.

I found that kind of curious.

I never find anything curious. So I figure it's a time-travel issue, or a me issue. Now, I'm not pulling a Mary Sue thing here, but I *am* the vampire queen. One of my best friends killed himself so that Evil Me from the Future (EMFTF, pronounced "emftf") wouldn't turn him into a horrid nasty Marc Thing.

So, yeah. I'm pretty sure it's not all about me, but it's definitely a lot about me.

So. Time to get to work.

Don't get too comfy being dead, Marc.

I'm coming.

CHAPTER
TWO

"What are you talking about, she's dead?"

"Betsy, I've got a zillion things to do, what with creating life and all, so could you pay attention when I talk? Did you not see my lips moving?"

They're always moving, I thought but did not say. Jessica was too cold except when she was too hot, and she was starving except when she was throwing up or, worse, starving *while* throwing up (I didn't even want to think how that was possible). She was angry and she was joyful. She was tearful and she was enraged. She was pissed and she was venomous. She was pissed except when she was crying and—God please help us all—crying-pissed was the worst. The very worst. My super vamp powers were no match for crying-pissed.

Wrong again, I realized, remembering what I'd over-heard last night from two floors away. When Jessica wasn't eating or pissed or nesting or pissed or nagging, she was horny. Sometimes eating olives stuffed with garlic made her horny. Worst yet: she was often all those things at once, nesting and horny and pissed and horny and hungry and horny. Nobody was brave enough to touch the olive jar in the kitchen. And poor Detective Nick/Dick was starting to shamble about the place with the nine-hundred-yard stare.

"Well, look." I was afraid to. Look at what? At her? Why? Maybe she was wearing her giant, yellow and blue circus-tent shirt in a terrifying attempt to seduce me. The thought made me want to simultaneously burst into gales of laughter and throw up in my mouth. "She is."

I peeked, prepared for the worst. Prepregnancy Jess had nothing in the knockers department, and that was no longer the case. Luckily, seduction wasn't on her mind right now.

We stared down at the body with more than a little surprise. "What happened?"

"No idea. I was headed to the basement and I almost tripped over the body." Jessica patted her gigantic belly. Like the stairway wasn't dusty and dark and claustrophobic enough without The Fetus of the Darned hogging her stom-ach and also most of the stairwell. "I could have broken my neck! Do you know what a fall could have done to me at this stage of my pregnancy?"

Nothing. Nothing at all; the Michelin Man had less padding. I didn't say anything, though. I wasn't ever going to be lauded for my genius, but that didn't mean I was an *utter* dumbass.

This is going to sound terrible (even for me), but you know that series *Game of Thrones*? I guess the show did so well that now there are books about the *Game of Thrones.* Or maybe the books came first—I dunno. I quit reading fantasy before I was voting age. There was just too much of "I shall draw the mystical sword of Eldenwurst, thus named Soulsucker, and with mine eldritch blade will smite all enemies of the fey, but fear not, all ye who tremble before Soulsucker, I shall rule with a just hand and also the council of Geeks, now ye and ye, bring me fifty virgins and lots of mead." Those books lose me right around chapter two. Anyway, I'd never read the books, but the show was pretty cool, and I got hooked on it.

No. That wasn't true. Marc had a huge crush on the Khal Drogo character, and *he* got me hooked on it. So he'd come off shift from the ER and we'd raid the DVR and rhapsodize about Drogo's unbelievable shoulders and what a doucheboat Viserys was.

Wow, getting ahead of myself more than usual . . . okay, so, in the first season of *Game of Thrones*, the unborn baby of one of the main characters was called The Stallion Who Mounted the World, a scary yet cool nickname. Jessica was sporting The Belly That Ate the World. She claimed she wasn't due until summer, but I had my doubts. She was just . . . gigantic. Gah: Twins? Triplets? Just what this place needed, three pissed-off newborns continually crying and pooping.

"I'm glad you didn't trip." I sighed and glanced back down at the dead cat. "She's looked better." An understatement. Giselle didn't look like she was sleeping; dead bodies never looked like they were sleeping.

And Giselle, the cat who'd gotten me into this whole vampire queen mess in the first place, was most definitely not sleeping. Her eyes were cloudy slits. Her mouth was frozen, half-open, and she was thin, but not dangerously so . . . she'd always been scrawny. And she was old . . . I'd had her for over ten years. She just showed up one day and refused to leave, so I got in the habit of feeding and sheltering her. I guess that's how babies and roommates show up, too. You feed 'em and they just never leave.

For ten years we pretended the other one didn't exist. Our only interactions were during meal times. (Hers. Not mine.) And since I'd moved us into the mansion way back when, plenty of other people were happy to take over the chore. The mansion was so big, my pet (except I'd never really had that warm connection to her, and you couldn't say I was her pet: see above, lack of connection) and I would go days without seeing each other, which suited us both.

I'd been killed the first time trying to coax Giselle into coming out of bad weather. I wasn't paying attention during the snowstorm while I coaxed, and got creamed by a Pontiac Aztek. Giselle, natch, scampered off without a scratch. She was the only thing in my life that found my resurrection boring.

Now here I was, looking down at her skinny dead body and realizing I had one more task to finish before I could consider all my pet responsibilities fulfilled.

"Ugh."

"Yeah."

"Are there shovels in the shed?"

"Several."

"There are? Really?" What terrible news; I couldn't pull the old "I can't do this unpleasant chore even though I really want to because we don't have the right equipment" ploy. Another wonderful day in a shit week. Month, come to think of it!

Giselle, you insensitive jerk, you couldn't have done this a month ago? Or a month later? You gotta do it now, while fate and/or karma is really piling it on, and Jessica wouldn't have pedis without me, and we'd burned out the motor on one of the smoothie blenders? Typical cat: not one thought for how her death would inconvenience me. Andrew Vachss, the best noir-ey writer in the history of the genre, called

cats the lap dancers of the animal world. Give them attention, they're there. Stop, they're outta there.

Well, she was outta here, all right.

"Next time," I announced, "I'm getting a dog."

Jessica snorted. She knew that was a lie. She knew why
it was a lie, too, but was too nice to call me on it just then.
"If memory serves, you didn't exactly *get* Giselle."

"Your memory serves." I bent and gingerly picked up
the body, then held it at arm's length like a luau platter.
"Yuck."

"Oh, will you suck it up? You've seen how many hid-
eously mangled dead vampires, never mind mangled regular
people (who were bad, but still mangled), and friends have
been shot in front of you and/or killed themselves in your
house, but you're squicking out over a cat? *That* cat? Hey, I
just said 'suck' to a vampire." Weirdly, that seemed to please
her. "That's all you've been doing lately, complaining about
how awful it is to be white and pretty and rich and married
to the hottest guy in the state of Minnesota. Okay, Marc *did*
kill himself," she admitted. "*That* you can bitch about."

I gave her a look, but decided not to shove her down the
stairs. *She's creating life, she's creating life. Oh, and she stuck
with me when I came back from the dead. Also: creating life.* "Can
you go grab me an old sheet or pillowcase or something?"

"Sure." My hugely pregnant pal was looking right at me,

her brown eyes thoughtful. Since she was a couple of steps above, I started to get scared. If she tripped, she'd kill us both. "Sorry about this, Betsy. And sorry about a couple of seconds ago. My back feels like someone's resting a set of barbells on it, and the barbells are on fire. It's not doing much for my mood. And you know . . ." She let out such a gusty sigh, I wondered if she'd float off the stairs like Mary Poppins. "The random deaths and stuff."

I waved it away, all of it, along with my fears of being squashed to death by a pregnant woman while clutching the dead body of my cat and fretting over my lack of pedicures. "Par for the corpse. Whoa. At least that didn't come off as a Freudian slip or anything." Had I said that? Had I *really*?

She giggled, thank God, then turned and started climbing the stairs again. Nonpregnant Jessica was rail thin and favored nail polish in colors like Day-Glo Orange or Aged Chartreuse (which, in case you're wondering, looks like vomit dried on a nail bed). Pregnant Jessica was not rail thin. At all. Quite the opposite of rail thin. What would that be, bovine fat? And she was avoiding all the chemicals she could. *All* of 'em! Which was only impossible.

So among other things, she wouldn't go near a salon (or sushi, of all things . . . like eighty-zillion Japanese women didn't eat sushi when they were knocked up?), which was a personal disaster for me. She was using all-natural deodorant (the kind that didn't work) and natural hair product (the kind that made her look like a pissed-off Rastafarian), and when I gently suggested a fetal-friendly salon massage, she slammed the door in my face (so to speak). All of this to say: this sucks. Who goes to a salon alone? Big-time boring. If Marc were still here, he'd love—

Never mind.

I followed her up the stairs, lugging my dead cat. If I was smarter, or nicer, I'd think something like, *It's sad that the cat keeled over, but Jessica's baby will be born soon and out of death comes life, a full circle of life, hakuna matata and suchlike.*

But I'm not smart, or nice, so what I thought was: *And the hits, they keep on coming. Nobody ever considers my feelings when they decide to keel over and die on the basement stairs. And the second I'm confronted with an evil poopie diaper, I'm going to go right out of my teeny tiny mind.*

Still: if our situations were reversed, I'd want Giselle to bury me. Wait. I absolutely wouldn't, since half the time I had no idea if I was dead-for-real and could wake up screaming on an autopsy table or, worse, sleep through Macy's annual shoe sale, so I wouldn't trust a cat to know, either. Shit, *coroners* sometimes couldn't tell. I actually knew that for a fact; it was a horrible thing to know for a fact: at least two certified medical examiners hadn't been able to tell if I was dead.

Besides, our situations weren't reversed. And I could whine and bitch until the sun rose and set and rose again, and it'd still be my responsibility.

So after Jessica got me a yellowed pillowcase, I stuffed Giselle into it and out I went, into the deep November cold, searching for some meaning in all the crazy shit that had been happening since Giselle got me killed a few years ago. And I was also searching for a shovel. And after this yuck-o errand, I would be searching for a booze smoothie.

Ah, the glamorous life of a vampire queen.

CHAPTER
THREE

All sheds smell the same. Even though I hadn't been in all sheds, I had confidence making that claim. Dirt and paint, and grass cuttings and mouse poop. Once out in the getting-deep-in-a-hurry twilight typical of late fall in Minnesota, I circled around to the backyard and into the shed, then set my bag o' cat on the dirt floor to begin poking around.

The shed was as creaky and old as the mansion, which had been built in 1860 or 1720 or 1410 or something like that. And I figured the last time the shed had been cleaned was while Lincoln was still walking around on the planet.

Also, like all sheds, it was magical in that once you got inside the thing, it seemed much, much bigger. *It's like a ballroom in here!* A filthy ballroom that smelled like mouse poop and had a dirt floor. I couldn't tell if this chore was more annoying due to enhanced vampiric senses, or because I was an indifferent homeowner. There was probably another reason it was annoying, too . . . right! My cat was dead.

I found a shovel-sized piece of rust, grabbed the pillowcase, and went to the far backyard. Though I had zero interest in doing my chores, I couldn't fault the mansion for its size and beauty, and I liked that the yard was huge, not one of the postage-stamp ones . . . a good trick in a city the size of St. Paul.

I walked toward a couple of the big old oak trees in the left corner . . . they were naked now, but in the summer and fall they were pretty great. If Giselle had ever expressed a desire to be buried (by me), I liked to think she'd have asked for this corner.

It had been a mild fall, and there were only a couple of inches of snow, but the ground was frozen. Normally it'd be a bitch to dig, but I had confidence in my weird undead strength. There were a few upsides to being the queen of all vampires.

(I was almost getting to the point where I could think of myself with that title and not go into gales of amazed laughter. Give me another seventy or eighty years, and I might be able to pull it off with my puh-puh-puh-poker face.)

Me being me, I tended to focus more on the downside.

Stupid strength of the damned was on the list along with *stupid superhearing* and *stupid keen sense of smell.* Also me being me, the downside list was much, much longer. And as the shovel slid through frozen dirt like a smoothie blade through a raspberry, another one came to me. One I'd stupidly discounted when I took on my duties as the undertaker of the dead cat who'd gotten me killed and then inconveniently died on our stairs. The dogs. They were a *huuuuge* downside.

And here they came, thundering toward me in a slobbering charge.

CHAPTER
FOUR

Several neighborhood dogs (I'd guess maybe eight thousand) were sprinting and yowling in my direction. It could have been a terrifying sight and, for many poor dumb stupid slobs, would have been. But I, Elizabeth Taylor, courageous vampire queen, knew they were no match for my awesomeness, and thus I showed no fear and no hesitation. Firmly grasping the handle of the shovel-sized piece of rust, I bravely faced the oncoming charge of my fur-covered drooling nemeses . . .

Well, no. Dropped the shovel and ran like hell for the back door is what I did, with the hounds of heck slobbering at my heels. I was not a dog person. I wasn't a cat person, either. I was a Betsy person. And believe me: taking care of myself—feeding and clothing myself and putting a roof over my head, and keeping myself from being killed (again) and out of divorce court—was enough of a challenge without throwing domestic animals into the mix. Or wild ones, even.

Stupid *Book of the Dead*, with its stupid predictions and the way it stupidly drives people who read it insane which is so stupid, and warning me that stupid dogs will constantly want to drool on me 'cuz I'm soooo speshul.

How fast could dumb drooley dogs run, anyway? I was superhuman, dammit, I shouldn't even be worried about how this race would end. Let's see, like the movie said, "The fugitive has been on the run for ninety minutes . . . average foot speed over uneven ground barring injuries is four miles an hour. That gives us a radius of six miles." Just when I forgot what a radius was and how to calculate it, movies saved me again.

"What I want from each and every one of you . . ." Am I the only one who thought Deputy Gerard must be the biggest pain-in-the-ass boss ever? Come on: think me up a donut with sprinkles? Really? Bet he gooses the office staff at the U.S. Marshall's office, too. ". . . is a hard target search of every gas station, residence, warehouse, farmhouse, henhouse, outhouse, and dog—"

Right, dogs, *that's* what I should be focused on. Bleah, I could smell them. I didn't dare risk a glance, but my nose risked a glance, and it was awful. Horrible, horrible enhanced

vampire senses! Wet fur and dog spit and—was that . . . ?
It was! Poop!

I lunged for the front porch (didn't bother with the back
door, which was small and always locked; it'd slow me down
before saving me), made a clutch for the big heavy door
knocker, then skidded right past the front door, slamming
into the three-foot-high wooden post partition. And I did
it so hard, my feet shot through the wood and I found
myself up to my shins in splinters. Ow! Ow! God *damn* it!
I wrestled free of the porch's hungry grip, creating a shower
of wood splinters that pattered all around me. *This wasn't
over, porch! Time for round two! See you in hell, porch!*

"Open up! Dog emergency! Level nine!" Wait. There
were a lot of them. It might be a level ten.

I managed to scramble to my feet and lurch toward the
door, but falling ass over teakettle had cost me seconds,
thus I was engulfed.

"Nnnnnnn! Geh! Geh off! Off! Gehhh!" I howled and
pounded on the door, which was the size of a walk-in freezer
door and about as strong. And why was I pounding on it?
Who'd locked it behind me, anyway? We let bad guys walk
in with guns every second Wednesday, we printed our
address in national newsletters, werewolves routinely
dropped by and tried to kill us, psychos routinely dropped
by and tried to kill us, the friggin' Antichrist had her own
set of keys to our home (and she always apologized from

outside before she used them, because the Antichrist routinely channeled Miss Manners), but now, *now* my roomies were all security-conscious? I bet it was Jessica, that gestating bitch. "Let me in! You guys! C'mon, open up! I was just burying the stupid cat, I didn't think I needed my keys!"

A deeply amused, laugh-choked voice drifted from the dog-free side: "What . . . is . . . the password?"

"You fucker, open this door!"

"That," the king of the vampires replied, "was last week's password."

"Sinclair!"

"Also incorrect."

"You shit! You think there won't be giant payback for this? There will be major giant payback, asshat! Enjoy sleeping on the couch for the next *five decades*." I risked a glance over my shoulder, not letting up the hammering. They were everywhere! They were going to get drool and fur all over my shoes! Then they would poop, which also would get all over my shoes! I was living one of my worst nightmares, though usually in that dream I was naked, except for shoes I knew were goners, like how you know terrible things in your dreams. Things that are all the more horrifying because you also know, in your dream, that you can't stop it. Nothing can stop it. Poop everywhere. Poop-smeared Prada. Everywhere. *My God, my God, why hast thou forsaken me?*

"You realize you're not in any actual danger, darling."

"Sez you, butt monkey! Open! This! Door! That's a royal command, buddy, from your queen. Who is allowed to give royal commands and also allowed to kill you and *eat* you if you disobey, and I don't mean that in a sexy way, either!"

The door opened so quickly I fell into our entryway, shrieking all the way down. "Die! Die! Die! D—oh. I'm inside now."

Sinclair shut the door, and I heard the thud-thud of a couple of the dogs not being able to stop in time and running into the door. Heh. Stupid dogs. "Why didn't I try the royal-command thing first?" I groaned from my splayed position on the floor.

My ferociously handsome, smart, hot, evil husband was looking down at me from his six-foot-plus height, faultlessly dressed in a navy blue Hugo Boss suit, a crisp pale blue dress shirt, and the tie Marc

(*O God. Marc.*)

had given him as a gag gift: it had a navy background and the standard physician's eye chart in white. "Read the second line from the bottom" . . . like that. "Because, my heart, you so rarely think of yourself as our queen."

"Huh?" The tie had surprised me; I wasn't the only one missing Marc, and should try harder to keep that in mind. "Oh, right, why I should've tried the command thing first."

"Yes indeed, my own. You should have."

"Really, Sink Lair?" I rolled over and glared at him. "Are you really gonna compound your gross evil errors by lecturing me into a boredom coma and then not helping me up?"

"Oh, never." He smiled and stuck out his hand. "As your subject and your husband and your cosovereign—"

"How can you be my subject and my cosovereign?"

"—lecturing you is my prerogative, and only mine. Unless, of course, you count your dear mother. Or Jessica. Or—"

"Please make it stop," I begged no one in particular. I grabbed his outstretched hand and used it to haul myself to my feet. It might have been how Jack felt climbing the beanstalk. Sinclair was really tall. Climbing him to the top took forever. "And in case you didn't hear all my yelling—"

"All of St. Paul heard it, darling."

"I hate you, you treacherous jerk."

"Ah, but I love you, my dearest queen."

"You should save time," I threatened, "and make up one of the sofas now as opposed to waiting until dawn."

"How is it outside?" he asked, a rare look on his face. It took me a second to place it. Nostalgic? No. Wistful. Yeah, that was it. Sinclair had grown up on a farm some fifteen decades ago (or however long ago he'd lived before he'd died, I could never remember), and missed sunshine like I missed a new spring collection the autumn before. "Is it very cold?"

"Sure, but I'm always cold." I instantly forgave him his

asshat-ery. I tried not to take for granted the things I could do that no other vampire could, but I messed it up sometimes. Sure, I was constantly bitching to myself the whole time I was looking for shovels and racing away from a canine lynch mob, but at least I could go out. At least I could stand in a backyard during the day and ponder which tree to inter my cat beneath. At least I could be snuck up on by sneaky dumb dogs in broad daylight. At least I could feel the sun on my face and not burst into flames.

Sinclair, though . . . my husband was the strongest vampire I knew (also the sexiest, and most irritating), but he couldn't do any of those things.

I'm not sure what you're up to, God, but some of it seems pretty mean. Why don't you lay off for a while?

I still prayed. Sure I did.

I just wasn't sure anyone was listening anymore.

CHAPTER
FIVE

After sulking for three hours and twenty minutes, I decided
Sink Lair should bang me. Because I realized that five
minutes into my 3.20 sulk I was probably punishing myself
more. So I begrudgingly accepted his apology, then let him
fuck my brains loose.

That oughta learn him.

"Ummmm," the vampire said sometime later.

"Yeah, what you said. Ummm, I agree. One of these days
we're gonna really hurt each other. Or break the bed again.
Or not be paying attention and break the window again,
and then fall out of the window. Again. Thank goodness the
sun was down." I shuddered . . . Jessica had had a complete

hormonal meltdown over the broken window, claiming that The Belly That Ate the World would one day be playing in the yard, and she wouldn't stand for him toddling over broken glass. No one dared argue, or point out that of course by then we'd have the glass cleaned up . . . no. Nope. We'd all fled, my husband leading the charge. Wise man. We were the king and queen of the undead, and we were scared to death of a skinny woman who was maybe 101 pounds dripping wet . . . when she wasn't gestating, anyway.

"You're still chilled." He propped himself up on an elbow and stroked my back. I'd sort of passed out facedown right around the time my third orgasm raced through my limbs. Chilled? Numb? Satiated? Freaked? Still smelling dog? Yeah.

"I forgot. Or never noticed." It could be either . . . since I'd died the first time, I was always cold. It was impossible to look sexy in wool knee socks, by the way. Scarlett Johansson could not look sexy in my navy and red striped wool socks. Which was all I was wearing right now. Sinclair bitched, to no avail. I would tolerate all kinds of nonsense, except having freezing cold feet during sex. "You did a good job trying to warm me up."

His knuckles were stroking my spine. "Yes indeed. It was kind of you to cut your sul—"

"Careful," I warned. "One of the parlors can still be turned into your permanent sleeping residence at half a moment's notice."

"—ah—your quiet time. Kind of you to cut it short by . . ." He squinted at his watch, the only thing he was wearing. "Two hours! What can I say, my own, but that I feel blessed."

"Blessed. Sated. You say toe-mah-toe, I say drop dead." I yawned into the pillow. "Stupid dogs."

"Why were you out there at all?"

"Jess didn't tell you? Giselle died."

"Ah . . ."

"My cat."

"Oh?" Sinclair hadn't had much use for my antisocial (even for a cat) cat. She, natch, hadn't much use for my dead husband. I doubt they'd even crossed paths in this place more than half a dozen times. "I'm . . . sorry?"

"Yeah, I'll take that. She was a pet, if not a terribly beloved one."

"Ah, but if memory serves, she is responsible for your journey from your world to mine."

"Well . . . yeah. Except . . ." I thought about it for a minute. I'd been thinking about it, for a lot longer. Meanwhile, Sinclair was still stroking up and down my back, which was—there was no other word—delicious. "If I was supposed to be the vampire queen, if the Book of the Dead saw all this coming, I would have died, anyway, right around then—around my thirtieth birthday. Right? Because I was able to come back . . . the way I came back . . . you know, able to be in sunlight and not a total savage when it came to drinking blood . . ."

"Not a *total* savage," he teased.

"The Fiends had already nibbled on me outside Khan's—the Mongolian barbecue place on 494. They'd—infected me, I guess? So I would have died somehow right around then. Right? If I hadn't tried to go after the cat in a snow-storm, I would have slipped while crossing against the light, or fallen down the stairs looking for the *TV Guide* and bro-ken my neck, or gone off the road and frozen to death in a snowbank on the way to the Mall of America . . . right?"

"I imagine." Sinclair looked a little appalled at how I'd reeled off all sorts of dumb ways to die. "Yes."

"So no matter how it was gonna happen, it *was* gonna happen."

"Yes."

"So what chance do any of us have," I griped, "if it's all ordained? Except it's not. Because Marc's dead . . . and not vampire dead. *Dead* dead. And it's all a mess, and I don't know how to fix any of it."

"My own, you must give yourself more credit. What Marc did, he did on his own. He chose it. And as wretched as it is to be in this house without him—"

Wretched? Wow. I knew my husband had liked Marc well enough, but was still surprised at the hole the big idiot left when he OD'd.

"—we must respect his choice. I know you wish to fix it, but perhaps this is the event you must leave alone. You have inadvertently changed the timeline once, and we have no real concept of what damage has or has not been done. I tell you in all truth, my queen, I fear what havoc you may wreak when you really set your mind to such things."

"Anything sounds bad when you say it . . . say it like that." I tried a smile and burst into tears instead, startling both of us.

"My dearest, my own queen, please don't." Sinclair hated it when I cried. For someone who tolerated multiple trag-edies in life, and tons more *after* life, for someone who could take a bullet to the heart and come away from it only mildly irked, my husband went to pieces when I cried. He tended to have the Fred Flintstone reaction: "Who made ya cry? I'll murder him in the head!" Sort of comforting and Nean-derthal at the same time.

"I'm sorry," I said, sobbing harder. "I didn't know I was going to do this. Stupid cat! Stupid dogs!"

"I am sure your shoes are fine," he soothed. "I let you in before the neighborhood pack could defile them."

"It's not that." For once in my life, I didn't give a tin shit about my shoes.

"I know," he replied sadly. "A poor attempt to distract you. You must not do this to yourself, Elizabeth. Marc made his own choice. No one blames you."

Wrong. *I* blamed me.

"I don't know what to do. I want to fix it—but like you said, what if things get more fucked up? But I don't like lying around like a coward, hoping things will just work themselves out. Because they *don't*, Sinclair. They *get* worked out, y'know?"

"Yes."

So I bitched and griped and cried, and my husband held me and soothed me, and the whole time I was thinking, thinking, thinking.

I wasn't queen by accident. Some of this shit was supposed to happen. Just like some of it *wasn't* supposed to happen. And letting Marc stay OD'd was at the top of my "not supposed to happen" list. He had killed himself to save himself . . . he had OD'd so he wouldn't end up the Marc Thing, so he wouldn't be an insane vampire five centuries down the line.

Okay, fine. So: figure out how to bring him back . . . and never, ever turn him into a vampire. Why did we think one thing precluded the other? Him *not* being dead only meant exactly that: he wasn't dead. It didn't promise he'd end up the Marc Thing. Besides, that had been in the old timeline. Which I'd changed, as my husband pointed out, without even trying.

So: what could I do when I *did* try?

Time to find out. Past time, frankly.

CHAPTER
SIX

It's funny . . . life can sneak up on you. Your own life can do that. Because when you're inside all the weird stressful awful things that are happening, you can't see the big picture.

But when you finally realize, when you get a chance, a glimpse, to really see the mess you've made . . . it's like it's happening all over again, only more terrible because you can see that, bad as you thought it was before, it's much, much worse when you see just how much wreckage is in the middle of your life.

Some of my friends were dead. Some of them didn't remember me (or remember a different me) because I accidentally changed the timeline. Some of them were well on their way to insanity, and some of them never, ever wavered in their love and loyalty to me, not for a second. Not for a blink.

Stepping back, thinking about that . . . it's so fucking depressing, you know?

Which brings me to milk-shake time.

"Smoothies aren't going to do it," I announced, heading for the freezer for my go-to staple: half a gallon of Breyers Vanilla Fudge Twirl. Predeath, my go-to had been Hershey bars with almonds, or my mom's risotto. I had been a simple, uncomplicated girl. Once.

Adding to my annoyance (which had never been difficult, since I had always been a bitchy girl), I first had to haul out half a dozen bottles of Tina's weird, weird vodkas before I could extract the Precious. Just reading the labels was enough to make me shudder, but I also had to handle the things: hot pepper, three olives (like one olive wasn't vile enough), root beer (good God!), triple-shot espresso (so you could take something that will make you sleepy and spazz you out at the same time), Absolut LA (which boasted acai and blueberry, and thus was good for you, except for the fact that it was alcohol, which is *poisonous*), and plenty others too hideous to mention, all nestled together like some unholy frozen army of booze. No, wait . . . Three Olives was a brand, not a flavor. The flavor was tomato. Why, why had someone decided to invent flavored vodka? *This changed nothing!*

Finally, after a nice crop of frostbite was no doubt gonna show up any second, I found my go-to and restacked all the booze . . . upside down, so Tina would have to reach in and haul each one out to check the flavor. Ha! More proof that it doesn't pay to mess with the vampire queen. My wickedness and lust for cold-blooded vengeance were endless.

The door swung in, and there was Jessica. For a woman who claimed she couldn't hear me when I tried to explain why it was perfectly okay for a woman in her last trimester to wear high heels, she had no trouble hearing the fridge or freezer open from several rooms, or blocks, away. "Oh boy," she said, seeing the blender and ice cream. "Pretty serious, huh?"

"Yeah, so let me get to work and then we'll have a family meeting."

It was out before I realized I'd thought it, never mind said it. And it was fine. Better than fine: it was *right.* Family meeting. Well . . . yeah. If these guys weren't my family, what was any of it for? Jessica had always been my sister, and Nick loved me (I was pretty sure . . . he didn't hate and fear me, at least) because Jessica did, and I knew Tina loved me, too.

Maybe even Garrett, the Fiend formerly known as George, and his girlfriend, the bitchy werewolf Antonia, did. (What? She *was* a werewolf. And she was also bitchy. Grumpiest person I had ever, ever met. Because in death, I was fated to be surrounded by weirdos.)

For sure they liked me. I didn't think that was my considerable vanity talking, either: they'd moved from their lives to our lives to hell and then back to our lives. Of course, I *did* rescue Antonia from hell, so maybe that's why they were hanging around, but like I said, that prob'ly meant they liked me. Or at least didn't loathe and fear me. (I'll take it. Believe me. And how sad is that?)

As for Sink Lair, his love had never been in question, though I was too bubble-brained and pissed to catch on right away, or realize I loved him back with everything. So, yep, my husband absolutely loved me.

(I wasn't quite sure about my sister Laura, the Antichrist.)

The coolest thing was how Jessica didn't blink, or pause. Just took a step back while holding the kitchen door and yelled, "Milk shakes, idiots!"

I had to take a few seconds and pretend to be busy dumping scoops of ice cream into the blender, so she couldn't see my face. I didn't leak tears anymore, but any girlfriend can tell at a glance when you're upset or touched or pissed.

After a few seconds I was able to turn my back when I went to the fridge, and no longer had to pretend. Because now I had a whole new problem: where were my candy bars? My precious delectable Hershey bars, always kept in the fridge (room temp chocolate = yuck) so I could chop them and dump them into a blender with the Precious and a generous splash of whole milk, were not in their appointed spot!

"This is not the right time for me to deal with this," I growled, pawing past gallons of milk, some sticks of butter, Jessica's vile ginger ale (with actual lumps of ginger in it, which did not belong in ginger ale!), a few boxes of leftover Chinese takeout (who was eating *that*, I had no idea), a bottle of blueberry vodka (what, the freezer wasn't enough, fer Chrissake?), a box of Godiva cookies (pretty decent chocolate, but useless for my needs), and a couple of tins of Giselle's cat food. Ouch. Another of my many character flaws: I was a little slow to do my share of the upkeep around here.

"All right, first off, remind me to clean out the fridge," I said into the fridge, still hunting. "This is just sad, and also gross. And second, if one of you amoral thieving shit-heads filched my Hershey's, there will be *blood* on the *streets*, I swear it, *blood* on the *st*—oh, there they are." Why they were in the door slot for eggs I did not know and did not give one shit.

I heard the *fwoomp* of the kitchen door swinging open, and looked up in time to see Antonia and Garrett walk in. Sinclair and Jessica were right behind them, and Nick/Dick was behind *them*.

"Oh, good," I said, grateful. Sometimes it could take over half an hour just to round everybody up.

"Uh-oh," Nick said, eyeing the Precious and grinning. It was weird that he didn't hate me in this timeline. The way I remembered it, he had made Jessica pick between him and me . . . and she picked me! (I couldn't believe it, either.) But that had never happened now. So . . . had it never happened? Even though I could remember? Because it was so awkward and awful? Ow, I'm hurting my brain. "Bringing out the big guns, vampire queen."

And that! What was that? He said it, but not in a mean way. In a happy way. Like me being a vampire was a good thing. Like it hadn't ruined his life.

I don't like being confused and angry!

"You keep shooting me these incredulous glances," he continued (happily!). "I take it in the old timeline we weren't close?"

"Uh, she wasn't pregnant, and you weren't living here." To put it mildly. Also, I accidentally tortured you and then my husband did, too. Oops! "But we've got weirder problems."

"Yeah. Like how she's not dead anymore." He pointed at Antonia, who'd gone to the booze freezer for a drink, and was now knocking back espresso vodka in a milk glass.

"Weirder than that, even."

Antonia chortled in mid-gulp. Her black rat's-nest hair was its usual unkempt mess . . . on a good day, Antonia looked like a witch having a bad day. Not that she wasn't gorgeous—she was. Sickeningly so, what with the black masses of tumbled and tousled hair and the pale skin and the burning werewolf-y eyes. But she was weird. All werewolves were.

"Not weirder than that," Jessica mock-gasped. "Nothing could be weirder than that."

"What's weird about it? I left. Now I'm back. Don't throw me a party."

"Don't worry."

Antonia glanced around. "Where's Tina?"

See, see? Nothing about Marc being dead. Nothing about hell. Just "time for booze and then I think I'll bang my man for a while, don't wait up and ha ha, I scored more free vodka off Tina, and oh by the way, where is she?"

"Everything's better now," Garrett said with a sweet smile. But I expected his reaction, too. Garrett was a little . . . off. He'd been a Fiend (a vampire deliberately starved until it went feral and bitchy) for decades, and had been dead going on a hundred years. That had shattered any vibrancy of personality he'd ever had in life. He'd been a shell of a vamp until Antonia swooped into his pants. I mean, his life.

Garrett looked at the world with envious simplicity: life without Antonia wasn't worth living. Antonia was back. Knit one, purl two. All was well. Again: envious simplicity.

But I was starting to wonder. We sometimes wrote him off as a mindless savage who can cast on, knit, and then purl while blindfolded. But I tended to forget, even though he brings out my protective side, that Garrett wasn't a kid, and hadn't been one for close to a hundred years. And if I ever wanted to make my very own serial killer, putting someone through all that Garrett had endured was as close to a fool-proof recipe as I could get. I knew there wasn't much he wouldn't do to protect Antonia. I also knew he was a liar and a coward.

I guess seeing the Marc Thing a few days ago was giving me some unwanted perspective on "it's always the quiet ones." And this is the part where, if this was a movie and I was a sensible (yet hot) heroine, I'd make a vow to "get to the bottom of this." Then I'd haul out another chestnut by adding, "This isn't over." By which I'd really mean, it's over. I mean, who has the energy?

Spreadsheets. That's what we needed. Some kind of written record of all the weird stuff we should never lose track of no matter how busy or life-or-death things got. Then when things were settled (however briefly), I could look on my Spreadsheet O'Evil and Scary and say, "That's right, I caught Garrett in some lies and he tricked me into going to hell and I also know he's killed more people than Hot Pockets . . . maybe we should follow up and do a little investigation?"

It would be easy! Which was the flaw. Too easy, if anything, because such things tended to get shoved out of my brain when the Big Bad of the week reared its—

"—much of a problem, right?"

"Yeah, but with this particular problem," I said, "it's time to get moving. We can't just lie around working on spreadsheets, people!"

"Uh, what?"

"Never mind. Here it is: I've been sitting around long enough."

"Does this have anything to do with how much you hate Thanksgiving?" Nick/Dick asked.

"Don't speak to me about That Holiday."

"Does this mean you're not going to make a cornucopia for the dining room?"

"I'd rather gargle gasoline and then light up a cigarette."

Sinclair laughed. "What an . . . interesting mental image that makes."

"And I'll save plenty of gas for you, too," I threatened. My parents had gotten divorced in November. Jessica's parents were killed in November. The Ant was born in November! April was *not* the cruelest month. "So you'd better stay on your toes, pal."

"This," my husband commented, sounding not at all perturbed at the thought of being burned alive, "will be the third time this week I have fallen in love with the queen all over again."

"And it's only Saturday," Jessica pointed out.

"Is it really?" I was amazed. It felt like eight years had gone by. Too much happening and not much time to soak it up. "Oh, crap. So Thanksgiving is next week already?" No wonder my teeth were on edge. "God, that sounds ominous. It's a whole damn holiday lurking in next week's calendar. Just waiting to pounce."

"It's turkey and football," Nick/Dick said, exasperated.

"With a side helping of genocide," Antonia snickered. She had by now drained her glass. "You think it's bad here? Try New England this time of year. It's all Thanksgiving and Pilgrims all the time out there."

"Gross," I said, appalled. Ye gods, I'd never thought of it, but she was right: Thanksgiving must be pure heck if you hated it and yet were surrounded by it. "Remind me to count my blessings."

"Why?" She was rolling sky blue yarn so fast her fingers were a blur. "You never do, anyway."

"Can we get back to the matter at hand if it's not too much trouble? Like I said, weird stuff is going on, and it's time to fix it. We're gonna fix it so *hard* . . ."

"What are we fixing?" Garrett asked. For him, that was practically a speech. A Gettysburg Address, even.

"Don't think I've forgotten about you," I warned, "but with Marc dead, I've gotta have my focus—"

"What *are* we fixing?" Nick/Dick interrupted. "Because this conversation is already making me nervous."

"Don't be nervous! Okay, I've gotta—remind me to talk to you guys about a spreadsheet later, but for now, there's nothing to be nervous about. 'Betsy can fix it' doesn't necessarily always translate to 'Betsy accidentally destroyed the relationship/mansion/Eastern Sea board/world.'" A short silence followed. "What? It doesn't. But I think I've got a good shot at fixing it."

"Fixing what? A spreadsheet?"

"No. Fixing—"

"Not Marc being dead," Jessica said, an expression of reproach on her face. "You're *not* talking about that."

"Oh yes I am." I must have been wearing one of those incredulous expressions Nick talked about. "What else do you think would be on my mind? The new Manolos? The fact that, incomprehensibly, Christian Louboutin doesn't exist in this timeline?"

"Well . . ."

Nick wasn't looking at me. Neither was Sinclair. Antonia tossed the now-round ball of yarn into Garrett's bag and began rolling a new ball of yarn. Garrett was carefully crocheting . . . uh . . . something red and blue and big (too big to be a potholder, too small to be a blanket . . . maybe a grill cover?). His lap was full of yarn; his entire attention appeared to be on the whatever-it-was he was making.

Only Jessica, who'd put up with my bushwah for almost two decades, had the courage to look me in the face and say, "Yeah, kinda. Why wouldn't you be worrying about shoes and their designers?"

"Well, you're totally wrong because . . . okay, that's a good point about Christian, but I can't fix that." Probably I couldn't fix it. I'd look into it, sure, but one nightmare at a time. "Marc, now, Marc maybe I can fix. I'm gonna try, at least."

"Why?"

"Hello! Queen of the vampires? Power over all the dead, or however the saying goes? Ring-a-ding-dinging a bell?"

"Not 'why,' why *you*? 'Why,' why would you *do* that?"

"Why wouldn't I do that?" Was Jessica's unborn baby eating her brain? She was normally quicker on the uptake. Was it just me, or were we all talking in riddles?

"Have you thought you might respect his choice?" Nick asked quietly.

"A braver man than I," Sinclair said, rolling his big dark eyes heavenward.

"Ah, shaddup already from you. Listen, Nick—"

"Dick."

"Stop it. Detective Berry, Marc killed himself because he was scared, I get that."

"Do you?"

"Don't talk . . ." I paused as Jessica judiciously hit the blender, which hummed and brayed and whirred for a good thirty seconds, an endless time in which my friends and I glared at each other. This hadn't taken long to get nasty. For me to turn it nasty, I guess it'd be fair to say. I continued as she poured milk shakes, as everyone took hasty slurps. ". . . like I'm stupid."

"No, we wouldn't want to do that." Like that! See? There was the Nick/Dick I knew, not the Mr. Happy Cop I'd been dealing with.

"Sure he was scared. He was scared of being the Marc Thing," I said, assuming the baby had also been dining on Nick's teeny brain cells as well. "Not scared to keep living. He loved it here."

"Betsy, you met him when he was about to jump off a building!"

"Well, yeah." Anything sounded bad when you said it like that. "But then he was better."

"Oh, so you cured his chronic depression? Is that one of your superpowers now?"

Hmm, no. But wouldn't it be cool? "Anything sounds bad when you say it—"

"He was a borderline alcoholic who couldn't stay sober. He was a gay man who never dated, a man who had no relationship with his father, his only family."

"We're his family."

He wasn't listening. He was leaning so far forward his suit jacket was open and I could see the gun clipped to his belt. "This was an unhappy man. For God's sake—sorry, Sinclair—I mean, for crying out loud, just let him rest in peace."

"Stop talking about him in the past tense!" Somehow I was on my feet and Nick/Dick was on his, and had backed up. Sinclair had moved across the table and was standing at my side, almost ready to block me. Like I was going to hurt Dickie/Nickie. And Antonia was now standing in front of me, like Dickie/Nickie was going to hurt *me*. I think it'd be safe to say we were all temporarily freaked.

"It seems I have not arrived in the nick of time," Tina said, standing in the kitchen doorway, holding it open with tented fingers and totally stealing that line from *Practical Magic*.

CHAPTER
SEVEN

"I wasn't going to hurt him."

"No, of course not."

"They're acting like I was going to hurt him. You are, too."

"No," my husband disagreed.

"Sinclair, you've got your arm around my elbow and you're propelling me out of the kitchen."

"No."

"You absolutely are, Sinclair."

"No."

"And Tina's right behind you!" Backing him up, like she always did. Or she was backing me up. Or she was helping him back me up. So that'd be . . . backing him up to back me up?

Anyway: they were hustling me up the stairs so fast, I was getting vertigo.

"We're not . . . I'm just, ah, pleased to see you, my queen."

"Spare me the crapola, Tina."

Tina was our assistant/subject/friend. She was Sinclair's majordomo—I've recently learned that's one word! (Oh, the things I've picked up in death . . . I could write a book. A funny, shallow book, which would be, incomprehensibly, a bestseller.)

Tina was my husband's superassistant, a secretary with power who occasionally carried a pistol. (So: best secretary ever! And since I used to be a bad one, I'd know.) Majordomo or, as she once teased last month (I think she was teasing), Major of the Mansion. Yeah, I know: I was scared to call her that if she was teasing, or if she was serious. Could *I* tease if she was serious about M of the M? What if I took it seriously when she was teasing? You see the sort of problems I have to deal with on a daily, nightmare-y basis.

So she was an assistant, but much, much more. Except I never knew just how much. Friends didn't call you "Your Majesty," and she'd saved my ass about nine times in the last couple of years. But she discouraged closeness. Chilly, and also insanely hot: Tina'd been killed in her teens during the Civil War, and dressed like an escapee from a Catholic school run by a *really* dirty old man. So chilly but hot. Distant but caring. Professional but familiar.

"We were having a family meeting," I explained, all the time being rushed to my room like a bad girl ("Bad vampire queen!"), "and things got a teensy bit heated, and then Sinclair freaked out, and that's when you came in. Cribbing lines from *Practical Magic,* I might add." It was Tina's favorite book, but not her favorite movie. Weirdo. Bullock and Kidman rocked that flick.

"It did seem a little tense in there."

"Tense? Try insane. They don't think I should save Marc."

"Can you save Marc?"

"You missed the 'duh, queen of the vampires, duh!' part of the meeting, because I established I was pretty sure I c—yeow!" A final shove up the stairs, a slam of the door, and now the three of us were in my bedroom.

I took a breath and tried to chill. "Seriously: why did you put me on the train to heck straight to my room?" (Having actually been to hell, I hardly ever used *hell* these days unless I was referring to hell.)

"You cannot, my own."

Tina nodded so hard she almost lost a hair ribbon. (See, see? A *hair ribbon?* She looked like a slutty hot extra from *Little House on the Prairie.*) "The king is right, Majesty, you cannot."

"Don't you two start." I scowled and flopped on the bed, leaned back on my elbows, and scowled more. "It's my fault Marc decided he had to give himself a dirt nap. I'm getting him out of said dirt nap, and I don't wanna hear from you two about it."

"Yes."

"Precisely," Sinclair said in almost the same breath.

"Uh . . . what?" I was usually braced for opposition, so when I didn't get it, it sometimes threw me off guard. "Sorry?"

"But you cannot."

"I'm confused," I admitted. Maybe less scowling, more paying attention? I guess it could work . . . couldn't hurt to try, right? "And too hungry to concentrate on your riddles. Dude, we haven't snacked on each other for two days. And my rapist-trolling was a bust last night. Stupid St. Paul low crime rate . . ." Rapists and cops: they were never around when you needed to complain about a parking ticket or lure a sexual offender into a dark alley to drink their blood and explain the concept of irony. Typical. I bounded off the bed and spotted the small bowl of cherries on the mantel—Jessica had been snacking and chatting in our room earlier, and must have forgotten the bowl.

I grabbed one, popped it into my mouth, and then gently bit down and sucked on the juice. It wasn't as good as I remembered eating them to be, and not nearly as thrilling as blood, but it was also better than nothing. I could think if I had something in my mouth. Uh. Maybe I should rephrase . . .

"We have to come up with a plan."

"Agreed."

"Oh. We *are* on the same page . . . that's always nice." I shifted the cherry to my other cheek. Chomp, suck. Admonish self to ignore urge to swallow, so as not to then be victim to the urge to vomit.

Sinclair smiled broadly. "It is, my own."

"And as their (ugh) king and queen, we gotta set a good example. Well, Garrett's king and queen. But the example-setting, that's gotta be the first thing." The enormous bedroom, bigger than the living room *and* master bedroom in my old house, suddenly felt too small—that was a first!—and I started to pace. "Then we gotta convince them that we actually know what we're doing. So we can do the second thing. The leading. If they know we've got the Marc Thing under control—whatever the Marc Thing's gonna *be*—they probably won't freak, right?"

Sinclair started to laugh. And Tina was looking at the ceiling, the mantel, the headboard . . . anywhere but at me.

"I know, it sounds kind of impossible, but Marc's counting on us to pull it off. At least I think he is. Wherever he is."

He was still laughing. And she still wouldn't look at me.

"What's the matter with you? I'm the one doing all the

thinking, and your big contribution is to chortle like a hyena. Handle your shit, Sink Lair."

"The stem," he managed, holding his stomach, "has been sticking out of your mouth during your entire discourse."

"Well, who gives a ripe shit?" I spit the pit, stem, and masticated cherry remains into my palm. "Focus, you two." Ewww. An average observer would think I was hanging on to a blood clot. "There's a garbage can around here some-where." I spied it, and tossed the clot. The cherry, I meant. "And I guess we'd better figure out what we're gonna tell the others."

"No, Majesty." Tina could finally look at me, which was a relief for both of us, I was sure.

"What?" "No" was not something I heard from her very often.

"No, you cannot talk to them about this." Sinclair and Tina were now nodding in unison. It was terrifying.

"Uh, what?"

"You cannot." He shrugged his broad shoulders, which looked especially yummy—Sinclair practically wore suits for robes, and had put on a nice dark one this evening. "They are good friends, and are loyal to us, but they are human. There are things they cannot understand. Not ever. You continually ask me why you must be the queen and I the king—we must for things like this."

"So . . . you're saying . . ." Careful. It could be a trap!

Though for what, I had no idea. ". . . that you support me in trying to bring Marc back to life, but that I shouldn't talk to Jess or Nick—"

"Dick, now that you've changed the timeline, Majesty."

"—never mind—or Antonia or Garrett, even though they're really weird?"

"Antonia isn't one of us." Ouch. Since Tina had been in a war to set people free, I was a little surprised at how quickly that came out of her mouth. "Garrett *is*, but he is also . . . different." To put it mildly. Hmm, I'm gonna regress for a second and wonder if Tina might be just the person to do the spreadsheet. So I decided not to point out to her that up until a few months ago, she had been on my back to kill him. That was interesting, how quickly Tina could erase people from an equation.

I'd have to really, really try to remember that.

They were with me. But not with the others . . . and so they strongly recommended I drop the Marc Thing for now. I could bring it back up soon enough when we had a plan or, even better, when we'd executed the plan I hadn't thought up yet, and could present Newly Alive Marc as a *fait accompli*.

I wasn't scared they were suggesting that course of action. I was scared because it sounded like a pretty good idea. So I dropped it.

For a while.

CHAPTER
EIGHT

For the third time in an hour and a half, I tripped on something, and nearly pitched headfirst into the attic stairwell. Cursing, I caught myself on the railing and hauled myself upright, then looked to see what had nearly killed me. A stool! Who puts a stool on stairs? *Who needs to use a stool on stairs?*

Stupid Jessica and her stupid nesting instincts, that was who. Post-meeting, and post-meeting-meeting, Nick/Dick had explained the thing to me. Nesting was this weird hideous thing pregnant women did when they sensed their giant bellies were getting ready to expel the kid into the world. Depending on the woman (and the unholiness of the baby, I s'pose), that meant anything from reorganizing the spice rack to combing through every room of an ancient mansion and stacking stuff in hallways and stairwells to be hauled or stored or burned or blown up.

And I kept tripping on the damned things! It was no good having super vamp eyesight when I wasn't paying attention to my surroundings. Which I hardly ever was. I had stuff to think about. Mostly I had to think about the fact that Tina and Sinclair were all, "Yay, Team Betsy, rah-rah, bring Marc back!" while also being all, "And shhhh! Leave the humans and weirdos out of it, it's our vampire awesomeness societal secret." I had no idea how to feel about that, and just *that* part of it, the not knowing how to feel? Scariest thing to happen all week. And it had been a shit week.

But fuck it. If Jessica was waiting for the Stool Fairy to lug things into the attic, the Stool Fairy was here. No longer queen of the vampires, nay, now I be Ye Olde Stoole Faerie. Screw bringing back the dead (and the first geek to holler, "Bring outcher dead!" like a "hi, I never had sex in high school" Python-channeling idiot was gonna get smooshed); I'd bring back the footstools. I'd open my own U-Haul franchise. It wasn't like it could be *more* stressful than the queen gig, right?

So I picked up the little thing—about a foot high and wide, and so banged up there was no way to tell what kind of wood it was . . . was rust a wood?—and stomped up the attic stairs. Time to use my stupid vampire strength for more than lugging six gallons of milk into the house at once. I'd haul *all* this icky crap into the attic. That ought to learn her . . . and the unborn kid, too. Never soon enough for the kid to learn whose house this was. Whose house it was now, anyway.

(Yes. I'll come clean: the baby wasn't even here yet and I was jealous of it. I kind of liked being first in Jessica's life since her worthless asshat parents died their richly deserved deaths. In another time, she'd picked me. Maybe here, with a baby, maybe in the future I was determined to prevent . . . she wouldn't.)

"Stupid babies," I muttered, plodding up the stairs, "ruining everything by being drooley and stupid. Except for BabyJon who is drooley, but not stupid. And how the heck am I gonna bring him back and also get through Thanksgiving? And my mom is dating! Ugh!" (I often bitched out loud to myself when no one I lived with wanted to hear it, which happened more often than you might think. No, really! And my baby bitching had nothing to do with how jealous I was that Jessica could make her body do something mine wouldn't . . . couldn't, since I woke up dead. No, really!) "Stupid moms who date stupid guys whose names rhyme with 'beehive.' Stupid Clive Liveley, who looks like a giant baby and wants to make out with my mom! And stupid Giselle the cat, who started all this by willfully choosing to drop—"

I stopped bitching. Stopped walking. Also stopped breathing (which I probably hadn't been doing, anyway). My heart? Yep: stopped.

Because Giselle the cat was spread out on a clean towel on a carefully scrubbed section of the attic floor in all her dead-yet-pissed glory. And Marc, my dead friend, was busily dissecting her.

He looked up. His green eyes blinked slowly at me, like an owl. "Now, don't freak out," Marc said.

But I did, anyway.

CHAPTER
NINE

"Who did it?" I screeched, pointing a shaking finger at him.
A shaking finger with chipped Marshmallow fingernail
polish (people have been *dying*, dammit, and Jess won't go
with me to the salon anymore; was it any wonder I needed
a touch-up? Not for what the pedicurist actually did to my
toes, but the pampering was essential to my mental well-
being.). "Who did that to you? Did you figure out how to
bring yourself back? If you did, you are *so dead*! You're
supposed to be dead until I'm damned good and ready to
bring you back!"

Marc opened his mouth.

"Do you have any fucking idea how hard this has all
been on me? Huh? I'm gonna guess *no*, dead guy! I'm gonna
guess you don't have the faintest clue!"

"Betsy—"

"I turn my back for five seconds and you kill yourself? That's the thanks for being one of the coolest roommates in the history of human habitation, huh? *No* regard for how that'd make me feel, huh? Like I don't have enough friends getting shot or ending up in hell or both? Huh? Oh, and that stupid nasty scary Marc Thing is *dead*, thanks to me, and you're welcome!" Oh. Except the reason the Marc Thing existed at all was also because of me. Icky stoic cranky Future Me.

Irrelevant! Marc had a lot of nerve being alive, and I was going to explain just how much in loud and shrill detail.

"Betsy—" He sort of flowed to his feet . . . not fast, not like a vampire moved, but slow and not-quite-graceful. Like when you've given yourself a pedi and you sort of roll over and carefully climb to your feet so you don't smear anything. You get there, the job gets done, but it's not the most beautiful way to move. That was how Marc moved now.

My mind was ticking off possibilities even as I bitched and yowled at my inconveniently resurrected friend. Not a vampire. Not human—no way . . . he didn't smell anything like his old cotton-and-blood-on-hospital-scrubs self. And you didn't "catch" being a werewolf from a bite; I'd found out a couple of years ago that either you were born a werewolf, or you weren't. Scratch lycanthropy. So that meant . . .

I brandished the stool at Marc like he was a zombie bull. "Back! Stay back! Do not lurch over here to try to eat my brains or I'll bash *yours* right in. Why? Why am I even surprised to run into another zombie in this same attic? Again?"

"Betsy—"

"Don't think," I warned, taking a big step back. I hate hate *hated* zombies, and the only reason I wasn't shitting myself in terror, other than the fact that I couldn't, was because he wasn't gross and goopy or trying to eat my brains. And because it was Marc. "Don't think I won't kill you again, buster. I'll jam this stool up your ass so far you'll barf splinters for a week! And then I'll really make you sorry!"

"I believe you," he said dryly. He'd stopped coming for me, just stood there with his hands up in the universal please-don't-shoot-me-in-the-face position. His hands were bloody—no. The surgical gloves on his hands were bloody. Because he'd been—he'd been— "Listen, Betsy, I—"

"Oh my God! What have you been doing up here?" My brain was still cycling through reasons, and not liking anything it was coming up with. I stared at the cat with fresh horror, then back at Marc, who was staring at the floor in . . . what? Shame? Hunger? Anger? "Why? Oh, Marc, what are you doing here, and why are you cutting up my

dead cat? How could you do this to me?" I wailed, then flung myself facedown on the floorboards
(ow!)
and burst into tears.

CHAPTER
TEN

It wasn't entirely Sink Lair's fault. But I didn't figure that out
'til later. At the time, things were kind of an undead gross
weird shocking scary mess. And they'd been bad enough
before my husband literally burst in on the scene.

So anyway, Sinclair hurtled through the attic door and
galloped up the stairs, and because he heard me screaming
and yelling and crying, and because he knew it wasn't at
him, he took all seventeen of the stairs in about half a second.

Then he burst into the attic just in time to see a zombie
with bloody hands looming over his wife. "Aw, c'mon, Betsy,
don't cry, I—glllkkkkk!"

"Never touch her," he said in a tone that would seem
friendly and conversational if you didn't know him, and
thus scared the shit out of at least two of us, "and explain

yourself. Right now. Do *not* lie: I know you are not a new subject."

Marc's zombie feet kicked and swung about a foot in the air—Sinclair already had several inches on the poor guy, and had now hoisted him in the air in what looked like the beginning of Make Marc My Personal Piñata.

"Glllkkk!"

"Get your hands off him!" In a more mercurial than usual swing, I went from scared and pissed and crying to scared and pissed and protective. "He wasn't doing anything except coming back from the dead without permission before I was ready and freaking me out by chopping up my dead cat after making me shake a stool in his direction to ward him off. Leggo!"

My shrill nagging had no effect. I jumped to my feet, silently groaning at the dust all over my wine-colored tights (the black mini was probably also a total loss), and tugged on Sinclair's arm. It was like tugging on a redwood and expecting it to come to dinner with you. Just. Wouldn't. Budge. Great: the one time I actually wanted vamp strength, I was tussling with a vamp stronger on his worst day than I was on my best.

"Let—ack—him—nng—go!" Ye gods, what did the man have in his pockets, gold bricks? "You better not . . . make . . . me . . . withhold . . . sex!" Please *please* don't make me withhold sex . . . if there was a merciful God (and I was starting to seriously question the guy's mercy), I wouldn't have to withhold sex.

I nearly fell on my ass (again) when Sinclair obeyed (again). I'd ponder what that meant later; for now I was just glad he'd put Marc down and I wasn't clinging to the inside of his arm like a damn kinkajou.

"What is going on?" Sinclair asked. He bent, hauled me to my feet with as much trouble as he'd have picking up a box of paper clips, then thrust me behind him in one slick move. I could admire the guy's sneaky deftness while being irritated that his Fred Flintstone side was showing. "Explain. Now."

"What, like *I* know? I came up here, and there he was, all reanimated and back from the grave and everything." I stood on tiptoe to peek at Marc over Sinclair's shoulder. "You're in a lot of trouble, pal!"

"Tell me," Marc said dryly. He took the chance to strip off his surgical gloves and fire them, without looking, at a nearby wastebasket. That was such a Marc-ism, a trick I'd seen him do a few times before, that some of my fear and anger ebbed, and I felt the first beginning gladness that my friend was walking and talking and firing rubber gloves at things without missing. "You want the long version or the short version?"

"I want the version where you start by saying, 'Then I stupidly OD'd in my bedroom so my roommate could find me and be totally *traumatized*' and finish with 'and then Sinclair shook me like a maraca.'"

He grinned, and it actually hurt my heart. If hearts could get cramps, mine did just then. I didn't know how to feel, which made it cramp more. "I stupidly OD'd in my bedroom, and then all of a sudden I was back here. In the mansion."

"You're saying," Sinclair began slowly, stepping to the side to block me when I tried to duck around him. "Ah . . . what are you saying?"

"I don't know what happened. I've got no idea how I ended up here. I'm saying I was kind of hoping you guys would."

Sinclair looked at me, and his usually excellent poker face was not home this evening; he looked as perplexed as I felt. We sort of stared at each other for a few seconds, and then stared at Marc.

"Well, heck," I said, figuring one of the three of us should probably say something. "I guess we'd better go talk to the others."

Marc sighed. Did that mean he needed to breathe? "They're not gonna like it."

They didn't.

CHAPTER
ELEVEN

Jessica screamed and screamed. She probably wanted to jump up and down as well, but couldn't reach escape velocity with The Belly That Ate the World. So she screamed some more as she stood in one spot.

"I can explain!" I shouted, trying to be heard over her air-raid-siren wails. "It's not what it looks like!"

"It looks like you resurrected Marc after you said you wouldn't!" Nick grabbed Jessica's shoulder and yanked back, so she was now behind him. His gun wasn't out, but his hand was on the butt and he never took his gaze off Marc, though he was talking to me. "That's what it looks like!"

"Okay, you're right!" I shouted back. "I can see why

you're confused! We'll have to straighten this whole thing out! So don't worry!"

"Bullshit don't worry! I've got some questions, Betsy! I thought we'd shelved this topic! And now I find you've brought Marc back from the dead!"

"It wasn't me! That's what I want to talk to you guys about! If we just—good God, Jess, take a breath before you pass out."

She stopped as suddenly as if I'd thrown a switch on her vocal cords. "What is this?" she asked hoarsely, pointing a shaking finger at Marc, who looked defiant and embarrassed and unhappy and hopeful all at once. "What's going on? Betsy? Why? Why'd you do it?"

"My queen did nothing," Sinclair said. He had a wary expression on his face, and Tina, who'd burst into the kitchen seconds after Jessica let loose with her first yowl, was rubbing her ears. Jess had lungs when she wanted 'em . . . the others hadn't ever seen this side of her before. Of course, they'd never met her scum-bucket parents, either. "But she—we—could not keep this new development from you."

"New development?" Nick/Dick asked, amazed. "Is that what this is? Because it looks more like a sign of the apocalypse to me."

"Please." I made a conscious effort not to roll my eyes.

"You think people running yellow lights are signs of the apocalypse."

"So here we are again," Sinclair finished, then added, "What a pity all the blenders are still dirty from our last meeting."

"That's why God made sinks and Dawn liquid soap," I snapped. "Would it kill you to grab a sponge?"

"It would not *kill* me," he admitted, "but I would find it unpleasant. Do you have any idea how many germs are lurking in a sponge at any given time?"

"Sinclair, I swear to God, you worry about the dumbest things at the dumbest times . . ." The only thing, the only good thing, about this kitchen confrontation was that Antonia and Garrett had flitted off somewhere, probably to a yarn shop, or to have sex in the spoon at the Walker Art Center. In November! Brrrr. But at least there were two less people to prevent from having hysterics. Try to prevent, anyway.

"Marc, what happened?" Jess was peeking at him from behind Nick/Dick. "Why did you do it? Why'd you come back? Oh, Marc . . ." She trailed off and her mouth turned down; her lips trembled despite her efforts to press them into a grim line. "How could you scare me like that? How could you scare *us*?"

Then she started to cry, and we started to feel really, really, really shitty. As for Marc, he looked so mortified I could tell he was wishing he could disappear down a hole/

grave/abandoned well just then. He took a slow step forward, but a look from Nick made him stop.

"Jess, please don't cry." He didn't touch her, but he made sort of pleading motions with his hands. "I don't know why I'm back. I know I should have stayed hidden—I know I should have stayed in the attic. I just—I was so . . ." He trailed off, then added with simple dignity, "I missed you guys. I was lonesome. And . . . it's kind of spooky up there in the dark by myself. It started to get to me after the first couple of days."

Okay, now *I* was gonna cry. The thought of my dear friend creeping around upstairs, hoping we didn't hear him but also hoping, just a little, that we would . . . Christ! Lonely and afraid. That was what being friends with me got you: premature death, followed by hiding in attics, screaming matches with friends, and being afraid . . . being afraid all the time.

"The first couple of . . . jeez. Wait. How long were you up there? You haven't even been dead a whole week."

"Because time is a wheel."

"What?" I wasn't sure I'd heard him correctly.

"What?" He seemed to shake himself. "I'll tell you everything," he promised, "but I don't know much about what happened. I was sort of hoping you guys might know."

"Why don't we all just . . . uh . . ." Tina gestured to the kitchen chairs, and we slowly went to them and settled ourselves. Marc stayed on his feet the longest, and then finally walked over to the last empty chair and sat. It didn't escape my attention that Nick had pushed Jessica into the seat farthest from the friendly neighborhood zombie. "Marc? Do you want to tell us what happened?"

"Not really," he sighed. "But I guess I'd better. Once upon a time . . ."

CHAPTER
TWELVE

"Once upon a time I met a pretty grotesque creature who was gonna be me in a few hundred years."

"This part we know," I said.

"My story, my rules," Marc snapped back, and I had to bite my lip so I wouldn't grin. For an evil undead shambling brain-chomping zombie, he sure sounded like my good friend. "Okay. So—"

"Where did you get the hospital scrubs?" Tina asked. She'd come late to our little "Welcome Home, Zombie Marc" party, and was wasting no time indulging her curiosity. "And how did you—"

"Will you guys give me five seconds, please? Cripes. *Anyway.* To save myself from becoming the Marc Thing—

great phrase, Betsy, it pretty perfectly sums up that guy's extreme awfulness—"

"It did, didn't it?" I was pleased; I so rarely was able to turn a phrase without using the word *asshat*. "He wasn't Marc-the-vampire, he was the Marc Thing. Yuck."

"Anyway, once he got done scaring the living shit out of me with his life story—his death story?—I pulled my bag and OD'd on morphine. Which, by the way, is pretty much the awesomest way to die."

"This is not a cautionary tale," Sinclair commented. "Those do not normally begin—or end—with *awesomest*."

"And thanks once again for offing yourself in our house, you inconsiderate asshat!" See? *Asshat* was my default. Hey, it worked for me, so what could I say?

"Will you guys shut the hell up so I can tell this?" Zombie Marc glared around at us, and there was some foot shuffling and stirring in seats but we were finally quiet enough to suit him. We weren't sure what would set him off into a brain-chomping frenzy, so we tried to sit still and pay attention. "*Anyway.* The last thing I remember from life was falling asleep in my bed as I tumbled into morphine's sweet, sweet embrace."

Annoyed once again ("Morphine's sweet embrace"—was he kidding us or what? "Morphine's sweet embrace" in *my house*?), I opened my mouth—only to shut it as Tina, Sinclair, and Jessica all glared at me. Phooey.

"And then I was in the attic. Alive. Except not."

"We never put you in the ground," Sinclair prompted.

"Now that I'd figured out on my own," Marc replied with an admirable lack of cutting sarcasm.

"You forbade a funeral—remember? You left me your papers and your girly journal."

"Betsy, come on. It's not a girly journal."

"It has. A pink. Cover."

He muttered something I didn't catch . . . a good trick, with my hearing. "Anyway," I continued, "what with it being late November and all—"

"Did I miss Thanksgiving? What's the date?"

"Unfortunately, Thanksgiving still looms over our lives like a scythe made of turkey drumsticks . . . it's this Thursday. But anyway, you—your dead body, I mean—were in a crypt, or whatever they call those places where they keep coffins until the ground's soft enough to dig up. And then you were here."

"The part in between is what we are keenly interested in," Sinclair said.

"I'll bet. Okay, so . . . I OD'd. And then I was in the attic."

"Yeah? And?" Jessica was looking less horrified and more interested. She still kept her distance, but who could blame her? "What happened?"

"Well, I had no idea how I'd gotten there, so I figured

it was a good time to lie low. I stayed up there for a couple of days, trying to think of what to do. I knew I wasn't alive anymore—I *felt* dead, you know? No, that's not right." He stared at his hands, the long slender fingers he'd used to fix broken bones and stitch up kids who fell down on playgrounds and pump his system with a lethal dose of morphine. "I felt different. I didn't feel alive—I saw things, smelled things in a different way . . . felt things in a different way." He paused, clearly struggling for a way to explain. "I wasn't rotting or craving brains or anything, but I knew I wasn't alive . . . the world just looked . . . I can't really explain . . . shit!" His fist dropped to the table and his body language was putting out "man, I'm sooo frustrated right now" vibes. "I'm not doing this very well."

"Take your time," Tina soothed.

"Screw that . . . what about my cat? Can we talk about my dead cat?"

"Oh my God." Jessica's hands went to her mouth. She saw Sinclair and Tina flinch. "I'm—I'm sorry, guys, I didn't—were you eating Giselle the cat? Were you eating her brains? You were, weren't you! Oh, Marc!"

"Gross, of course not!" Zombie Marc shot a reproving look at her. "I was just dissecting her so I wouldn't rot faster."

Nobody said anything. Probably because not a one of us had any idea what *to* say.

"Okay, I know that sounds bad," Marc began. "But—"

"So you wouldn't rot faster?" I practically screamed. "That's why you were up to your elbows in dead cat when I found you? To prevent rapid rotting? Because that's pretty bad, Marc, that's pretty damned awful!"

"I was only up to my wrists in your dead cat," he replied with simple dignity. "It wasn't like *she* cared."

"I cared!"

"I'm not defending it; I'm explaining it." I was pretty sure that was wrong . . . pretty sure he was doing, at best, both. "Look, I saw you go outside to bury her."

"How did you know just what she was doing?" Sinclair asked. He, Nick/Dick, and Tina were the only ones keeping their cool.

"Why else would she bring a pillowcase that obviously had something small in it, then find a shovel, then head to the back corner of the yard? I mean, I knew you weren't happy with all those velvet clogs in your closet, but I didn't think you'd decided to bury a few pairs."

"Logical." Sinclair (barely) kept the approval out of his tone.

"And then all the dogs . . . came. And they . . . um . . . chased Betsy. Chased her back . . . back into the house. She had to, um, bang on the door a lot while dogs were slobbering all over her."

"Are you trying not to laugh right now?" I asked, never more suspicious in my life.

"Of course not . . . this is a very serious . . . business . . . I felt for you while . . . all those dogs . . . um . . . chased you . . ."

Sinclair lost it. He started laughing so hard he tilted his chair so far back that two legs were off the floor. I had to resolutely squash the impulse to give his chair a kick and send him crashing to the kitchen tile. Jessica and Nick/Dick stared—my husband had a peculiar sense of humor, but hardly anyone but me ever heard him really laugh. Then Dickie/Nickie/Tavvi broke. Only Tina and Jessica remained impassive, but Jessica's mouth was twitching in a way I didn't like.

"Never mind the dogs!" I whined. "Get back to you lurking in our attic—*stop laughing!*"

"I wasn't." Marc cleared his throat. He didn't dare look at Sinclair, probably figuring that'd set them both off. Jerks! "You know how big the attic is . . . there are windows on all sides of the house. I could see everything from up there. I saw the—uh—"

"Hounds of heck."

"Right. They chased you inside, and nobody came back out for the cat. So I slipped outside and grabbed her."

"Okay, weird and gross. But why?"

"I get worse when I don't have something to do, or think about."

"Worse, how?"

"More dead," he replied simply.

"Um . . . could you clarify that one?" Dick asked. At least his hand wasn't on the butt of his gun anymore.

"I get slower and dumber. It's a lot harder to think. If I'm not keeping busy, I find all I want to do is sort of slump in a corner and listen to the mice fucking in the walls."

"I have no idea how to respond to that," Jessica admitted.

"Yeah, I don't blame you, Jess. If I keep busy, I keep . . . keep *myself*, I guess."

"Where did you get the scrubs?" Tina asked again.

"You guys hadn't packed up any of my stuff," he said, smiling a little. His brilliant green eyes held some of their old gleam. "I waited until everyone was out one night, then grabbed a bunch of my stuff and brought it to the attic. You guys never noticed."

"Careless of us," Tina murmured, and Sinclair nodded.

"We never even heard you moving around up there."

"We didn't hear the other zombie, either," I reminded them. Yes, in this wonderful life I'd made for myself after death, I'd encountered a zombie *before* Marc became one. "It must be a zombie power."

"I have no idea." Sinclair and Tina traded glances. "I know little about them," he admitted, and I knew that must have stuck in his craw. "Perhaps . . ."

I knew from "perhaps." My husband and sovereign, who

loved me beyond anything else, had a ruthless side. He was probably telling himself that Marc being a zombie was an excellent opportunity to learn all about them. Hey, look on the bright side, right? I could admire the trait, while at the same time fearing it was one I'd develop over the years.

God, I hoped not.

Marc shrugged. "I'm not judging. I'm glad you didn't get rid of my stuff, because it made things easier. I figured it was all still here because you're in denial, or because this has all happened too soon, or because you knew I'd be back." He looked right at me for that last one. "I wondered if it was all still there because you didn't expect me to stay dead—all-the-way-dead—for long."

"Marc—I was going to try—but I hadn't done any-thing." I shrugged helplessly. "Please don't think we didn't miss you and weren't thinking about you all the time because we *were* thinking about you all the time, Sinclair can tell you I've been crying my eyes out—"

"She has," he confirmed. "It's been distressing."

"—and we'd only just talked about it yesterday, but it didn't . . . um . . . we couldn't . . ."

"We were going to respect your choice," Nick/Dick said. "That's what Betsy's trying to pussyfoot around. We figured you knew what you were doing when you OD'd, and we were going to let sleeping zombies lie."

"Really?" Marc looked astonished.

"No, that's not true—I was absolutely going to figure out how to bring you back no matter what these guys said, but first I was gonna sort of let things sit. You know, let the others get used to the idea. Then later I was going to sneak off and resurrect you—uh, somehow—but then someone else did it, so I didn't have to."

"You *what?*"

Ulp. Jessica.

"*What?*"

Thanks to a terrifying mix of hormones, Jessica could go from zero to murderous rage in less than three seconds. It was like watching a fire consume your house: terrifying, but strangely beautiful, too.

"Let me rephrase," I began, but it was too late.

THIRTEEN

"Owwww, enough!" I batted the ice pack away. "I'm going to heal from this in half an hour; do I also have to heal the frostbite you're inflicting on my poor face?"

"She clocked you pretty good," Marc said, which was so obvious I was amazed he felt he needed to verbalize it.

"Tell me. For someone eating for eight, she can really move when she wants to." And she had. I'd been so astonished to see her leap from her chair, grab said chair, and bash me with said chair that I didn't duck, so the chair leg caught me spang across the temple. Some people see stars after a sharp blow to the head; I saw five Jessicas, all brandishing chairs and screaming at me. Scariest. Thing. Ever.

The next thing I knew I had ice on my face, and Jessica

had been hustled out of the kitchen by a rattled-yet-proud Nick/Dick.

"She did not take kindly to your revelation," Sinclair observed.

"I know . . . why are we all feeling the need to state the obvious? Can't blame her, either." I rubbed the side of my head. "It was really stupid of me to let that slip."

"Yes," Tina and Sinclair said in polite unison.

"And thanks for protecting me, you two," I snapped. "Good thing she didn't try to stake me, huh?"

"I have no desire to cross Jessica while she is in a family way," Tina said, and Sinclair nodded so hard I wondered if he'd made himself dizzy.

"She's rather terrifying these days," he said. He brushed his fingers across the lump on my head, and smiled. Against my will, I could feel my irritation start to fade. Dammit! Sometimes I wondered if Sinclair was a witch. "And you seem to have weathered the blow."

"Yeah, barely. Marc, stop with the ice pack! You're not a doctor anymore." Oops. Tactless. "Let me rephrase," I said, aware that rephrasing hadn't saved me from getting a chair smashed across my head by an enraged pregnant millionaire in desperate need of a pedicure. "I meant that you've got more important things to worry about."

"I'm legally dead," Marc mused. He'd given up with the

ice pack, and sat back down at the kitchen table. "What does that mean? Does my social security card work? Has my license to practice medicine been invalidated or revoked? How about my driver's license?"

"I had a lot of the same questions when I died the first time."

"So what happened?"

"Uh . . . nothing. The whole queen gig came up, so I never really had to worry about that stuff."

"Worry about what stuff?" Antonia had stepped into the kitchen, Garrett on her heels. They weren't carrying bags of yarn or needles or what-have-you, but they were both flushed and bright-eyed. "What's the vampire sewing circle bitching about now?"

"Ah-ha! You were having sex in the spoon, admit it!"

"Sure," she said, shrugging. Her black hair had been pulled back into a messy ponytail, which for Antonia was practically a smooth chignon. "Why d'you care? Aren't you dead?"

"Well, I'm a vampire, so technically—"

"Not you, moron." She pointed. "Him."

"Hi," Marc said. "I'm back."

She stepped closer, her nostrils flaring. "You're dead," she said, as if accusing him of drinking milk out of the carton.

"Yeah." He smiled and went for the lame joke: "But I got better. Time is a wheel."

"What? You said that before, I think."

"Said what?"

"What you just *said.*"

"What are you talking about?"

Before I could answer, Antonia was right up in his face. She was prowling around him, sniffing like a dog with a scent. Which, I s'pose, she kind of was. "You're not a vampire—you're not blank like these three."

"Blank? Oh, *very* nice, Antonia, just because we're not all shape-shifting seers who—"

"I mean vampires don't smell like anything, dummy. Why d'you think Pack members get so rattled around you? It's creepy, not knowing what dumbass move you're gonna pull."

"You know, some people are afraid of me." I tried not to whine, but didn't pull it off. "Some people wouldn't dare call me dummy, or dumbass, or idiot, or asshat, or moron, or dumb shit, or—"

"You're not one of *them,*" she continued, ignoring me so thoroughly I wondered if I was even in the room. "You're just a dead guy. Except you're walking around. Ummm . . . why?"

"Zombie?" Garrett asked. He'd walked right past Marc to rummage through the fridge. Since Antonia was alive, he didn't give a shit about what was happening in any other phase of his life. At most, Zombie Marc popping up was mildly curious. "Did you make him a zombie, Betsy?" He held up a can of V8. He was crazy for the stuff. I tried not to think about why. "Can I have this?"

"No."

"But it's not even the last one."

"No to me doing that, not no to the V8—drink all the V8 you want, what do I care? It wasn't me . . . it wasn't on purpose," I said. "In fact, I'm pretty sure I didn't have anything to do with it." *Pretty* sure. But I was getting a bad feeling. A bad intuition, call it. Because who could have done such a thing? The list of candidates was laughably short. And I was on that list.

So was my sister, the Antichrist.

"You're dead, but you don't smell bad," Antonia informed a bemused Marc. "There's no rot. There's not anything. You're just you. Only dead."

"Thanks for the analysis," he said wryly. "Welcome back from hell, by the way."

"Mmmmm." She looked at Sinclair and me. "I assume you two are on this?"

I opened my mouth to say, "Not a chance, so plan to stick around and help, for God's sake!" but Sinclair beat me to it with, "Assuredly." So I decided not to argue. For now.

"Antonia, there has not been time to address this, but I feel I must put it to you now: have you let your Pack know you're alive?"

"Nope! Too busy having sex in the Walker Center spoon, right?" God, I'd forgotten the pure pleasure of tattling. How come we have to give up all the fun things about being a kid when we grow up and die? "I bet it hasn't even occurred to you."

"It's none of your business, queen of the monkeys," she said with a scowl.

"Hey, hey," I warned. *Monkey* was the werewolf equivalent of *nigger*. "Put a lid on that Pack potty-mouth."

"Antonia," Sinclair said in a tone full of reproach. "It's not only careless to keep this from them, it's quite cruel."

"They weren't all that fond of me before I went to hell, and you both know it. So who cares?"

"Antonia." Sinclair knew she was right, but he also was a huge believer in all things family. His parents and sister had died when he was still in his teens. I think that was part of the reason he liked my mom so much. It didn't have as much to do with her as it did the fact that I still *had* a mom.

She rolled her eyes and stomped to the phone on the wall. "Fine, fine. You won't quit bitching until I do, so let's get this over with."

"Thank you so much for your cooperation."

She dialed, listened, then put her hand over the mouthpiece and said, "Got his voice mail . . . yeah, Michael? This is Antonia. Betsy went to hell and brought me back to life, so I'm alive again and living in the mansion in St. Paul with her and the rest of the weirdos. And I'm not dead anymore. Anybody you gave my stuff to had better cough it back up. So . . . just FYI." She hung up. "Happy?"

Sinclair was as horrified as I'd ever seen him. Which I understood because I was sure I had the identical expression on my face. "Oh, Antonia . . ." He shook his head. "You *cannot*."

"What?" She slashed her hand through the air like Sinclair was a giant fruit fly and had to be swatted away. "You butted into my business—"

"You live under my queen's roof," he said sharply, "and thus your business *is* my business, as are all things that happen in our home, and your liking of that fact is irrelevant."

"Fine, fine, don't get your undead skivvies out of joint. You said I should tell the family. I told the family. Are there any of those caramel brownies left? There better be. I'm starving."

"So . . ." I admired the shit out of her, while at the same time found her terrifying. Oh, and if anyone was keeping score, Antonia had been like this *before* she went to hell. "So, is it appealing to not be hindered by a conscience? I guess it is. It must be . . . So is sociopathy all it's cracked up to be?"

She rolled her eyes. "You just don't get it."

"Yep. I don't. Werewolves are weird."

"Come on," she said to Garrett, and he followed her out of the kitchen. "Way to not stay dead, jerk," was her parting comment to Marc.

Garrett's was, "Hi again. And bye."

I sighed and raked my fingers through my bangs. "Where were we?"

"Trying to figure out how I emerged from my dirt nap." Marc spotted the newspaper on the counter, got up, and grabbed it. "You guys done with this? I kind of need it."

"Nobody but Sink Lair reads newspapers, so yeah. What do you need it for? Are you potty training yourself? Eww, does that come with the whole zombie thing? *Are you potty training yourself in my attic?*"

"Gross. And no." I hadn't realized until that moment that a zombie could look reproving. "I don't think I can 'potty' anymore. But I need to keep busy," he replied, tucking the paper under his arm. "Dissecting the cat. Crossword puzzles. Sudoku. Stuff I have to think about."

"Okay." Weirdo. "Listen, I had a thought. I think it's time we tracked down the Antichrist. She's one of the people on my short list of who could have done this to Marc. And even if she didn't do it, she might have some ideas. Plus it's making me kind of nervous how she hasn't popped by or called in almost a week."

"Things were left somewhat tense between you," Sinclair pointed out, which was an astounding understatement.

"Things are always tense when the Antichrist is keeping secrets. Lucky for us she's a terrible liar." Secrets were, by definition, her mother's purview. So ask me how glad I was that *that* skipped a generation. "I'll call her again. I've been leaving messages—hi, how are you, started up any new timelines lately—like that. But if I ask her straight out to come over, or have us over, I think she'd do it."

She'd better. Because the last thing I wanted to do today was break into hell without an invitation . . . or an escort.

CHAPTER
FOURTEEN

Sinclair and I were rigid in our bed. For one of the very few times in our marriage, we had no interest in banging each other into semiconsciousness.

Nope. Thanks to the zombie who had the run of the house now, sex was the last thing on our minds.

"Okay, it's weird, right?" We were both staring at the ceiling. "It's just so creepy. He's our friend and I wanted him back—"

"Monkey's paw," Sinclair muttered.

"—but there's a *zombie* creeping around our *house*."

"He has to keep busy."

Boy, did he. Marc had explained that he needed tons of mental stimulation as a zombie, and thus was doing everything he could to keep his zombie brain sharp. Apparently the modern zombie fed from mentally taxing work (like accountants, I guess), which kept him from needing brains. Excuse me: Braaaaaaaains. Marc was a modern cuddly zombie as opposed to a revolting terrifying George Romero creation.

Okay. Fine. We could adapt. We had to adapt to weird stupid things all the time. But we still had the problem of knowing a zombie was creeping around the house trying to keep busy so he wouldn't rot.

I wriggled around on our new bed (Sinclair and I occasionally broke our beds, which was why we were on bed no. 7 . . . thank goodness Sinclair was rich!), which mussed our sheets.

"Now I'm apprehensive *and* my feet are cold," Sinclair sighed.

"You think I'm any happier? It's so creepy knowing he's creeping around being all creepy."

We stared at the ceiling for a few more minutes. "It may be psychological," Sinclair said.

"What the hell are you talking about?"

"I cannot actually hear anything. We did not know he was in the house before he revealed himself. Now we know he is not only here, he is a zombie. Perhaps our tension is psychological."

"I have no idea what you just said. Oh, fuck."

"Was that a request, or an epithet?"

"My mom's supposed to drop BabyJon off tomorrow." BabyJon was my half brother/ward/son, kinda. But because I was a vampire, and all sorts of bad shit tended to happen around me, I often fobbed him off on my poor mother. The good news was, she'd had to baby-sit so often she was actually getting attached to the kid. "This is gonna be so lame . . . hey, thanks for watching our baby yet again, and by the way, you can't drop him off because now there's a zombie in the house and we're not sure he can be trusted, here's more money for diapers. Ugh."

"The alternative is even less pleasant."

"Dammit!"

We stared at the ceiling some more. "At least Laura called me right back."

"Yes?"

"Yeah. But she wants to meet at this farm outside the Cities, God knows why." My husband flinched at the *G* word, and I muttered an apology. To all vampires except me, the *G* word was like the lash of a whip, or a summons to traffic court: unbearably painful. "She said she's got stuff to show me and she wanted to meet on neutral territory. So some farm on the outskirts of Mendota Heights qualifies, I guess."

"I shall accompany you."

"Figured as much."

We examined the ceiling in silence for a few seconds,

broken by Sinclair's hopeful "Perhaps, to take our mind off the problem, we could—"

"Uh, no. It's just too weird. I won't be able to not hear him while we're—nope. Sorry."

"I suppose you're right."

Stupid Thanksgiving.

CHAPTER
FIFTEEN

"It's here, okay? Turn left here, that's what her directions say."

"Her directions do not say anything; they read."

"Oh, you're channeling Alec Baldwin in *Malice* now?"

"I do not know what that means."

"Means you're being a jerk."

"Is that more or less desirable than being a bitch?"

"God God God God God God God."

"Stop that at once!" My husband shuddered all over and we nearly went into a ditch. Served him right for taking the Volkswagen. He had a garage full of really cool cars and he picked the Jetta? The romance was dead. "Really, Elizabeth. That is beneath you."

"Ha! Shows what you know. There's not much that's beneath me." Wait. Did I just insult myself?

"Indeed," he muttered, *finally* turning left. We were in the boonies somewhere south of Mendota Heights, and the farm my sister wanted to meet us at looked deserted.

And it wasn't much of a farm, either. There were no barns, no outbuildings of any kind except a big cream-colored garage, no livestock, no hay sheds, no corn cribs, no bores (except the one I was married to—hee!). Just a garage, a driveway, a short sidewalk leading to the house, and the house: two stories, cream siding with dark blue shutters. The place was dark except for what I assumed was the living room.

"Why'd Laura want to meet us here?"

"I dare not guess."

"Well, dare not to park crooked again, too."

"I have never once parked 'crooked.'"

"Except for last week."

"I was following the lines! That was a forty-five-degree parking spot!"

"Crooked. Very, very crooked is what it was, Sink Lair, crooked beyond belief, as crooked as your dark, dark heart, and you just can't admit it, can you, how crooked it was?"

"Darling, do shut up." I could actually see his teeth in a snarl as he stomped on the brake and jerked the parking brake so hard I heard the metal groan.

"We should probably have sex pretty soon."

"Agreed. Just not with each other." He flung himself out

94

of the car and slammed the door so hard, the entire Jetta rocked.

"Oh, *real* mature!" I shouted at his back. I considered sticking my tongue out at him, then figured one of us ought to act like a grown-up. Proof! Proof things had gone from bad to terrible: when I was the one trying to set the example of adult behavior.

Marc being a zombie was ruining my life. Also my sex life. I unbuckled my seat belt (old habits died, etc.) and followed my bitchy husband up the driveway. "This isn't a farm, this is just a house and a big smelly garage out in the country," I whined. "With dogs . . . I can hear yelping. Gross. Stupid farm dogs."

"Perhaps the Antichrist does not understand what a farm is."

"Oh, that makes a lot of sense," I snapped. "She might be the AC, but she grew up on Planet Earth just like you and me. She grew up in Minnesota! Gah, all I can smell is poop."

Sink Lair muttered something I couldn't quite catch . . . luckily for him.

"Her car is here," he said, eyeing the modest black Ford Fusion. "And there's a light on in the house."

"Great job, Nancy Drew!"

He ignored me. "Curious . . . why such a large garage for such a small house?"

"Yeah, that's the question that's burning me up inside, too . . . come *on,* we don't want to be *late.*"

He was standing stock-still, sniffing like . . . well, like Antonia did when she was scoping out Zombie Marc.

"Are you going to stand in the yard all damn night?" I could hear how shrill and bitchy I was, but couldn't seem to stop. Who would have thought that *not* banging my husband would be so bad for our sex life? "Laura's waiting, and we've got mysteries to solve and bad shit to stop, so c'mon already."

"Ah," he said, then flipped the latch on the garage door and slid it open. The smell of poop got much worse, much quicker.

"Wait!" I cried.

"See?" he said with the first happy smile I'd seen all night. He gestured and—*what* the?—bowed a little.

"Don't!" Seconds too late, I figured it out. "Sinclair, you crumb! It's not a *farm* farm, it's a puppy farm, do *not* open that door any—"

Too late.

CHAPTER
SIXTEEN

What sounded and smelled like a hundred black Lab puppies swarmed over me, barking shrill puppy barks and licking everything they could reach and suffocating me with their foul puppy breath.

My cardigan! My Etienne Aigners! If one of those mangy little monsters so much as *thought* about taking a chomp on my shoes . . . oooh, just picturing it made me feel like I was going insane.

And Sinclair had *made this happen.* The betrayal! He really screwed me after he didn't screw me, the treacherous bastard.

"Get them off. Get them off! Argh, it feels like they're crawling all over me! Is this what withdrawal is like? Oh, those poor drug addicts! Why are you just standing there, you rat bastard? Help!"

While I writhed in a sea of puppies, the king of the vampires fell to his knees. His sinister plan had worked beautifully, and he was so delighted he gave in completely. For a guy who prided himself on keeping things under control, he was letting loose an awful lot this week.

"Stop it! You bum! Ack, get away . . ."

He'd collapsed to his knees and was holding his stomach while bellowing laughter. Every time he tried to get up and help me, he fell back down again. This only increased my puppy-induced fury.

A velvety black ear slipped into my mouth, probably because I was screeching threats at my husband, the puppies, the stars, the Antichrist for picking such a dreadful meeting place, and any bugs or telemarketers in the vicinity. I puffed it back out with a breath and struggled to sit up. Did I . . . was that? It was! My left shin was warm and wet. "Oh, Goddammit! That's it. Gloves off. I'm gonna pull a Cruella de Vil and skin each of you. Starting with you!" I told Sinclair, and he finally stopped laughing.

"Now, darling," he said reprovingly. "There is no need—"

"Don't 'darling' me, butt monkey. You *knew* what would happen. You figured out what this place was, and you deliberately—get *away*!" I yelled at the puppies, and several of them scampered back toward the garage. Of course, several more ignored me and collapsed on their fat puppy butts, looking up at me with their puppy tongues hanging out of their puppy mouths. "Dogs and zombies. That's what this Thanksgiving has for us, Sink Lair. Dogs and zombies."

"Perhaps you might consider seeing if they bend to your will," he suggested.

"Shut up."

"Now, Elizabeth. You yourself said this sort of, uh, event . . ." The corner of his mouth twitched, but he managed to keep the grin off his face. If he'd still been human, his eyes would have watered with the effort. "This sort of thing did not happen to you in life. Perhaps you can control them in death."

"I can't even control my split ends, never mind the hounds of heck."

He blinked. "I have no idea what that means. But as I said—"

"I wasn't listening."

"Perhaps you could dominate them."

"I'm *still* not listening."

"Oh, you're here," the Antichrist said. No doubt roused by my bitter screams of hatred, she'd come out of the house and was standing on the porch. She was pretty focused, too: she was looking straight at me, like Sinclair wasn't there and, weirder, like thirty-some puppies weren't, either. "Good. We've got to talk."

"Boy, do we," I said. "Also, do you know a good divorce attorney?"

Sinclair ignored me and was (ugh!) holding two of the black Lab puppies, which seemed delighted to be in his arms, judging from all the wriggling and licking. "They shall be mine," he said, delighted, "and I shall name them Fur and Burr."

"And the horror continues. Fur and Burr? Be serious. Uh . . . Laura . . . you wanna help us wrangle some of these dogs?" They were annoying, but that didn't mean I wanted them to get lost or wander onto a highway and get squashed.

"Okay." Laura came down the steps, crossed the driveway, and absently scooped up two more puppies. I'd rarely seen her look so solemn. And given that the Antichrist loved puppies, shelters, orphans, lemonade, babies, marshmallows, and the homeless, it was weird that she wasn't going deep into cuddle mode. "But then we've got to talk."

"That's not all we've gotta do," I muttered, aiming a kick at the vampire king, who easily dodged, and walked toward the house talking in a low voice to Fur and Burr.

CHAPTER
SEVENTEEN

The Antichrist, in addition to her many other odious qualities, was stunning.

Yeah. Completely thoroughly gorgeous. My half sister (we had the same dad) looked better on her worst day in torn jeans and with dirty hair than I looked in my wedding gown. I was pretty sure she'd never had a pimple. She had skin that would put an Irish milkmaid to shame, was leggy and statuesque (over six feet!), with long blond hair the color of corn silk and with nary a single split end. Eyes the color of a cloudless spring sky . . . except when she was having a bad day. Then her eyes went poison green, and her hair deepened to red. So, gorgeous while being evil, just a different kind of gorgeous. And in hell, she had long gorgeous brown wings with which she could fly and in general just be the most gorgeous thing you've ever seen, ever.

But such are the challenges I, as vampire queen, must face. So when my husband and I (and Burr and Fur) went into the little farmhouse, it was to find the Antichrist in black leggings, a St. Olaf sweatshirt (weird, since I was pretty sure she was a U of M student), muddy tennis shoes (we were on a puppy farm, so I let that pass), and one of her adopted dad's old winter jackets. Her hair was yanked back in a messy ponytail, and her face was pale. Even for a blond Minnesotan. And gorgeous, of course. Proof! Proof she had sinister supernatural powers; no woman should look gorgeous with messy hair and a sweatshirt!

"Do you know who lives here?"

Fine, thanks, and you? But I played along; Sinclair had exhausted my bitch reserves for the time being. "Someone who really, really likes black Labs?"

"Jon Delk."

I waited for the name to mean something. My sister was getting good at interpreting my blank expressions, because she patiently prompted, "Of the Blade Warriors?"

I snorted. *That* Jon Delk. He and a few other weirdos had started their very own vampire-killing club a couple of years ago, complete with the *de rigueur* priest-as-team-leader and mysterious financial backer who turned out to be a villain. (Yawn.) Sinclair and I had encouraged their little club of vamp haters to disband and behave, or at least behave, and they had all gone back to their lives after the villain was trounced.

Jon had sort of fallen for me . . . yes, I know, it's all about me, but it really was, and he did fall for me—I can't help it if men sometimes find me irresistible. Which was why he couldn't stand Sinclair (tonight, though, I could see the logic behind the dislike).

Even worse, I'd given Jon-boy my life story, which he wrote down and then sold to a publisher. But not before Sinclair mind-raped him into forgetting it was *my* story. So in a short time Jon went from loving me and hating my husband to hating me. And hating my husband (the latter I totally get now). And I couldn't blame him. The whole mess was avoidable, and entirely on me.

In the old timeline, though, Jon lived on his grandparents' farm. Which was an actual *farm*. And not outside Mendota Heights . . . it was in North Dakota, a fourteen-hour drive from the mansion. He did not live on a puppy farm just outside the Twin Cities.

"See anything unusual about the place?" the Antichrist asked.

"He really likes vampires now?" I guessed, eyeing the Dracula posters, the stacks and stacks of vampire books, the *Sweet Valley High Vampires* posters, several action figures with fangs . . . it was like being trapped in eBay's forbidden basement.

"No, *everybody* really likes vampires. In this timeline, he wrote your life story and it went on to be a big hit, prompting all sorts of other books about modern flaky selfish—"

"Hey!"

"—sorry—hip vampires to hit the shelves. Which spawned movies. Which spawned TV shows. Vampires are huge now, Betsy. Huuuuuge. And Jon Delk started it all. That's what *he* thinks. Except *you* did. You started it all. Your stupid story started it all."

"Okay." I took another look around the living room. No signs that Jon lived with his folks. This was the lair of a single (geeky) man. "So where is he?"

"Book tour. And then he's off to L.A. to oversee the TV series they're making based on his books. Because vampires are huge now."

"Okay." I traded glances with Sinclair. Burr was snoring; Fur looked like she was going to start any second, if her glazed puppy eyes were any indication. Sinclair, I was relieved to see, looked as puzzled as I felt. "And we should be terrified because . . ."

Laura folded her arms across her smudged sweatshirt. She could pull off imposing, even dressed like she was on a prom committee, and she was pulling it off now. I was starting to get nervous, with no idea why, which made me irritable *and* nervous. "Vampires were not huge before we screwed up the timeline."

"Yes, I remember." Specifically, I remembered thinking, I'm the queen of the vampires? *Vampires?* How thoroughly lame.

"But they are now."

"Uh-huh."

"Because of us."

I glanced at Sinclair again. *Um . . . help?*

My own, I do not see the danger here . . .

Our telepathic link had been many things to me: cool, weird, big-time hot. This time it was comforting . . . as dim as I knew I could be, at least I wasn't the only one in the room without a clue. There was comfort in our mutual ignorance.

It's nice not to be the only stupid one in the room.

I do not know that I would have phrased it quite like that . . .

"Betsy!" Laura made a grabbing motion, and I knew in her mind she'd seized my shoulders and was shaking me like a maraca. "Think! You've accidentally made vampires into the new big trendy thing! They are *huge* now, and it's only gonna get worse!"

"Worse how?" Merchandising to go with, I dunno, movie rights? Vampire iPod apps? Vampire beach towels? Vampire tote bags? Half of Barnes and Noble dedicated to all things vampire: cookbooks, teen-angst stories, bookmarks? "What, exactly, is the danger here?"

If anything, vampires being cool and trendy might actually make our lives easier . . .

Do not think like that, my own! Sinclair, I realized, was finally getting it. That made two of us, and neither of them was me.

"I think this is the beginning . . ." Laura raked her fingers through her ponytail, mussing it even more. Why? Why did she treat her hair like this and never get split ends? "I think this might lead to your eventual takeover."

"Not mine . . . you mean . . ." It was too awful to think about, never mind say out loud, but I did, anyway. "Ancient Betsy? You think vampires being trendy somehow leads to Ancient Me taking over the country after that future nuclear winter thing?"

"Yes. That's what I think."

I looked at the Antichrist. She looked back at me. We both looked at the vampire king, who was cradling Fur and Burr and looking at us.

"Well, shit," I said, because really, what else was there to say?

CHAPTER
EIGHTEEN

"Sinclair."

More silence. Ye gods. The sexiest coolest most maddening man I'd ever met, a guy I loved more than my own life, and he was sulking. Over Fur and Burr! Yerrggh, I could still smell the little monsters all over him.

"Sinclair, you couldn't just steal those puppies."

Nothing. Argh, he *knew* I hated the silent treatment. I'd honestly rather be at a poetry reading. Or scrubbing toilets at the airport. The silent treatment was just so . . . silent. The only thing it left me with were my thoughts. And that was awful.

"Come on! Count up all the reasons this is a terrible idea: we don't have leashes, we don't have puppy chow, we don't know what shots they've had and if they need more, we're not set up for puppies, what with all the vampires and zombies and werewolves living at the mansion these—"

"Zombie, singular. Werewolf, singular."

"We're not set up for it! Plus we live in a big gorgeous expensive mansion full to the attic with antiques and old wood and also the undead . . . can you imagine the havoc two puppies could wreak?"

From the slight smile on his face, he could. Meanwhile, just the *thought* of what those two could get up to with their puppy shenanigans left me cold(er) all over. Giselle wasn't the, um, cuddliest pet, but she knew where to poop and she stayed the hell out of my way. As a return courtesy, I stayed the hell out of hers. It worked! It was, come to think of it, a perfect relationship . . .

"Okay, shouldn't have used that last as an example. You should see your eyes, man, they lit up like a pinball machine!"

"My eyes do not light up."

"Oh yes they do. Listen, back to my point—"

"Your interminable point."

"You know how needy dogs are . . . someone's always got to walk them or play with them or give them shots or . . . you know . . . all the dog stuff you've gotta do with dogs all the time, and how's that gonna work? Sinclair, you can't go out during the day without doing an impression of a comet hitting the earth's atmosphere! You can't take care of puppies. And are they really your puppies if someone else is doing all the work?"

The second it was out, I wished I could take it back. Wished I'd never opened my stupid flapping mouth in the first place. I was the only vampire who could bear sunlight. And my husband, my king, the child of farmers and the earth and the sun, missed sunlight almost as much as he missed his long-dead family. If he'd been born during the right decade, he could have been a flower child, that's how into nature the poor schmuck was.

"Point," was all he said.

I still felt shitty, though. And the best way to leave my *faux pas* in the dust was to barrel on ahead to the next *faux pas*, to wit: "And—and they aren't our puppies to take, anyway. What's poor Jon Delk gonna think when he gets back from his eleventh huge book tour only to find he's two dogs short? Didn't we do enough to almost ruin his life in the old timeline? Now we've gotta steal dogs in the new one? Hmm . . . Delk running to me was actually a good thing . . . that's so weird, me being an asset and not the other thing."

"I doubt he would notice . . . he *left* them."

I could almost hear his teeth grinding, which was a scary thought. I tucked my legs beneath me so I could face him. "Now, come on. You heard Laura . . . he's got dog sitters or whatever coming over four times a day for feedings and walks and, I dunno, puppy pedicures and stuff. We're lucky we missed them."

"*They're* lucky."

"Stop that. Jon set all that stuff up before he even left for the first city on his tour." Laura had known all about Jon's book tour and dog-sitting plans. When I asked her how she'd stumbled across all this, I'd gotten a mysterious, "I followed some bread crumbs my mother left," for an answer. Which didn't make me feel any better, or more secure, but I had other things to obsess over.

"Besides," I summed up, "we've got bigger problems. Vampires are trendy now."

"Truly a nightmare vision of a horrifying future."

"Well. Yeah." We really needed to have sex soon. Almost everything he said was pissing me off, and I was sure almost everything *I* said was pissing *him* off. More so than usual, even. Terrifying thought. "And we've still got to figure out Marc's deal. And his dad."

"Sorry?" Sinclair stopped glaring through the windshield long enough to look at me. "His father?"

"Well, yeah. Did we even notify him that Marc was dead? I didn't. I didn't have that homophobic idiot's address or anything, and frankly, I was too busy feeling sorry for myself to look. Marc didn't leave a will, just his journal. He forbade a funeral—he wasn't even buried (and now we know why). Only now Marc's . . . back. So do we tell his dad, Colonel Homophobia? Or not?"

"Likely we should ask Marc," he said, looking thoughtful. "Interesting that we *can* ask Marc, but it does not change the fact . . ."

"We fucked up."

"We were careless," he amended. "But not without cause."

"*So* with cause. We had tons of cause! But it's another one of the little details that always seem to bite us on the ass. If I were gonna take over the world—and I won't—but if I was—and I'm not—I'd hire a whole team of people whose only job would be taking care of the ass-biting details I always forget about."

"A whole team, beloved?"

"A squadron."

"The ass-biting team?"

"A *battalion*."

He laughed, and I did, too. So it was a little better. For a while.

CHAPTER
NINETEEN

"You stupid, stupid, stupid woman." It was safe to say the Antichrist was displeased. "After what we saw in the future, and the past? Oh, Betsy! How could you be so stupid?"

"Hey, hey! Two *stupid*s are all you're gonna need to cover my many mental deficiencies. And I didn't do"—I pointed to Marc—"that. In fact, I was wondering if you did it. Look! Look at what you may or may not have done, you bad, bad Antichrist!"

"I have a name," Marc the Zombie said.

"See? He's talking and he has a name! The dead guy is talking and has a name . . . somebody has to answer for this grossness."

The zombie looked irked. "Well, I love you, too, Betsy."

I shrugged my shoulders in apology. "I know, sorry, but

you know what I mean, Marc—the main reason you let yourself be seen was so you could find out the answers to those exact same questions, so this is a bad time to get picky. Now shush. The grown-ups are talking."

"This is bad." Laura sat down so quickly, I had the feeling it was plop onto the sofa or fall down. Poor kid . . . I knew how she felt. "This is . . ."

"Bad?" Marc asked politely.

"Do the others . . ." Laura asked in a near whisper, glancing toward the entrance hall. We were in the first parlor off the hall, with almost the whole rest of the house beyond that parlor. "Do they know about this?"

"Oh yeah. No need to lower your voice. Like, at all."

"Oh." She thought about it for a second, then looked alarmed. *"Oh."*

"Yeah. See, Jessica knows so much she brained me with a kitchen chair, and Nick/Dick's kept her out of the way ever since. I won't say I didn't have it coming, but it was still pretty rude. Antonia knows so much she didn't give a shit, and Garrett knows so much he was politely interested for half a second and then ran off to crochet a grill cover or whatever the heck he's working on now."

"Oh my God." At Sinclair's near-imperceptible flinch (was it me, or was he getting better at handling the *G* word?), Laura managed a smile. "Sorry, Eric. But this . . ."

"Let me guess. It's bad?" Marc asked.

"Sorry." The Antichrist was huge with the apologies. And you'd never get a more beautifully written thank-you note than the one Laura popped in the mail on real stationery. "Marc . . . please don't misunderstand . . . I'm glad for you—I—" She raised her arms, and he slowly crossed the room to her, bent, and gave her a stiff hug. She didn't stand, just sort of halfheartedly raised her arms and hugged-shrugged back. I couldn't tell if the awkward body language was because he had to move his creaky zombie arms, or because he was embarrassed and unsure how hard to hug her back. Or even if he should have hugged at all. I've seen hugs between people suing each other that had more warmth and spontaneity. "Are *you* glad for you?"

Really good question, one I was instantly embarrassed not to have thought of. So I gave Marc my full attention.

"Glad?" Marc had been the one to let us in; he knew we were meeting Laura and knew the three of us were coming back to the mansion. He knew the plan was to shock Laura with . . . well . . . *him.* Exhibit A: Behold and ye shall see before ye a zombie. Now take it back, ye sinner!

And it had worked. Laura had been plenty shocked. But not shocked enough, I guess, or about the right things. We weren't any closer to knowing what had happened than we were before she'd walked into our house. *"Glad?"*

"Uh," was as far as I got before the zombie blew.

"I am not *glad*! I am *pissed*, okay? Okay? I killed myself to avoid all kinds of *bullshit*! And what did I get after I killed myself? *More bullshit!* I am very far from glad right now! I am all the way around the world from glad! Okay, Laura? Okay?"

"Yes," she whispered, and looked at the floor.

"Oh, hell," Marc said, and rubbed his eyes. He was dressed in new scrubs—he must have absconded with, like, a dozen pairs, and his hair was military-neat. Knowing how much he loved to change his look—buzz cut to mullet to Caesar haircut to the Hugh Jackman—I felt even more sorry for him. Who cared about a zombie's hair, anyway? And could he even change it anymore?

"Right, Betsy?"

"Huh?"

"I'm so sorry."

"Oh. Well, that's okay." What did Marc have to be sorry for?

"Laura, I just—I can see by your face you can't—I didn't really have a plan for what to do if you weren't the one who did this. And you're clearly not."

Say it twice. The daughter of the Lord of Lies was a laughably bad liar, even by omission. She could barely maintain eye contact if she was trying to cheat at Monopoly (nobody gets *that* many Get Out of Jail Free cards in one lousy game . . . who did the Antichrist think she was dealing with?).

Besides, if she *had* done it, she wouldn't have covered it up. If she had done it, she wouldn't lie about it. And it was obvious she had no idea what had happened to Marc . . . or what to do next.

"Marc, I was very sorry about what happened to you—that other you—"

"The Marc Thing," I prompted.

"Right . . . I was sorry about that. And I was sorry you—you hurt yourself." She'd been a little more than sorry. More like distraught at the thought of Marc being in her mother's clutches—burning in hell, in other words—because he'd killed himself. Though after what I'd seen the past few years, I was no longer certain who went to hell and why. I doubted Marc would have burned for eternity, suicide or not. If God isn't around to lend a hand, what was so bad about trying to fix your own life? Or death?

"And I—it's nice to see you," Laura continued, sounding like she was coughing up the words, "but I—I'm not sure—okay, this is going to sound terrible, but you're an abomination now."

"You're right," I told my sister. "It sounds terrible."

"That's not to say I don't still like you as a friend," she added quickly.

"And an abomination!" I added brightly. "*I* love you as an abomination. Speaking of the *A* word, Antichrist, what does that make *you*?"

"You stay out of this!" she snapped.

"Ooooh, did that one sting a little?" Marc shot me a grin and I instantly felt much better. And how lame was that? I had to be mean to my sister to feel better about myself. Where was an After-School Special when I needed one? "Sorry. So . . . you, the Antichrist, were talking to Marc, the abomination, about how you felt about him being an abomination. And . . . go."

"Shut up," she said helplessly, and covered her face with her hands.

Temper, temper, my queen. But his feelings—smug and amused—didn't match his tone. In my head. Yeah, I know how it sounds.

She's so fucking quick to hit people with the judgment stick! Makes me nuts. She's no angel. She's, um, half angel.

My husband laughed in my head, which had the dual attraction of giving me an idea, and making me feel better.

"So you should come over for Thanksgiving," I blurted out.

Shocked silence. Staring eyes. Horrified expressions.

"No, really. It'll be . . ." A disaster. A boneheaded idea. A clusterfuck. A Republican back in the White House. "Fun?"

"But you hate—"

"Hate!" Marc added.

"Darling Queen, you loathe Thanksgiving."

"Well, now I don't!" I snapped, annoyed they weren't embracing my brainstorm. I didn't get a lot of them. They could at least get on board when I did.

"Since wh—"

"It's a family holiday, right? Well. We're all family. Even the ones we aren't married to or the ones who have the same dads and we've had a hard time lately and I want us all to have Thanksgiving together as a family because, dammit, we're a family! So we're gonna give thanks for that! On Thanksgiving! Obey me!"

"Because it *sounds* like you're planning to kill us in our sleep," Marc replied, still looking perplexed. "And I'm okay with that, by the way. In fact, I need to talk to you, Betsy."

"My parents will be doing Meals on Wheels like every Thanksgiving," the Antichrist said, "but I could come over for the dinner. If that's okay." She gave me such a hopeful, pleased smile that I was instantly ashamed I had never thought of it before. All the Antichrist had ever wanted was to belong. And of course, she didn't, and wouldn't ever. Not really.

"So it's settled." Yeesh. What had I done in my moment of reckless madness? Every Native American was turning in their grave right this second. Oh, wait . . . only the dead ones were doing that. "It's a done deal. We can't escape now." Hmm. Better rephrase before I spring it on Antonia and Garrett. Dickie/Nickie/Tavvi wouldn't care as long as Jessica didn't. And Jessica, I knew, would be in. Still rightfully pissed at me, The Belly That Ate the World would never turn down a free meal loaded with carbs.

"Ah, Laura," Sinclair said, extending a long-fingered hand in her direction. She looked up, then took his hand and he pulled her smoothly to her feet. "Come, let's have a drink in the kitchen."

"You know I don't drink," she said, but started to follow him as he led her out of the parlor.

"Yes, yes, I know you are a teetotaler until you are of legal age, which I find quite admirable, but that doesn't mean you can't have a glass of chai, or a shake."

"Strawberry?" the Antichrist said brightly while the king of the vampires led her out like a cosseted child.

"Oh yes," he promised, and out the door they went.

"Okay, Marc, I just had an—whoa."

Marc had also gotten up, and swiftly crossed the room until he was looming in front of me. I mean standing. Marc didn't *loom.* He was a good zombie. Guy! He was a good guy. That's what I meant. That wasn't some sort of psychological slipup.

It wasn't!

"You have to kill me, Betsy, because time is a wheel."

"Um . . . what?"

"You have to kill me! I'm no good at it myself, clearly," he snapped. "So you're gonna do it."

"Then *I'm* gonna need a drink. And I'm sick of hearing about that wheel you're obsessed with."

"What?"

"Forget it."

Where? Where had it all gone wrong? Oh, right. The minute I woke up dead.

God, you sick fuck, we are gonna have such a talk when I catch up to you . . .

CHAPTER
TWENTY

"You've got to thoroughly kill me. No half-assed Betsy stunts."

"Hey!"

"I've got to be *really* dead," he continued, ignoring my outraged yelp. "And since we've got the weight of about a hundred zombie movies on our side, I'm thinking decapitation."

"Marc, I didn't not bring you back to life just to kill you."

"Yeah, but we still don't know who did it, right? So we're right back where we started."

"But you won't be the Marc Thing now."

"Who says? Maybe shambling around in your wake for a few hundred years will turn me into something even worse."

I shuddered. No chance.

"Try, just this one time, Betsy, try to put yourself in

someone else's Marc Jacobses. I killed myself to avoid the future. So think what it must be like to find out I'm even more repulsive than a fucking psycho vampire!"

"But you aren't. Repulsive, I mean." He really wasn't. He didn't rot or stink. He didn't lurch around the house after physical brains; he just wanted mental stimulation. In fact, I could see no sign of even the slightest decomp . . . and sadly I knew what stages of decomposition looked like. "Now that I've gotten over my gross shock, I—I think it's kind of cool that you're back."

"You dumbass! Name one good thing about being a zombie."

"You can't die again." It was what my mom had loved about me coming back as a vampire . . . she'd never again have to worry about me being a victim of a ten-car mash-up, or a date rapist.

He raised his eyebrows. "Wanna bet? See, that's where you come in."

"I think you'd better think this through."

He began to pace. "A vampire, okay. Not being able to eat solid food looked like a downer, but on the other hand, I'm best friends with the queen of the vamps! Being a vampire would have been very cool. Until I met the Marc Thing."

"Really?" I said, pleased. "Best friends? Aw, Marc, I love you, too."

"Will you focus, you undead bitch?" he cried.

"Say it, don't spray it," I muttered, refusing to look at him.

"But this?" He gestured to his mild-mannered, nonrotting self. "I've got to constantly find this interesting to keep my brain occupied."

"Just like you did in life. It's true!" I added as he opened his mouth to bitch more. "You were always chasing excitement. This is nothing new."

"And how will I ever find a guy who wants to be with a *corpse*, for God's sake?"

Okay. He had me there.

"Right," he said, correctly reading my expression. "I can't have a relationship and I can't be a doctor. So what's left for me but pain and betrayal and going crazy? I don't sleep, Betsy, have you noticed?"

"I'm sure I would have eventually."

"I don't sleep, and my skills are getting atrophied. I'm fucking useless to you—and me—like this."

I couldn't stand to hear him talk about himself with such loathing. "Marc, you have worth!" I thumped my fist against his chest to make my point. "You're still a doctor, you're just a dead doctor. You can still—"

"Cut up dead cats?"

"Provide really, really advanced first aid. Maybe you can't do surgery or stuff like that, but you can still help people in trouble . . . and I bet you could talk a layman through something complex. You're *not* some worthless rotting zombie . . . we need you!"

"I don't give a shit; I'm not hanging around like an extra in a George Romero vehicle. So c'mon. Let's figure this out. How will you kill me?"

"I'm not. Listen, we'll figure something out, okay? How do you not get that this is a gift?"

"A gift?" he yowled. "Oh my God. Just when I was pretty sure you couldn't get any dumber."

"Insulting me won't get you what you want," I snapped.

"Oh yeah?" Up went his dark brows again. "It's your fault there isn't a single Christian Louboutin pump anywhere on the planet."

"That's . . . don't. Don't say that."

"This Christian guy was all you could babble about when you came back from hell, but he's nowhere to be found because *you* fucked up the timeline."

"That's not—"

"All those sexy high heels he thought up are gone and, worse, won't ever be, and instead you've got a closet full of velvet clogs and it's all your fault."

"You don't say that ever!"

"And your hair," Zombie Marc concluded, "looks stupid. Nobody's doing red lowlights anymore. So: stupid *and* dated. Grrggh! Argh! Hey, wait," he gurgled. "Things're going dark! Maybe this'll work. Margle! Sqzz hrdr."

This. This was what my life had become. I was strangling my zombie roommate over clogs and highlights. And he'd had trouble getting laid *before* he died. After a sweet moment of feeling his esophagus crackle under my fingers, I let go.

"Dammit! Look what you almost made me do. That was just plain stupid."

"I know. I mean, why would that have even worked?" he mused, rubbing his throat. "You could have crushed my trachea and I'd still be walking and talking. No, decapitation is the way to go."

"Don't tease me about crushing your trachea," I muttered.

"Ah, decapitation," a most unwelcome voice said. "One of the classics."

We looked. Lounging indolently on the two-seat sofa in a navy blue Donna Karan suit, sheer black hose, and breathtaking *peau de soie* black fuck-me heels was Satan herself.

"Well, *great*," was all I could come up with.

"So it's true." The devil, who looked like Lena Olin—she had the cougar thing *down*—looked irked. "You're supposed to be somewhere else, boy," she told Marc. "You are *not* supposed to be here, in the state you are in, right now. It's all wrong." She shook her head. "I might have known you'd screw it up."

"Ha ha, Lena Olin, shows what you know. I didn't have anything to do with *that*." I pointed triumphantly at Marc.

"You did, actually." She crossed her legs and admired the toes of her beautiful shoes. Then she looked at Marc. "What do you have to say for yourself, boy?"

"That I really want someone to kill me right now, and if you've got a minute . . ."

"I can't touch you, and you damned well know it," Satan

snapped. "You're hers now, and I can't—wait. Ahhh . . . you don't know that yet. None of you nitwits know that yet." She sighed, aggrieved. "Ask me how much I loathe time travel."

"Is that why you popped in from hell? To bitch?"

"No, mostly to see for myself. Unfortunately, the rumors were true."

"What rumors?"

"Mother!" Laura had rushed back to the parlor, Sinclair right behind her, so quickly I barely had time to realize they were back in the room before my sister was screeching at her mother. "Get out of here! This has nothing to do with you!"

"Wrong, wrong, wrong." She eyed Laura's old sweatshirt and muddy shoes. "You're looking . . . ah . . . frumpy."

"Go *away*, Mother."

"But I have to be here when she finds out. Well, perhaps I don't have to," the devil admitted, "but I must insist on watching the whole sordid scene." Then she tittered. *Tittered.*

Sinclair was stepping in front of me, which sometimes made me feel cherished, and other times—like now—made me feel like he was crowding me into a corner. I put a hand on his shoulder and shoved him aside. "It's fine, Sinclair, we're all fine, and Satan here was just hopping back on her broomstick to go back to hell or Newark or wherever."

"A New Jersey joke?" Satan rolled her eyes. "At least no one has ever tried *that* before."

"Doesn't my nasty stepmother have something else on your schedule for today?" Antonia Taylor—the Ant—was Laura's biological mother and my stepmother, or had been in life. In death she was Satan's assistant, or whatever the hell she does down there in hell. Which made my brain hurt. First, what were the odds that I'd have two Antonias in my life? Second, what were the odds that if I called one of them Antonia-from-hell, *it wasn't specific enough*? "Anything else?"

"Sadly, no." The devil looked right at Laura. "Are you going to tell her, or shall I?"

"Mother, *don't*. I told you I'd handle it."

"Well, thus far, you haven't."

"It's been less than a week!" she howled.

"Time isn't always on your side, Laura, even if you're a time traveler."

"Okay, at least that wasn't cryptic and weird. Get thee behind us, Satan. We've got stuff to take care of, and your name was nowhere on the guest list for my Thanksgiving party."

Satan wrinkled her adorable nose. "But you loathe Thanksgiving."

"Never mind! Get the heck out of my house!"

"Indeed," Sinclair said, trying once again to shove me behind him.

"Oh, but this concerns you, too, Eric. You most of all, I think."

"Mother. Don't do it."

Satan's demeanor lost all playfulness; now she was giving off all the warmth of an ice sculpture. "Then you'd best get to it, daughter."

There was a long silence while mother and daughter locked gazes, broken by Marc's puzzled, "What's she talking about? What's wrong? Uh, besides all the obvious stuff . . ."

Laura dropped her gaze and slowly turned so she was facing the three of us. "I didn't want to meet at the farm—"

"Puppy farm," I interrupted, still annoyed at the puppy hair that was now everywhere.

"Just to talk about Jon Delk. I also wanted to come back here with you to talk about this." She ducked out of the parlor, and I could hear her rummaging around in one of the coat closets in the huge entryway, and then she came back carrying—ugh—the Book of the Dead. "We've got to talk about this."

"Gross! Why? Jeez, Laura—sorry, Sinclair—jeepers, Laura, you and I bounced all over time, and in and out of hell, so I could learn to read the stupid thing without going batshit nutballs, then you *steal* it and refuse to give it back. Except now, less than a week later, you *did* bring it back. After stashing it in a coat closet?"

"Thank you so much for the recap, Vampire Queen."

"Pipe down, Lena Olin. So why, Laura? Just what is it about this nasty thing that's got you so freaked out?"

"Besides the obvious," Marc added.

Even now, feeling our impatience, feeling the devil's ire, Laura couldn't seem to spit it out. We watched her struggle with the words, and when they finally came, it's like they were wrenched out of her. Torn from her.

"Betsy, in the future, *you* write the Book of the Dead."

I laughed.

"No, really. Then you ask the devil to put it back in time, so the first vampires find it and keep passing it down through the ages. It's not a book that tells your future . . . it's a book that lists your past, because you wrote it in the future, when you already knew everything."

I laughed harder. Oh, this was rich! I couldn't even write a grocery list, never mind *that* nasty thing.

"And the reason you did that—do that—is because the Book is Sinclair."

"Like . . . about Sinclair?" Marc asked.

"No. It *is* Sinclair. It's his skin the Book is written on."

I stopped laughing.

CHAPTER
TWENTY-TWO

Okay. Okay. Okay. It'll be okay. Just . . . stay calm. It'll be okay. It's okay. Okay. It's fine. It's okay. She's wrong, is all, or lying. She's not just a liar, she's the daughter of the lord of them. She's got bad intel, is all. I don't kill Sinclair and skin him and turn him into the Book of the Dead. I don't don't don't don't don't.

Nope. Shake it somewhere else, Satan, 'cuz this vampire queen isn't buying.

Okay. Okay! It felt good to have that settled.

I ran from the room and lunged for the closet. I could feel someone come in and stand behind me, but I had more pressing matters to deal with. I yanked open the closet door, groped for the nearest receptacle (sadly, it was a Beverly Feldman shoe box I'd stashed right after UPS dropped it off), tore the lid off, and threw up all over a lovely pair of pewter-colored gladiator sandals.

CHAPTER
TWENTY-THREE

I'd run out and barfed and run back in so quickly, they were all standing right where I'd left them.

It wasn't true.

It *wasn't*.

"You can talk until you drop dead," I told the devil, furtively wiping my mouth—probably time to lay off the banana chocolate smoothies for a while—"and it won't change a thing. You'll never make me believe it. Hear me? Never. Shit, Satan, I wouldn't believe you if you told me the ground gets wet when it rains."

"Then believe me," someone said.

We looked.

Ancient Me was standing in the doorway. "I did it. You will do it."

I did the only sensible thing. I ran out and threw up again.

CHAPTER
TWENTY-FOUR

I staggered back into the parlor, weaving like a coked-up runway model. "This is the worst dream I've ever had."

"You think you know fear?" Ancient Me asked. "I'm going through all this a second time. As if the first wasn't horrific enough." She glared at Satan. "I'm beginning to wish I'd never asked you for that favor."

"That would be two of us, Betsy."

"Don't call me that, it's infantile, you know I loathe it," Ancient Betsy shot back.

"I do know you loathe it," Satan agreed cheerfully. "Yes."

"And that right there is the source of your problems," Laura pointed out.

Meanwhile, Marc and Sinclair were looking from me to Ancient Me and then back to me again. "Okay," Marc finally said, "don't kill me yet, because this just got really interesting. So we'll put my murder on the back burner for now. And no wonder the Book of the Dead follows you everywhere! It's *Sinclair*!"

"It's *not* Sinclair!"

"It absolutely is Sinclair," Ancient Me confirmed.

"Why are you here?" I cried. "Don't you have a future wasteland to lord over?"

Ancient Betsy, wearing yet another awful gray sweater dress with pilled elbows and a ragged hem that dropped a few inches past her knees, looked more ticked than ever. "Because of you, numbskull. You'll have to fix this. I can't, more's the pity."

"How am I supposed to—"

"I. Don't. Know!" Ancient Me snapped. "But you had better figure out a way. *You're* the one screwing up the timeline. My memories haven't been reliable since you two showed up in my present." She jabbed a bony, unpolished finger in my general direction. "Your future."

"Okay, first? Buff the nails, Decrepit Me."

"I'm not decrepit; we look exactly alike."

"Except for your eyes," Sinclair said quietly. "Your eyes are not at all the same."

"*You* shut up." Now that bony finger was pointing at my beloved husband. "Quite a lot of this is your fault."

"Oh, sure, blame the victim! Buff, okay? It's not hard,

and you'll feel better about yourself. You don't even have to do polish, just a top coat."

"My world is a nightmare of post-apocalyptic forever-storm."

"And who's fault is *that*?"

"*So fix it!*" Ancient Me screamed. It was so loud and piercing, I nearly heard glass cracking. No, wait . . . that was probably just my eardrum blowing up. "Do you hear, you stupid mewling foolish idiotic girl? Fix it! Save him! Save *us*!"

She seemed almost appalled she'd had a screaming tantrum, because she visibly calmed herself—a good trick, one I might have to learn, or would learn—and then looked around the room at all of us and said, "You're a stupid, stupid girl. But you might pull it off. And Marc." She nodded at him and he nodded back, looking wary.

"Uh . . . yeah, um, Queen Elizabeth?"

"That's a good look for you. It suits you. And you're welcome." Then she looked at the devil, who was wearing the expression of someone who thought something was gonna be a big joke . . . only to find the joke was on her. It was an expression I hoped to see on Satan's face a few more times. The devil looking discomfited was hilarious. "Get me out of here. Right now."

Satan shrugged, and they both disappeared.

"Ancient Betsy must have brought me back!" Marc cried

when the stench of brimstone faded. Okay, there hadn't been any brimstone, but the two of them disappeared in an appropriately sinister way. "She must have gotten the devil to bring her here, find my body, and resurrect me."

"Yeah. It was a short list." I explained that I'd made the list not long after my attic breakdown in front of Zombie Marc. "Me. Laura. Or Ancient Me. And I knew it wasn't me. And then we knew it wasn't Laura. So . . ." I shrugged. "Like the Bad Book says, *the Queene shalt noe the dead.*"

"Well done, my queen." Sinclair looked and sounded impressed. Which made me feel awful. I didn't want to be logical and calm and smart. I didn't want to grow into the talking ice sculpture that was Ancient Me. I wanted to be a flapping dumbass. I wanted to be the kind of person who was so dumb, when they played Russian Roulette they loaded all the chambers. I did *not* want to be smart. Not if it meant being her. Never, never her.

Sinclair seemed to read my expression pretty accurately, because he added, "I do not believe it. You could never hurt me, as I could never hurt you. I do not believe it."

"You do, too!"

"Very well." He instantly reversed course, the better to soothe you with, my dear. "I am not afraid."

"Well, you would be if you'd been paying any attention the last five years." I sniffed, comforted. "What are we going to do, Eric?"

"Truly things have come to a wretched pass." He put his hands over his heart and made like he was going to swoon. "Calling me by my first name, almost as if we were husband and wife. The horror of it!"

"Shut your cake slot, Sink Lair."

"Much better." Weirdly, he did seem relieved.

"We'll fix it, Betsy. Of course, I have no idea how . . ." Marc was stroking his chin and looking thoughtful. And Laura looked like she'd been given a death-row reprieve. "But we will."

"We absolutely will," Laura agreed. "Betsy, I'm so sorry about keeping this from you . . . I couldn't tell you. I thought I could fix it—head it off—if I kept the Book from you while I figured out what to do, but my mother jumped in with both feet and . . . and . . ."

"I don't blame you, Laura." Though in that moment with Sinclair I had forgotten she and Marc were even in the room. "I know you wanted to help. I shouldn't have assumed you'd gone klepto out of spite." I looked around the room at the glum faces. "C'mon, guys! It's not the end of the world. At least, not yet."

They obviously didn't believe me, but were too polite to tell me to my face. So I forced brisk cheer into my tone, as much for my own sake as theirs. If I didn't fake cheer, I was gonna go into some very real hysterics, possibly for several months.

"I'll tell you what. We're gonna fix this. And here's the fun fact: I don't give a tin shit how many laws we have to break or how much blood we have to drink. If we have to lie, we're gonna do it."

Marc was rubbing his temples and staring at the floor. "Time is a wheel."

"Don't start with the wheel . . . if we have to cheat, we're gonna do it."

He rubbed harder. "There's something familiar about this . . ."

"As God is my witness, Sinclair will never be skinned again!"

"That is sweet, my own." Which sounded sincere until Sink Lair lifted a hand to his mouth to turn his laugh into a cough ("Hee-hhmmphhhh!") and then fake-cleared his throat. (Or would it be *faux* cleared? Jessica's the one who took French, I'd have to ask her . . .) "I think I just fell in love with you all over again."

"Gone with the Wind!" Marc shouted, leaping to his zombie feet. "You're cribbing prose from the estate of Margaret Mitchell, you thieving whore!"

"Am not. And I am *not* a thief. Okay, I am. Who cares? Focus, Lazarus. We'll fix it. It's gonna be fixed. Okay?"

I forced a smile. They did, too, and their smiles were about as real as mine.

CHAPTER
TWENTY-FIVE

Hours later, when we were alone, Sinclair reached for me, and I clung to him. Things started to get naked when we both heard Marc shambling around the house, no doubt looking for a project. A door to paint. A shelf to straighten. A dead cat to dissect.

"Odd how now that we know he is here, we cannot *not* hear him."

"I can't," I groaned, letting go and stepping back. "Sinclair, I can't. There's a wide-awake zombie running around, and I apparently have you skinned and then write a book out of you."

"Not conducive to horniness," he admitted, and since it was the first time he'd used that word, I had to laugh.

Then we both went to bed, and pretended to try to go to sleep. Him with his thoughts, and me with mine.

I reviewed my to-do list:

1) Save Marc
2) Save the future
3) Buy frozen strawberries
4) Save myself and/or kill myself
5) Remind the Ant she's stuck with that dumb pineapple-colored shellacked hairstyle for all eternity
6) Pick up BabyJon after future is saved (unless I've killed myself)
7) Hit Macy's for semiannual shoe sale

A lot to do! Better get started. Or at least, I'd better do more than I had so far. And I instantly forced myself not to think about BabyJon or my mom. They were out of this, they would know nothing about any of this disaster until it was fixed, or I was out of the picture. It was something so fundamental, I knew without taking a poll that everyone in the house would agree. So: no Mom and no BabyJon. Maybe forever, if things went the way I was afraid they would.

I thought about the BabyJon from the future—he had been the best thing about the future. A handsome, charm-

ing grown man. Kind and big-hearted. Blessedly normal—
not a vampire, not anything supernatural as far as Laura
and I could tell.

"Holy God! BabyJon!"

*"Aw, man." Gorgeous Grown BabyJon covered his face, then
dropped his hands and shook his head. "I outgrew that nickname
a while ago, Mom."*

"Mom?"

*"Okay, technically you're my big sister—like you're Aunt
Laura's big sister—"*

"Aunt L—"

*"But I grew up calling you Mom. But if that's freaking you
out, since I'm still shitting in my crib where you come from—"*

"That's a weird way to put it," Laura said.

*"Look, I'll try to master the whole toilet thing as quickly as I
can, but bottom line, right now in your when, I'm suffering the
heartbreak of fecal and urinary incontinence." He threw up his
hands. "I'm owning it, okay? Don't judge."*

*It was too much. I burst out laughing. And BabyJon—Jon, I
s'pose—joined me. It was kind of nice. I remembered it for a long
time, because it was about the only nice moment we had the ninety
minutes we were there.*

I tossed and wriggled and tossed some more. Sinclair lay
like a six-foot-four stone beside me. Meditating, or thinking

hard, or zonked for the day. I didn't know. What I did know was that for one of the few times in my undead existence, I couldn't conk out. Shit, half the time I'd just flop over wherever I was when the sun came up—much to the amusement of pretty much the entire household.

Great. Of all the stupid times to evolve . . .

Please God it's not true. Please God it's a trick. Please.

I'll do anything. Anything to save him, even if it means putting a bullet in my mouth. But c'mon, God, I can't do it alone. Help a vampire queen out, willya? Help me and I'll owe you a big favor. Help me and in return, I'll . . . I tried to think of something worth bargaining for. *I know! I'll use some of Sink Lair's vast amount of money and buy a Payless Shoe franchise. And work in it. Every day, I'll work in it. I'll pull double shifts in the motherfucker from now until the end of the universe. I'll sell cheap knockoffs to everyone who comes in the door. I'll have those silly "buy one pair, get the second half off" sales. If he'll live. If I don't kill him.*

Please God it's not true.

As for what Sinclair was thinking, I had no idea. Our telepathic link was down, or he was keeping his thoughts from me. I couldn't blame him. I wouldn't blame him.

But it hurt, anyway.

CHAPTER
TWENTY-SIX

Sinclair was gone when I woke up at 4:45 p.m. He didn't have to sleep all day; he could be out and about in daylight, so long as daylight didn't touch him. He was often in his office on the first floor, or reading something stuffy and moth-nibbled in the library. I had no desire, none at all, to look for him. Shit, after what we'd found out last night, I could barely look *at* him.

I heard footsteps, pained, labored, waddling footsteps, and then a knock on the door, which opened at once at my weary, "C'mon in, Jess."

She stood framed in the doorway in all her enormity, holding a six-inch sub from Subway in each hand. "Laura told us," she began. "How can we help?"

Like the cool, collected undead monarch I was, I thanked

her politely. By which I mean I let out a cry and launched myself at her, then started sniveling on her shoulder. She staggered back a step, then regained her equilibrium.

"What am I gonna do? What am I gonna do?"

"You'll figure it out, Bets. You're not alone." Lettuce from her sandwiches dribbled down my back as she soothed me with onion breath. "We'll all help. We will. It's a trick. Got to be—you'd never hurt Sinclair. And even if you were capable of—of that, it's nothing that has already happened. Only something that might, but you're forewarned and all. Okay?"

"Okay . . . ow!"

"What?"

"Your sto—your, um, adorable baby just kicked me."

"Welcome to my pregnant world," she replied, unperturbed.

Pass. I straightened from her sandwich-ey, baby-kicking embrace and brushed a tomato slice out of my hair. "Thanks. I know it's a cliché, but I really needed that."

"No problem."

"And you've got a point. I'd never hurt him. And as for the Book of the Dead? This doesn't seem like a me kind of thing to do. First off, why human skin? What, OfficeMax was closed? I wrote it in the future . . . plastic and paper suddenly weren't available?"

"I'm convinced."

"And I'm sorry about before."

"Current events—future events—gave us all some perspective, I think," she said, smiling.

"Laura told you?"

"Yeah. She was just leaving when I came downstairs. She told me the whole weird thing."

"That was . . . helpful."

"Sure. She's your sister."

"And the Antichrist."

"And your sister," Jess said patiently. "You know she cares, even if she's kind of conflicted about vampires."

"She's not around so much these days. She's spending a lot of time in hell. And maybe even worse places . . . she's not like us, Jess."

"*You're* not like us, Bets." She said it with a smile, but she still said it.

"Okay, good point." One I occasionally hated, but this wasn't the time to quibble. "But where is she when she's not here? And where's hell, exactly? When Laura teleports or evilly beams herself or whatever—which she's gotten very good at very quickly—where does she go?"

"Unknown."

"What, unknown? That's it, Spock? That's all you've got?"

"Betsy, what do you want from me? Some things, they're just not explainable or understandable. Hell is where hell is because that's where hell *is*. Satan does what she does because that's her nature. Laura can teleport through space and time and sometimes has wings and sometimes doesn't and can make weapons made of hellfire that nobody can touch except you by thinking them up, and there is no logical explanation for any of it."

"Lame."

"Make a list of questions and ask God when you see him."

"Oh, I have been. I've got *plenty* to ask that absentee landlord of a deity."

"You should just ask Laura those things. I bet she'd tell you."

"I'm kind of scared you're right."

"Oh. You're asking me questions because you're not sure you want the answers. *That's* a little on the lame side."

"Yeah . . . listen, do you know where Marc is? I have to go talk to him right away."

"Got a plan already, huh?" she said, sounding impressed. "Good. Um, I don't know where he is. I've kind of been avoiding him, what with how he makes my skin crawl and all."

"Jessica." I couldn't always pull off a reproachful tone, being such a disaster as a human being and a bigger disaster as a vampire queen, but this time I could. "Come on. It's not his fault. In fact, it's Ancient Betsy's fault."

"Think I don't know that? I got the whole skinny this morning. I didn't say it was his fault. But come on. I'm gonna have a baby! A tender, delicious baby no zombie could resist."

"He's not that kind of zombie," I said, exasperated. Not as long as there were dead cats around, anyway. And the *People* "Second Look" page. ("Find the differences in these two pictures!") And the *NYT* crossword.

"Girly-o, I am taking no chances. None. Now Dickie, his thinking's different, he *has* been hanging around Marc, but only to find out ways to control him or defeat him in the guise of guy talk . . . like that. Once a cop, right?"

"Don't call him Dickie. Gross."

"It's his name, shithead." She said that with total kindness. And she pulled it off every time, too. She was the one person who could always say the worst, most truthful things about me right to my face and I'd almost never get pissed. Maybe it was her superpower. That and being rich. And huge.

"Don't care, it's weird, I gotta go find Marc. Thanks again. Oh. Here, you dropped a cucumber slice." I picked it up and handed it to her, then left so I wouldn't see what she did with it.

CHAPTER
TWENTY-SEVEN

I found our friendly neighborhood zombie in the kitchen, where he was dismantling our toaster. "Don't start," he said without looking up. There were screwdrivers and other shiny things scattered all over the near counter. "It's not like you eat toast or bagels, anyway."

"Like I care what you're doing with an appliance? If you're looking for more braaaaain stimulation, how about tackling some of my laundry?"

Marc laughed, the first genuine laugh I'd heard from the guy since he went toes up in his bedroom last week. He set down the screwdriver and picked up a water glass filled with clear blue liquid. Half of it went down his throat in a few thirsty gulps, and then he picked up the tool again.

"I think you should lay off the Windex."

"This is crème de cacao, dope. My seventh. It's five o'clock somewhere, right?" He checked his watch. "Actually, it's five right now. What kind of a world am I living in when I can't get drunk after I'm raised from the dead?"

"Uh, but you've kind of had a problem in the past. With the booze." I could never figure out if he'd been an alcoholic or just a shitty drunk. Months would go by and he wouldn't touch a drop. Then he'd go on a two-day bender. Sometimes he went to AA meetings, and sometimes he didn't. I'm embarrassed to say I was always caught up in my own drama to worry about anyone else's. He was a grown man, I reasoned, and a doctor—much smarter than me! Looking out for him, taking his inventory, well . . . not my job.

I know. Pretty shitty, right?

"Not that it's any of my business," I added somewhat lamely. "Uh . . . I think. But you did have kind of a problem, right?"

"Yeah. When I was alive. I'm dead now; booze can't hurt me. Cigarettes: nope. I could inject myself with a pure strain of the AIDS virus and not even catch a head cold. And tell me this, Betsy: What's wrong with getting drunk after I've died? Huh?"

"I think you'd better lay off the Windex a lot."

"Forget it. What's up?"

"Where is everyone?"

"Well, Detective Dick, whom I've decided you should

call DeeDee, made sure I had plenty to occupy my mind this afternoon before he headed off to catch bad guys. Jessica's been careful to stay the hell away from me. Sinclair's holed up in the library, and Antonia and Garrett haven't come down from their bedroom yet."

"Good. That's perfect."

"I dunno about perfect, but you gotta admire their stamina."

"Not them, idiot! It's good no one's around." I plopped into a chair across from him. He was wearing chocolate brown scrubs today, his hair was clean but messy, and he worked steadily while we talked. "You remember you asked me to kill you?"

"It was less than fifteen hours ago. Of course I remember."

"Time for you to return the favor."

"But you never actually got around to killing m—"

"Time to return the favor!"

I told him how it was. I was sort of amazed at how quickly I could run down all the problems of my life that began after my life ended.

"Hmmm." He paused in his work and set the tool down again. "That's your plan?"

"It's all I've got so far."

"We'd better get it right."

"Yeah."

"You're really hard to kill."

"Yeah."

"The last thing we want is you crawling back from the grave."

"Gross."

"That'd be . . . just a disaster. So we have to thoroughly kill you. Decapitation or something."

"Or something," I agreed. Boy oh boy. God has the *weirdest* sense of humor. The Big Guy had some serious explaining to do. I guess the good news was, I'd be asking Him questions way sooner than I thought.

This. This is what my life was now. Getting decapitated so I could pin God down on a few issues actually sounded like a good plan.

"Funny how things work out."

"Huh?"

"Well. When you and I met, I was getting ready to jump off a tall building. Then we talked about you killing me just last night, and now you're asking me to kill you. Full circle."

"Lovely."

"What about chopping you up into bits and, I dunno, burning the body?"

"*Burning* me?" I was appalled. Stupid, but there it was. Dammit, I wanted to leave behind a good-looking corpse. One possibly without a head. "Not a chance! Forget it."

"Okay, okay. It's your grisly death, I guess."

"You're damned right it is! Look, I've given my suicide/murder a lot of thought."

"Well," he began cheerfully, "there's a first time for—"

"Shut up. I want to make myself good and dead . . . with no coming back. So I should sneak onto a construction site and blow myself up with site explosives or be dropped into the middle of the Atlantic wearing only cement boots or fall on purpose into an incinerator. No, wait, then I'm burned again . . . anyway, overkill is gonna be just right."

"This is the weirdest conversation I've ever had," he said, sounding more than cheery—downright happy, in fact.

"Glad I could bring some sunshine into your zombie existence. And listen, Sinclair can*not* know about this."

"No shit."

"Good, we're on the same page. He won't approve at all. He'll be downright tiresome about it . . . I'm gonna have to try really hard not to even think about it. Argh." I rubbed my eyes. "This is getting complicated."

"Complicated is good."

"Said the zombie," I replied dryly, and the zombie laughed and agreed with me.

CHAPTER
TWENTY-EIGHT

We'd gotten off the subject of my murder, and I was just telling Marc to keep his screwdriver away from my iPod charger when Ancient Me walked in. I was on my feet in less than a second.

"Why. Are you wearing. My clothes?"

"My clothes, too," she said.

"Oh, *hell* no!"

She crossed to the cupboard where we kept the tall glasses, grabbed one, then went to the fridge and rummaged for a carton of milk like she owned the place or something. Oh, wait . . .

Screw it. "Ever hear of asking? Bad enough you're a foul undead dictator from the World on Ice, but you don't remember your manners?"

"It's also my house," she pointed out so calmly I wanted to rip out her highlights. "I know what you're thinking, and it's a good way to get your neck broken."

"Wow," Marc said respectfully. "All we need is a tumbleweed blowing through here and it's High Noon. Or High Late Afternoon."

"I thought you left."

"I did leave. Now I'm back."

"Why?"

She sat down across from Marc, who looked alternately fretful and thrilled. "I'm waiting for you to do something. Or not do something."

"Well, at least I don't get cryptic in my decrepitude. Get lost, this is a private meeting."

"Or I could get lost," Marc offered. "If this is private vampire queen stuff. I can wreck this toaster anywhere."

"You can stay because I don't know you."

"Uh . . . what?"

"I don't know you." Ancient Betsy sounded almost bored. "You were never a zombie in my timeline. Never. You're the wild card now, Marc. I don't know how to play you."

"He's not yours to play, he's *mine*," I said sharply. Oops! "Um, I'll rephrase—"

"No need, since I agree a zillion percent," Marc said, grinning.

"Will you get lost already? This is private roommate

meeting stuff. Also, it triggers my vomit reflex just being in the same room with you."

"Do you think it's any easier for me?" she asked sharply. She'd pulled her hair back into a low bun on the back of her neck, a dreadful look for us that made us look like we were growing a tumor of hair back there, and was dressed in one of my J.Jill purple sweaters and one of my pairs of black leggings. "Do you think I enjoy being here around people who, in my time, are long dead, or worse?"

"Boo fucking hoo. How about how I feel, knowing what you—we'll do to Sinclair?"

"You think I like seeing my husband as he once was? Brave and honorable and—"

"Stop!" Marc was holding up one hand like a zombie traffic cop. "You two could take the gold and silver in the Self-absorbed Olympiad, but I'm not sure which of you would walk away with the gold. Let's agree that it's hell for both of you, okay?"

At once Ancient Me smiled, and really, it changed her face. Or her eyes. It was hard to describe . . . she seemed younger and happier all at once. It was almost as unnerving as her ice-sculpture thing. "I've missed you, Marc."

"Well, thanks, I guess. But listen, I hope you don't want any sympathy from me. I had a long talk with the Marc Thing, so I know some of the baaaaad shit you were up to. Will get up to."

"And that's why you killed yourself."

"Yeah, but it didn't take."

"Except you didn't."

"What?" we said in unison. "Could you drop the cryptic crap for five seconds?" I added.

"Don't you understand? That's why I'm here. *He's* why I'm here." She pointed at Marc. "He was never a zombie in my timeline! Not once, not for half a day or half a second. He was a vampire in my timeline, and now, in the new one, he's a zombie."

"Well . . . because of you, though, right?" Marc asked, sounding as tentative and unsure as I felt.

"Yes, but it didn't happen like that in my memories. Do you truly not understand the significance? Satan's afraid, Garrett is more cunning than he ever was in my time, shoe designers will never have been born . . ." Creaky Me paused, and a spasm of pain crossed her face . . . the first "human" thing I'd seen her do. But she made the expression go away and came back as bitchy and unpleasant as ever. "When Tweedle Dum and Tweedle Dumbass showed up in their future/my present, things started changing. Now Marc will never be a vampire. And that's *wrong*. What I did to the other you was wrong." She had now focused her full attention on Marc, who was staring at her like a deer gazing into the lights of an oncoming semi loaded with hogs. "Very wrong, and the fact that in my time you'd slaughtered indiscriminately, that you were too dangerous to let loose while too valuable to kill—"

"I really don't want to hear this," he whispered. "I got enough of it from the other guy."

"Slaughtered indiscriminately?" Whoa. Had Wrinkly Me kept Marc penned up because of something bad *he'd* done? "You know what? I don't care. It hasn't happened yet, and I'm fixing it so it won't." Somehow.

"At last we have goals in common. I persuaded the devil to take me back, and I resurrected Marc as atonement for what he had done to me and to others, and for what I had done to him. You changed things, however inadvertently. I'm changing things, too, but on purpose . . . and only as a reaction to what *you* have changed. And though I loathe telling you something so shameful and personal, I only had the courage to try because you did things when you were in my present/your future that *had not happened*. You said and did things I had no memory of doing or saying when I was"—she flapped a hand casually in my direction—"you."

"Well, great. Thanks for the road trip to the past, we've got it all under control—"

"Ha."

"So run along or drop dead again or whatever it is you do when you're not stealing my clothes and sneaking around resurrecting my friends."

"Satan is afraid of you."

"And saying stuff like *that*! Stop it, will you?" I was tempted to beg. And shoot her. Or shoot her and then beg. Or just shoot her. A lot. In the forehead. A lot.

"Don't you find that at all interesting?"

"More annoying, I bet, than interesting," Marc volunteered.

"When I was you, I didn't truly understand the breadth and width of my power. I was constantly underestimating myself. It wasn't until years later that I realized I'd been my own biggest obstacle all along."

"What a lovely story," I said with *faux* admiration. "Does it end with you coughing up blood?"

"They're tools."

"What? Are you talking about actual tools, like the screwdriver, or are you being insulting again?"

She glanced at the ceiling as if praying for help from a higher power. "Try to pay attention. Your abilities. The strength, the speed, the fast healing. Those are the tools that can save you—and him, and them—but without the skill and experience to back it up, they're tools that could get you killed. Get them killed."

"You're the tool that could get you killed." Okay . . . immature, but so satisfying. Though I could see her point. How many times had I hesitated, or not even known what to do, because I was a thirty-year-old unemployed secretary who'd never taken a martial arts class?

"Until you have the experience, you have to look to your strengths. You do have some, you know."

Marc was nodding like Ancient Betsy was making sense. "You need a Yoda! A vampire Yoda."

"I can't think of anything I need less. I really can't." Herpes flare-up? IRS audit? Both were better options than fuzzy undead Yodas cluttering up my mansion, and also my psyche.

"You aren't suggesting I become her vampire Yoda?"

"Um . . ."

"No," she and I said in perfect appalled unison.

"Don't get your fangs in a twist. It was just a thought."

"A dreadful one." She sucked down half her milk in three gulps. "Ahhh. I miss fresh milk." She looked up at us, then at Marc. "You look pretty good for a shambling zombie nearly a week dead."

"Yeah."

"Want to know why?"

"Uh . . . *yeah*."

"It's probably a trick," I warned him. "Don't trust her. Remember the Marc Thing!"

"What Marc became was as much his fault as mine," she snapped. She made another of those visible efforts to calm down. "It's because she loves you . . ." Pointing at (ulp!) me. "And she's close."

"I don't follow."

"Me, neither, and I'm supposed to be the neighborhood expert in this stuff."

"Pity the neighborhood."

"Cow!"

"Dolt."

"Ladies! C'mon. What are you talking about, Ancie— um, Elizabeth?"

She sighed, as if greatly put upon. It was all for show, though . . . she didn't have to breathe, much less let out with the long-suffering sigh. "As long as you're in general proximity with her, as long as she loves you, you'll always be freshly dead. As in seconds dead . . . maybe only half a second dead. You've noticed you can think and feel, right? You're keeping busy . . . staying occupied. So you're not decomposing. But if you were to, say, move to London, you'd start deteriorating. Always rotting, never all-the-way dead. If she ever decided you were more trouble than you're worth, however, if she no longer subconsciously values you, the rot steps up."

While Marc mulled that over, I asked, "But that poor zombie from the future . . . she was a mess." She sure had been. And Ancient Me used zombies for slave labor in the future. Raised the dead and put them to work. Sweatshops! Of zombies!

She shrugged. "Well. I didn't know that woman. I didn't care about her. Why should it matter if she's a shambling mess, as long as the work gets done?"

"And just like that, I start not liking you again," Marc said, giving her a cold stare.

Ancient Betsy took it pretty well, I figured, since she yawned in response. "As I said earlier, which I will reiterate because you have the attention span of a fruit fly, I'm waiting. I'll know when it's time to leave. Until then, you'll have to put up with me."

"Want to bet?" I snapped.

"Uh, Betsy . . . Betsys . . . this is no time for a catfight. Or a vampire queen fight. Especially since it seems like you've got some of the same goals."

"Barf."

"I suppose." She drank the rest of her milk, then studied her empty glass for a moment, and asked in a surprisingly diffident tone, "When is Jessica due?"

"Next—" Marc began.

"None of your fucking business."

My venom didn't seem to bother her at all. Of course not. She'd dealt with much worse. She usually *was* what was much worse. "She's happy, though? With that man?"

"Sure." *"That man"?*

"I didn't expect that," she said in such a low voice, I had the impression she was talking to herself more than us. "That's . . . nice. It's really nice." She looked at me again, and her eyes lost that look Sinclair had immediately noticed. For a second it was like I was looking at me, and not a shark with my face. "You've got to figure it out. You've got to fix it . . . I don't want to go back to that."

"You get that you're not the victim here, right?"

She didn't rise to it. Just looked at me with eyes exactly like mine and near whispered, "Please help me. Please help yourself." She didn't even flinch when the glass exploded between her fingers, just looked at the mess of shattered glass splinters and milk and a little bit of her sluggish vamp blood. "Damn."

"Let me take a look," Marc said, extending his hand. He'd said it with such authority that even as she let him grab her by the wrist, she looked bemused. "Huh. Not too bad. Let's get it rinsed out first."

"I'll be fine. You must know that."

"Humor the Walking Dead Doc, willya? This is the perfect way for me to keep busy. It's not like if I fuck up I could do any real damage to you."

"How comforting," she said wryly, but suffered herself to be pulled to her feet, and obediently followed him to the bathroom down the hall, the one with the first aid kit.

Then I was in the kitchen by myself, with toaster innards all over the table and a mess of glass splinters and milk.

What just happened?

CHAPTER
TWENTY-NINE

"So she managed to stop being evil for three seconds and begged you to help her?" Jessica was strolling beside me down the aisle, popping green grapes into her mouth. "Weird. Or a trick. Or a weird trick."

"Tell me," I said gloomily. "I think I like Wrinkly Me better when she's being an imperious asshat."

"Glad I was napping and missed it."

Say it twice, honey. "Yeah. I sort of wish *I'd* missed it."

"Nope. That's why you get all the queen perks." She popped another grape into her mouth. "Comes with the job."

"Oh, perks? Is that what those are?" I reached out a hand and tumbled two cans of cranberry jelly into our cart. "Perks, my luscious white butt."

"Don't make me think about your butt. No, not that kind. Get the real stuff."

I eyed the two cans rolling around with the can of sweet potatoes. "That is the real stuff."

"Cranberries are not can-shaped. *Ergo*, those aren't proper cranberries."

I thought about running her down with the cart, then reconsidered. Probably couldn't displace her mass with one measly grocery cart, anyway. "I'm hanging on by a thread here, Jess. A goddamn thread."

"Oh, here we go."

"I've gotta keep Zombie Marc occupied while Decrepit Me is slumming in her past for mysterious reasons she won't explain while you're furiously gestating, Sinclair's hiding from me so I don't accidentally skin him and then write on him, Nick keeps changing his name, I stupidly decided to host Thanksgiving, my mom's dating a guy who looks like a giant baby, and I haven't seen my brother-slash-foster son in days and don't dare let him anywhere near the mansion right now. A goddamn thread!"

"Canned cranberries are lame."

"Canned cranberries are the only thing I like about Thanksgiving." I whipped two more cans into the cart. "Canned cranberries are the only thing letting me hang on to the shreds of my so-called sanity."

"At least buy real sweet potatoes."

"Canned sweet potatoes are real, you enormous harpy!" She shook the bag of grapes, now half empty, at me. "Are you trying to make me body conscious? I'm creating life here."

"Yeah, listen, that reminds me. There's no way in heck you can be due next summer."

"Sure I can."

"Jessica. Seriously. Look at you—and I say this with love—but look at you. You're huge!"

"Maybe I got my dates mixed up." She shrugged. Gulp, gulp, and more grapes disappeared down her gullet. What the heck . . . if she didn't care, then I didn't, either. She probably did have her dates mixed up, what with all the weirdness that had been in our lives the last few years.

"This is the kind of thing we need to put on the spreadsheet."

"What the hell are you talking about?"

"Never mind, we'll talk about it later. Because right now, I've got bigger problems." I glanced at her belly. Bigger emotionally, not bigger physically, clearly . . . "Ooooh over, I gotta grab a turkey."

"Do you even know how to make a turkey?"

"God makes turkeys, not me. I know how to cook 'em, though." I'd gone through a Martha Stewart phase after I dropped out of college. Jessica (who'd been majoring in psych at the time) explained that I was trying to control my environment, since I felt so out of control after getting kicked out. I mean, dropping out.

I also knew how to make "real" cranberry sauce, but then found out the real stuff is overrated. Who wants to spend the night picking cranberry skins out of your teeth? Blurgh. A wiggly can-shaped pile of cranberry jelly was the way to go.

"Oh, come on! A Butterball?"

"It's a turkey, Jess. We need one. And here's a bunch of 'em." I pawed through the frozen carcasses. "Let's see, you're supposed to figure on a pound per person, except the dead people won't eat. So . . . um . . . Nick/Dick, and my mom, and BabyJon (but he's barely onto solid foods), and you'll eat about nine pounds, but Sinclair and Marc and Garrett and I won't, so that's . . . um . . ." Math had never been a go-to skill of mine. Did I forget to carry the 1? ". . . um . . ."

"Not a Butterball. At least get a fresh one. Or maybe kosher?"

"To get a fresh one would mean I would have decided two weeks ago to host T'giving, ordered a fresh one, and in general be an organized, responsible person. What, out of anything you've seen since we were in junior high, would suggest—"

"Right. Sorry. But Butterballs are so dry and boring."

"Turkey is dry and boring; don't blame the brand. Stop being a rich snob." Given that she *was* rich, I almost never had to say that. Jessica lived in skinny jeans (long before they were trendy, and now again after they weren't) and T-shirts. We used to share a duplex in Apple Valley, and shopped at discount grocery stores like Cub and Rainbow.

She could have bought a new Ferrari every month once she passed her driver's license exam, but stuck with fuel-efficient four-doors like Toyota Camrys and Ford Fusions. The only reason she picked the mansion was because our old house had termites, and she figured a vampire queen should have a den, a basement lair, multiple guest rooms for entertaining, and a huge attic occasionally infested with zombies.

"I'm not being a snob. I'm pretty sure. I'm just trying to be superhealthy for the baby."

"Or babies." Triplets would explain the gut. So would septuplets.

"Baby," Jessica corrected firmly.

I grabbed a 10-pound turkey and dropped it into the cart. My cart was pissing me off—one of those sneaky carts that seem fine at first, but then you find out one of the wheels sticks, so you have to pay attention or you'll run into—

"Sorry," I told the thirty-something woman steering one of those huge carts that lets the parent strap both kids into a big plastic contraption hooked up to the grocery cart. Nobody asked me, but wouldn't it be easier to just leave the rug rats in a freezing cold car while you got the holiday shopping done? "Uh, Happy Thanksgiving."

"Yeah, right," she replied with the exact right amount of tired despair. Here was a kindred spirit, between the Butterballs and the twenty-foot stuffing display. Which reminded me.

"Stove Top! Oh worse, Stove Top *Mushroom*? Come *on*, Bets. Are you trying to make this the least interesting meal ever?"

"It takes five minutes and nobody gives a shit, Jessica. This is not New England. This is Minnesota, and we've all got more important things to do than make homemade oyster stuffing with walnuts and, I dunno, Craisins."

"Oooh. Craisins! That sounds good."

I was slumped over my cart, resting my chin on the steering wheel and steering with my elbows. "The problem is, I don't have a plan. I don't even have a plan to come up with a plan. The only thing I see ahead is nothing."

"Yeah, well." She'd finished the grapes and was looking around at the various food displays. She spied a baking display and helped herself to a 24-ounce bag of chocolate chips. "That's your thing. You sort of do everything by the hair of your ass. And sometimes it even works out."

"And sometimes people die. I just can't get it together this time. I'm Maverick after Goose bit the big one at Miramar."

"A *Top Gun* reference? Seriously?"

"I've lost my wingman," I griped, struggling with the cart before it could veer and clip someone else—thank goodness for vampire strength! "And now I enjoy standing around in my tidy whities staring at my mirrored reflection as Tom Skerritt checks out my butt!"

"Oh, the humanity."

"Why can't that bitch just *tell* me? Huh? Fuck all that mysterious-visitor crap. Just *tell* me what went wrong and how to fix it."

"That bitch, Satan? That bitch, Elderly Betsy? That bitch, the Anti—"

"Elderly Betsy. In the movies they're always 'Oooh, we gotta watch out we don't make a paradox so I'm just gonna be all cryptic and unhelpful,' and then everyone's mystified when things don't work out. I should just get my hands on her, find a blowtorch or something, and get busy until she tells me how to fix everything."

"Gross."

"Yeah, but effective, maybe."

"No, gross, and also that sets you on the road to Evil Town, which I know you're trying to avoid."

"Let me have my dreams," I sighed, and she left me to my morbid, torture-filled fantasies.

CHAPTER
THIRTY

When we got back, I'd managed to put a few of my problems behind me to rave about the Lifetime Special *du jour*. Since I wasn't having sex, and since I didn't have a plan, and since there was a zombie creeping around, I was watching an unusual amount of television this month.

"Okay, so then—check this—the heroine does this—"

"But I hate Rene Russo," Jess complained while I lugged bag after bag into the kitchen. "She was the least interesting thing in *Outbreak*. The monkey was a thousand times more interesting and it didn't have to emote. And when her character got sick, okay, everyone *else* who caught it, they're all bleeding out their ears and eyes, but she just sort of gets a mild flush. That's how you knew Rene Russo had the deadly plague. They put more blush on her."

"You'll like her in this, I bet. She did this remarkable thing. The killer called her and tried to get her to meet him, *alone*, and the *only witness* to his *hideous unspeakable crime* refused to do it."

"What?"

I was unloading bags, stacking cans and frozen birds and boxes of Stove Top on the counter. "Yeah. She wouldn't take off without a word to anyone to meet with the killer at midnight in the middle of a cornfield. Unprecedented! And then, when the killer tried to reschedule, she turned him down *again*. Yes!"

"That does sound kind of cool," Jess admitted.

"This time, though, she refused to leave the safety of her living room to meet up with a shady guy in an abandoned office building by a wharf where all the streetlights had been broken out. She said no. And she lived to testify! Unprecedented! So, yeah, I wanna reward that behavior. I'm renting everything Rene Russo ever touched."

"You're watching an unusual amount of TV these days."

"My thought exactly!"

"Remember your Denzel marathon?"

"One movie isn't a marathon," I corrected her, but I did remember. It was the day after Marc had killed himself, so I'd had to watch the movie three times in a row before I could even think about trying to do anything else: Feed. Cry. Rage. Think.

* * *

"*I don't need* Dead Man Walking*; I need* Man on Fire."

"When was the last time you slept?" Jessica asked quietly.

I ignored her, sorting through the DVDs. I needed the movie, not the book. The book was almost as much of a downer as *DMW*, which didn't mean it was a bad book, just one I wouldn't read twice. And not now, of all times.

The movie version, though: totally different story. Denzel Washington's character, Creasy, thought Dakota Fanning's character had been kidnapped (she had been) and murdered (she hadn't been). So he fucked with a bunch of bad guys and blew bad guys up and cut pieces off them and shot a few of them, and then he rescued Dakota Fanning and she got to go home to her mom. Yes, definitely a time to take *MoF* to heart as opposed to thinking about Sean Penn getting the needle while his nun friend watched helplessly and prayed and cried. "Where is the fucking thing? It was right here last week when Marc was teasing me about—about something else. Where the hell is it?"

"It's—it's here. See? You buried it by accident while you were looking."

"At least that's not a metaphor for anything awful," I muttered. "Are you gonna watch with me?"

"Betsy," my friend said, with an expression on her face

that meant she was picking her words with care, "Creasy died at the end. He saved the girl . . . and died."

I met her look. "So?"

She had nothing to say to that.

I guess I didn't, either.

"You should be glad I'm catching up on all the movies I never watch, what with dying and all."

"I'm kind of glad," Jess admitted so diffidently I had to smile.

"Movies? Cable television? Really? That's your priority at this time?"

Didn't even have to look. I just shoved cans into random cupboards. "Get bent, Wretched Me."

"For God's sake." Hmm. Nice to see Evil Old Me could still break the third commandment. Wait. Fifth? "I sent Marc back to help you."

"Some help!" I whipped around and glared. "He slunk around and giggled and freaked everybody out and scared our Marc into killing himself. And stop wearing my clothes!"

"Oh my God." Jessica was all big eyes and open mouth. "I'm seeing it and I don't believe it."

"Oh. Yes. Hello." Rude Elderly Me tipped a shallow nod in my (our) best friend's direction. "You're looking round."

I gripped the one can of cranberry jelly I hadn't put away. Right between the eyes . . . that ought to put a dent in her day. Not to mention her skull. "You watch how you talk to her, you clothes-grubbing harlot."

"I am here to—never mind why I'm here."

"See?" I said to Jessica, triumphant.

"Yeah, the coy thing is definitely annoying," my beloved brilliant best friend agreed.

"It's not only your turn to pull the freight, it's your damned job. What do you want me to do, tattoo instructions on your forehead?"

"You can't talk to you like that," Jessica scolded.

"You hear but you don't listen. You look but you don't see."

"I fart but don't stink. I shampoo but don't condition. What are you doing here? What am *I* doing here, you horrible decrepit thing?"

"Whoa," Marc said, shambling in. Okay, maybe not shambling. He walked pretty much like he had in life. I had to work on letting go of my zombie stereotyping. I'd hated the term *politically correct* long before it was trendy, but I had to get over that, too.

He didn't shamble, he didn't moan "Braaaaaains" while clutching at terrified roommates, he didn't stare vacantly (except when he was watching Drogo's scenes in *Game of Thrones*, but he'd done that in life, too) or hungrily (see above: only with *Game of Thrones*). He didn't do any of that stuff. He was a zombie, but he was still Marc. He was still my friend, and I was still his. As someone who resented being painted as a soulless bloodsucking dictator with a silly hard-on for good shoes (*it wasn't silly!*), you'd think I'd catch on to that stuff a little quicker.

He wasn't a terrifying *Pet Sematary* zombie . . . he didn't come back with demonic baggage. (And I'd thought toddlers were scary before I saw Gage Creed return from the grave.) He wasn't lurch-ey or clumsy; Ancient Me apparently knew her shit when it came to raising the dead—and keeping the dead.

At worst, he could be a speedy zombie. My God! I had hated the *Dawn of the Dead* remake zombies . . . they could run people down like a jaguar after a gazelle! I'd been so, so happy when movies and the TNT network went back to classic, shambling zombies.

"I forgot how much milling around we all did in the past," Ancient Me said, holding her head like she was getting a migraine. "All milling, no action. Until we were pushed to the wall. And then it was often too late."

"Okay, that was almost helpful." I could feel myself perking up. "If you could elaborate just a teensy bit . . ."

Before she could, a wild-eyed Nickie/Dickie/Tavvi burst through the kitchen door. "You didn't answer my texts!" he cried.

"What texts?" Jessica fished her phone out of her purse, then looked up with a grimace. "Sorry, Dickie."

"Ugh," I muttered.

"Sorry, *Dickie*, but I didn't know my phone was off." She stuck her tongue out at me. "It's his name. Suck it up."

"So you're okay?" He crossed the room and wrapped his arms around her. As much as he could, anyway. I had to applaud his heroic effort. "Jeez, don't do that. I was shitting bricks."

"Gross," Marc commented.

"Aw, it's cute," I teased. "In a nauseating overprotective and creepy way."

"And you!" The Artist Formerly Known as Nick let go of Jessica's "waist" and whipped around. "This is more or less your fault."

"Well, you're probably right," I admitted, "but I'm not sure why. Or what I can—"

"*He's* a zombie." Pointing to Marc, who shrugged, embarrassed. "Which is why *she's* here." Pointing to Ancient Me, who had never looked less interested in a person or what they were saying. "And now Satan is a pop-in guest? Fucking *Satan*?"

"She's never a guest! I only summoned her once; she almost always shows up on her own. Satan's the worst."

"And *he* might be skinned. By you!" Nick/Dick looked around the room in confusion before realizing Sinclair wasn't actually in the room. Now that was a frazzled cop. "And Antonia's back from hell, but your stepmother is still dead and in hell."

"Okay, those aren't entirely my fault," I began.

"In our home! Jesus Christ, Betsy, we're trying to have a baby here!"

"We?" *Don't look at his groin. Don't look at his groin. Don't mention that he doesn't have a vagina, so "we" is bullshit. This is not the time to mention your pet peeve about expectant fathers talking how "we" are having a baby. Don't. Don't.* "Um, sorry?"

"You're always sorry, Betsy, but things just keep getting weirder, don't they?"

"Huh." Ancient Betsy was staring thoughtfully at Dickie/ Nickie. "A backbone in both timelines. Interesting."

"*You* shut up."

"And a moron in both timelines," Ancient Me decided.

"This is on you," he said, pointing to (ulp!) me. "It all comes back to you. It always comes back to you."

"I'm pretty sure I'm the vic—"

"You were always going to go your own way."

"Maybe not always . . ."

He was in no mood to be coerced or distracted. Just held himself stiffly and stared at me with a gaze so fierce it nearly scorched me. "You were always going to fix things the way you liked them and to hell with the consequences."

"If you think *this* is how I like it, you're deranged."

"That's why you put it all off."

"Put what off?" I cried. To my annoyance, no one in the room seemed inclined to tiptoe out and leave Dick and me to thrash this out in privacy.

"Burying Marc!"

"Do not drag me into this," Zombie Marc began, but Dick/Nick was not about to be derailed.

"Classic Betsy: stall until something weirder happens, then do your own thing while we're looking the wrong way. You knew you were going to do something and you knew we wouldn't like it."

"Yeah, because that's how brilliant I secretly am. I'm so diabolical I planned for Marc to kill *himself* in November in Minnesota so his coffin wouldn't get sunk six feet and I could get my other self from a timeline I didn't intend to create to bring him back to life," I snapped. If only I *were* that diabolical a planner . . .

"You knew you were gonna do something."

Then I had my "you can't handle the truth" moment: "Okay, yeah. I was, and I knew you wouldn't be able to wrap your head around it. So I promised myself and Sinclair—"

"Sinclair!" he echoed, throwing his arms up like an NFL referee. *And . . . it's goooooooood! The Packers win the Super Bowl!* "Big part of the problem!"

"Don't start, Nick/Dick! I don't bust your balls because

of who you sleep with, and I expect the same goddamn courtesy."

"How many times? It's *Dick*. You're talking about courtesy and you haven't bothered to learn my fucking name."

Ow! He got me. Ignore it. Go for the throat! "So, yeah, I was always going to help Marc, and I was always not going to give a shit if you liked it or not." I managed to stop before, "So what're you gonna do about it, crybaby?"—but it was a near thing.

"My child will live in this house," he said. He sounded like he always did, but his eyes were slits of blue ice. I became morbidly aware of his badge, clipped to his belt, and his gun, which I knew was loaded. "Can you comprehend that, Betsy?"

"I'd never let anything happen to The Baby That Ate the World," I said, shocked. "The fact that you could even raise that as a concern makes me want to shove your teeth all the way down into your testicles."

"See? That's the sort of thing that makes it hard to like you."

"I'm very easy to like, shithead, you just gotta get your thumb out of your ass and see that!" Somehow we'd ended up nose to nose. In our kitchen. And despite accidentally making a timeline where he didn't hate me, he looked ready to draw down on me—and I was willing to bet he was pretty good with that gun in this timeline, too.

So there we were, ready to throw down in the middle of our grimy kitchen tile. With a rapidly thawing Butterball turkey as silent witness to the pre-Thanksgiving fight. Oh, and a bunch of our friends standing around trying not to look at either of us.

"Um . . . hi?"

And the Antichrist.

"This looks almost interesting."

And Satan.

"Neh? Buh?"

And BabyJon.

"Surprise! Guess who wanted to see his big sister!"

And my mom.

CHAPTER
THIRTY-ONE

"No. No." I tried to think of something to add to that. "Oh no. No."

My mom's smile sort of fell off her face when she got a good look at who was in the kitchen. "Ah," she began, not a little worried to see a police detective looking like he wanted to shoot her daughter in the face (and that just for starters). Then she noticed the zombie. "Ah? Marc? Betsy told me you were . . . ah . . ."

"I got better," he replied, the soul of politeness.

"And . . . Laura, hello."

"Hi, Mrs. Taylor," the Antichrist mumbled, taking a second from glaring at the devil to stare at the floor.

"And Jessica, you're looking . . . very, very healthy."

"Hi, Miz Taylor. We're, um, sort of in the middle of . . . uh . . . something?" She looked at me for help, but I was sort of frozen with the sheer horror of the moment.

My mom knew I was a vampire, but I hadn't had the time (or inclination, to be brutally blunt) to bring her up to speed on Satan, Zombie Marc . . . oh, all sorts of things. She knew I'd accidentally FUBARed the timeline, but didn't know many gory details beyond that. And I had *never* told her about Ancient Me, or the wretched future awaiting humanity. But I'd probably have to bring her up to speed right now, since there were two Betsy Taylors less than ten feet apart . . .

"Meh!" BabyJon was perched comfortably on Mom's hip, drooling and content, and reached chubby arms out to both Betsys. (That was a sentence I didn't think I'd ever have to say or write or think. Both Betsys? Why not just say both Michele Bachmanns? Both Kanye Wests?) "Beh? Muh! Geh-neh. Muh!"

"I'm confused," my mother said, looking from me to Ancient Me and back to me. "I'm sure there's some sort of supernatural/paranormal explanation, though. Which one of you do I need to scold for not returning my calls yesterday?"

Busted. I raised my hand. Ancient Me was, if anything, more shocked into immobility than I was. She just stared at my/our mom with eyes that got bigger and bigger.

Yet again the kitchen door swung open (I was so rattled,

I could barely concentrate on what was happening in the room, never mind also listen for footsteps) and Tina was framed, wild-eyed, in the doorway. Since she'd probably been reloading shells in the basement, she'd really flown up all those stairs. "Dr. Taylor, Her Majesty is very busy so please come with me right now I'm sorry she can't see you right—dammit."

"Nice try," I said, because it was. And I was doubly glad for the effort, because Jessica, Marc, and Dickie all got the giggles. "However this shakes out, I'm probably in huge trouble, but I appreciate the effort, Tina."

"Huge trouble," my mother agreed, managing to smile graciously at Tina and frown sternly at me with the same expression. Someone who didn't know her would worry she was having a stroke. "But I do see you're busy, and I shouldn't have just dropped by with the baby."

"He's my baby, Mom, of course you should have. I'm just sorry I can't take him back just now."

"Clearly not." She was trying to look at everyone in the room all at once. "I think that would be a very bad idea. But later, when you've taken care of business, you can plan on sitting down with your old mom—"

"You're not old." I smiled at her, my mother, whose fierce intellect was matched only by her diabolical sense of humor. My mother, who'd started going prematurely gray in high school but always looked good. "You'll never be old."

"—and telling me the whole odd story. Flatterer. But until then, I—yeee!"

She'd said "yeee!" because Ancient Me had crossed the room in half a blink, had flung herself at my/our mother and my/our son, and was holding them in a pretty firm clutch while muttering into her hair, "I'm sorry. I'm sorry. I'm so, so sorry, Mom. Please. I'm so sorry for what happened to you."

"I, uh, don't know where to look," Marc whispered.

"I'm not sure there's anywhere we *can* look," Jessica whispered back.

"Let go of her! Get your fucking hands off my mother!"

I'd started forward, only to be frozen by my mother's sharp, "Elizabeth Taylor!"

"Sorry, Mom—I told you to let go!"

Ancient Me looked up from embracing Mom. "Don't talk like that in front of her!"

"This . . . is . . . so . . . splendid," Satan sighed.

In evil, horrific unison: *"You shut up!"*

"Elizabeth! Elizabeths, I mean." Mom looked surprised at what she had just said, but rallied. "Ah, both of you, stop it. Grown women—"

"You don't know how grown," I tattled, pointing at Ancient Me.

"At least I'm an adult," Ancient Me fired back.

"And acting like children. Stop it at once. Think of the baby!"

"Meh," the baby added, swinging fat feet stuffed into tiny navy blue socks.

"Now, er, you two behave. Ah . . . do I know you, ma'am?"

"No," the devil replied. "But I know you, Dr. Taylor."

"Oh. You look familiar . . . there now, hon." Distracted (and who could blame her?), she patted Decrepit Me on the shoulder. "It's all right. Whatever happened, I know you did your best."

"I did," Ancient Me replied with an earnestness that would have been touching if she wasn't so gross and ancient and evil and wearing stolen clothes. "Only it wasn't good enough. And nothing seemed to go right after that." She glanced at Marc. "Not one thing."

"Irrelevant, if you gave it your best shot."

"I disagree, Mom."

"We'll talk about it another time."

"There is no other time." Was that . . . ah, man . . . did Decrepit Me's lower lip actually tremble? Oh my God, if that wicked bitch started to cry, I was going to lunge for Nick's gun. I wasn't sure who I'd shoot, but just getting my hands on a weapon sounded like a good idea. "There never was."

"Then you'd best work on the things you can actually fix, don't you think?"

Old Me bit her lip, then nodded.

Marc's hand shot up, like the kid in Algebra who wanted to know when the next pop quiz was. "Question?"

"She won't tell you," I said, shaking my head. "Whatever it is. She won't. She's gotta be all cryptic to protect the timeline that's already been hosed."

"Well, I do," Ancient Me said, having the audacity to sound hurt.

"Dr. Taylor, please allow me . . ." Tina stepped forward and relieved Mom of the diaper bag. "I'll be happy to show you to your car—"

"I know the way to my car, Tina," she replied, exasperated.

"So sorry Her Majesties can't assist you themselves at this time, but her—their—schedules are sure to clear up very soon."

"That's a lie," my mother said, smiling, but allowing Tina to herd her out, "and you know it."

"Don't forget, our house, Thanksgiving dinner, Thursday," I called after her.

"How could I? You hate—" And then the door mercifully swung shut.

I buried my head in my hands. "Jesus Christ."

"Say it twice," Ancient Me muttered. I bit my lip, hard, so I wouldn't laugh.

I much preferred loathing her to liking her. And I sure as shit did *not* want to feel sorry for her.

So how come I did?

Dammit.

CHAPTER
THIRTY-TWO

"I should pop by more often," the devil decided. *"That was fun."*

"Why *are* you here?" I asked, going from relieved to pissed. "Lose a bet?"

"Oh, just keeping an eye on things."

"You can't watch us on your plasma screen in hell?"

Satan shrugged. She was wearing a black suit this time— she didn't wear red anymore. She had told Laura it was beyond clichéd. "Next you'll want to see the pitchfork," was how she had put it. Hey, nothing wrong with the classics.

"It's not as much fun not being there when it hits the fan," Ancient Me pointed out.

Satan quit smirking and looked like someone had jammed a lemon through her teeth. "Touchier than usual, darling? Careful. Someone might think your faith has been shaken."

"*My* faith has never been an issue."

"What are we talking about?" Marc wondered aloud. "I'm having a little trouble keeping up with the cast of characters. Is there a reason why both Betsys and the devil and the Antichrist and Jessica and her belly—"

"Faith isn't anybody's issue," I said, exasperated. "We all know there's a God, we just can't be sure He's not on permanent vacation."

"Hold up," Nick/Dick said. "It's not that simple."

This time we all heard the footsteps. Someone in a hurry, not bothering to be quiet. I was almost afraid to see who was about to join the madness.

The door swung in. Antonia peeked in. "What the hell's going on in here?"

"We're having a debate," Satan said helpfully. "About—"

"Don't care." The door swung shut. The footsteps went the other way.

"I never thanked you for taking her off my hands," Satan commented.

"I *knew* you agreed too quickly."

"Yeah, great, listen—getting back to what we were talking about, I don't remember seeing a white light," Marc protested. "So we don't *know* there's a—"

"Oh, of course we do," I snapped.

This was a bad idea. A very bad idea. I knew better. We *all* knew better. We'd all been in chat rooms. Debates over religion were a baaaad plan. Next we could start chatting about abortion. And then politics . . . that'd go *great*. "We know there's a devil, right?"

"Here!" Satan said brightly, raising her hand.

"*Ergo* . . . right?"

"Huh. Well. I guess . . . but it seems like a cop-out." Marc was looking from Laura to Satan and back to Laura. "Knowing. You know?"

"It's worse than that."

"How can it be worse?" Nick had started making himself useful by putting away the rest of the groceries. Jessica had produced the sadly depleted bag of chocolate chips and started munching by the handful. "This thing people have had wars over. Slaughtered entire civilizations over . . . you just know. Kind of cool, maybe."

I shook my head. "You think it's easier, not just having faith in God but proof of God?" This time I did hear footsteps, and knew my husband was just outside the door. Tina must have given him a heads-up. "Not only do I *know* there's a God and a devil, I know *He* knows little kids starve to death and get raped. He knows there are suicide bombers and leukemia and plague. Shit, if you believe the Bible, He's *sent* plague."

"Okay . . ." Dick still looked doubtful, but I noticed

Marc was paying close attention. Made sense . . . he'd died, and by his own admission, there had been no white light. So what did that mean for him? For any of us?

Sinclair silently stepped into the room and nodded at me. I wasn't sure what that meant . . . he was still keeping his thoughts to himself. Smart man.

"God exists, and He's got a little explaining to do." Rattled by my husband's appearance, I tried to gather my thoughts. "I—I don't mean to rain on your parade, but I think in a lot of ways, it's worse to *know*. 'God works in mysterious ways'? More like, God's a dangerous lunatic and needs to be stopped."

"I didn't think of it like that." And Marc sounded like he hadn't wanted to think of it like that.

"Sorry," was all I could think of to add.

Satan was smiling at me. *Brrrr.* "So you're a dystheist."

"Yep. That's me all over." I wasn't gonna ask. I wasn't gonna ask. I wasn't—

"You think God exists, but isn't all good."

"Yes! Holy cow, I *am* a dys . . . dis . . . what you said I was. That's me all over: God's an omnipotent entity that is *so* powerful yet disliked, like the DMV."

"I'm not saying this isn't interesting," Jessica began, sitting down and sighing with audible relief once she was off her feet, "but maybe we could make some sandwiches or something while we crush each other's deeply held beliefs?"

"Interesting that you should feel that way about God, when you're the one running around mucking up the time-line." The devil made this observation in a perfectly pleasant tone of voice.

"Well . . . I . . . um . . ." Damn. She had me there. Stupid impressive-looking black Donna Karan suit.

"He has an entire universe to look after. You only need tend to the needs of the undead."

"And it's ridiculous that I should have to do that," I added. At their stares and raised eyebrows I added, "What? I've always maintained it's ridiculous that a thirty-year-old unemployed office worker has to be the boss of a bunch of ancient vampires, all old enough to be their own mommies."

"You're wrong," Ancient Me said. She'd poured herself another glass of milk . . . hope she was a little more careful with that one. "They need a leader . . . a good one, not another Nostro. Otherwise . . ." She shrugged and took a sip.

"Seriously? You guys?" Jessica wriggled in the wooden kitchen chair. "We're really gonna keep debating about God and the universe and vampire bosses and stuff? What are we, freshmen in college?"

"Otherwise what?" Sinclair asked Ancient Me.

"Otherwise the future," she replied, and took another sip. I had the distinct impression she was rattled to be talking to him.

She is, my own.

Ah-ha! There he was.

"The bottom line is, you had no business to be screwing with the timeline." Unfortunately, she wasn't at all rattled to be talking to me. "Either of you." She nodded at Laura.

"Hey, I'm with you! I'm with you, for once, a hundred percent." I turned to address the group—and what a group!—as a whole. "You guys. Haven't I been saying it all along? Isn't it just the most fundamental thing you've ever heard? I, Elizabeth Taylor—"

"Oooh, she's calling herself by her full name and also referring to herself in the third person." Jessica looked at once interested and terrified. "Brace yourself. This will not be cool."

"—should not be the boss of you! Any of you! I have never, *ever* refuted that."

"You've also never accepted it. Instead of hiding from your—"

"If you say 'destiny' like we're stuck in some lame made-for-TV sci-fi geektacular miniseries, I won't be responsible for what I do to your face."

"—responsibilities, you should embrace them. You don't want to rule? Boo fucking hoo. You're the queen. You don't want the timeline to be changed? Tough nuts; it is, so you'll have to deal with it. Not talk about it. Not bitch about it. Not wish it hadn't happened. Deal with it *now*. You want other people to police themselves? If we could do that, every cop on the planet would be out of work . . . would have *been* out of work for centuries. We needed cops a thousand years ago and we need them now and we'll need them five hundred years from now and a thousand years from now. And do any of you know why?"

Satan raised her hand. Luckily, Ancient Lecturing Me ignored her. "Because as a species, we are not toilet trained! Betsy: either you are, or you aren't."

"Toilet trained?"

"In charge. So: yes or no? Are you, or aren't you? That's it." She finished her milk and set down the glass. She stood. "That's all there is."

And walked out.

"Maybe a ham sandwich?" Jessica asked. "Or an omelet? Who wants eggs?"

No one wanted eggs.

CHAPTER
THIRTY-THREE

"The second least annoying person has left," Satan informed us, "so I will, too. Remember what we discussed." And she blinked right out of sight.

"I hope she was talking to *you*," I said to Laura.

Marc stared, then shook his head. Nick actually rubbed his eyes like it hurt to see someone teleport out of his kitchen. "I'm never gonna get used to that," he said, still rubbing. "Satan in our kitchen. And religious debates."

"I hope not, because what does it say about us if this is just an ordinary day?"

"An ordinary day sounds good, babe." Nick bent and kissed Jess on the lips twice: *Smek! Smek!* "Let's have one soon. I gotta crash." He yawned. "Gotta go interview a bunch more witnesses later . . . there's nonparanormal crime going on once in a while . . ." He left the kitchen, half talking to himself.

"You know, the old Nick would have shot me after that argument about me always planning to help Marc," I commented.

"That *was* the old Nick," Jessica said. "It's like Old You said . . . the timeline's changed. This is how things are. Suck it up."

"Do *not* take her side."

"I'm not, but I know good advice when I hear it."

"Do not! Maybe. Look, I can't deal with that now . . . Laura? Why were you and the devil even hanging out, anyway? Why'd you both show up here?"

"She was showing me more of hell. And then I . . . wanted to see you."

I nearly swallowed my tongue in sympathy-gagging. "Sorry. That sounds like the opposite of a fun evening."

"It's actually quite fascinating."

"Touring hell."

"Yes."

"Fascinating."

"Yes."

"Have you—" *Lost your damned mind? Gone rabid? OD'd on Green Tea Frappes at Starbucks?* My brain got too crowded, so my tongue was sort of hung up for a moment. Which was when Sinclair came up behind me and rubbed my shoulders.

Softly, softly, my own.

She's losing it! I don't have time for the Antichrist to get all nostalgic and go to hell for Mommy and Me classes!

Laughter in my head, followed by more, *That is the opposite of softly, softly.*

Well. At least he wasn't hiding from me anymore.

I was not hiding. I was researching.

I had a rare moment of maturity and let that one pass. "Why'd you want to see me?"

"I talked to my folks, my adopted folks, and they're fine if I bow out of Meals on Wheels early to have Thanksgiving here. And then I ran into your mom—"

"My mom!" I groaned and resisted the urge to slap my own forehead. "My mom walked in on the middle of all that weirdness!"

"She did really good, though."

"Laura, you're an angel—"

"Half angel," she corrected, smiling.

"—but you can't make me feel better about that."

"It could have been worse."

"How, Jess?"

"Could've been your dad."

"Oooh." Good point. My dad, when he'd been alive, had not handled confrontations, the paranormal, family fights, or changes to the tax code at all well. I'd explained to him that I had come back from the dead as a vampire, the same thing I'd told my mother, and he reacted to that by hiding from me until he died in a stupid car vs. garbage truck accident. "Really good point." It was stupid, but I could feel myself cheer up.

"You will explain to your mother at the right time. She is a woman of rare intelligence and understanding."

"Suck-up." Sinclair loved his mother-in-law. And she thought he was pretty neat-o, too. God help me should I succeed in skinning him; my mom wouldn't stand for it.

"Indeed. Which is why *you* will explain. I will be elsewhere. With all respect to your mother, I am certain it hasn't escaped your notice that she is, on occasion, capable of Olympian levels of stubbornness."

"Yeah . . ."

"And temper."

"Yeah."

"Suffice it to say, those qualities did not skip a generation."

"What's *that*—"

"So it's best you two sort this out yourselves. Meanwhile . . ." Turning courteously to Laura. "How was hell?"

"Besides all burning lakes of fire and stuff," Jess added, then yawned. "And give us the CliffsNotes version . . . I'm overdue for my nap."

"Yeah, she's only had three today," Marc teased. He got to his feet and ambled over to the sink, where several glasses were clean and gleaming in the dish drainer, and the blender was set up and ready to go. "You guys . . ."

"Yeah," several of us said. Taking it as a matter of course, Marc was already digging bags of frozen berries out of the freezer. Would he fix one for himself? He didn't have to eat or drink anymore. I didn't need to drink smoothies, but I still liked how they tasted. I'd have to get him alone later, find out what was up with zombie taste buds.

"I thought of this earlier, but you weren't around." I turned to my sister. "So, tell me if this is right. If Lucifer Corningware—"

"Morningstar," Laura corrected, and the corner of her mouth twitched.

"Right, sorry—I flunked Sunday school."

"You never went to Sunday school."

"Did, too! I'm pretty sure . . . can we please stay on point? So as I was saying before the Antichrist butted in for the zillionth time—"

"Oh, boy," the Antichrist said.

"—if Lucifer is God's direct creation—she calls Him Father, right? She's always bitching about her Father—okay, that means Lucy was one of the first things God even made, right? Maybe even before Adam and Eve?"

"Yesssss," Laura said cautiously, not sure where I was going.

"Then that means . . . God . . . is your grandpa!"

"Lame," Marc said.

"He is your kin, but I am your Father," Laura murmured. At my stare, she said, "It's a line from *The Stand.*"

"Great. If, while we're saving Sinclair and the future and me—though I think I can cross saving Marc off my list now—and we need someone to come up with random Stephen King quotes, I'll get in touch with you immediately. In the meantime, let's focus, people! No, Marc, no more bananas! Please, I'm begging you, just keep it simple. Strawberries. Pleeeeeeeese. The queen of all vamps is begging you, only strawberries!"

"Only if you cross me off your list in pencil, not pen. I might still need saving in the future."

"Slave driver," I muttered.

"That's why your mom shows you stuff down there, right?" Jess asked. "If hell is 'down there.'"

"It's another dimension," Laura began.

"Never mind hell." I knew it was rude, but didn't care. Talking about hell when Laura was ambivalent about the worst place in existence made me nervous. And I had enough things making me nervous this month. "I'm just glad you're out of there."

"But not for long, right?" Jess asked, heartlessly scaring the shit out of me. "Because you're sort of the heir apparent, right, Laura?"

"No she isn't."

"My queen," Sinclair began with great care.

"She isn't."

"Betsy." She was gazing at me with those incredible blue eyes, radiating pure calm, and I was still scared half to death. "You know I am. I'm the only one in the universe who could even think of taking my mother's job."

"It's not the dumbest idea in the world," my traitorous whore of a best friend said.

"It's absolutely the dumbest idea in the world!" I nearly shrieked. "Have you lost your mind? Laura has spent her entire life *not* following in her mother's hoofsteps!"

"Heh," Marc said. "Hoofsteps." Then he pressed Liquefy. He often did that if he thought the argument *du jour* was getting too heated. But nobody had trouble hearing my screams over the buzz-saw blender.

"She spent her life loathing what her mother stands for! She's not the Antichrist, she's the *Anti*-Antichrist!"

"O-*kay*," Jessica said, rubbing her left ear. "Re*lax*."

"I'll relax when you stop calmly explaining why it's so logical for Laura to take over hell, you traitorous whore!"

"Now you're just being mean," she reproached. "You wait until I tell your mom how you talk to pregnant women."

"Not all of 'em. Just you. And don't you dare go telling my mom." I thought I'd been scared three minutes ago? Nothing compared to the thought of enduring a lecture on etiquette from the terrifying relentless Dr. Taylor, who was fairly unphased to run into two of me, but plenty pissed when I lost my temper and acted like a brat.

Brrrr!

"Betsy, come on." Laura was trying to sound reasonable. And maybe she did sound reasonable. But I had no interest in what the Antichrist thought was reasonable. The devil was the devil. Laura was . . . was Laura. My little sister. A good person (when she wasn't executing rogue vamps or serial killers, or trying to kill me in a fit of rage. Hey, nobody was perfect.). *Not* destined to run hell. "My mother hasn't had a day off ever. She's never had a vacation ever."

"So tell her to register a grievance with the union." I was utterly unable to summon even the teensiest amount of pity or empathy for the devil. Y'know . . . because she was *the devil*.

"You're making jokes—"

"Not really."

"—but there's no one for her to turn to. Don't you get it? There's no one else. No one but me."

"Uh, no." I didn't like where this was going. At all. And Sinclair had gone dead quiet in my brain again. His face had all the expression of an Easter Island statue.

"Even if I hated her—"

"You do hate her!"

"—I don't know that I could abandon her once I realized

why I was here," she continued. "D'you know I'm one of the few people who actually knows the answer to the eternal question—"

Do you want fries with that?

"—why am I here?"

"Listen to me, Laura. Very carefully. Okay? Watch my lips: you are not the temp worker of the damned."

"More jokes," she sighed.

"I am absolutely not joking!"

"C'mon, guys. Ease up." Marc was shoving small juice glasses oozing with smoothies at all of us. "Have a drink. We're just shooting the shit, nobody's taking over hell right this second."

"Or ever."

"Right this second," he said again, in case I hadn't heard him two seconds ago. "Besides, Betsy, I think you might be projecting."

"Oh, really, Dr. Zombie?"

"And when you think you're cornered, or wrong, you lash out and say mean things," he added, looking pretty pious for a fucking *zombie*.

"Shut up, you reject from a George Romero wet dream."

"Elizabeth."

"And you can shut up, too," I added, knowing I was acting like a brat, a bitch, and helpless to stop. Or maybe I didn't want to stop. Hurting my friends' feelings sometimes seemed worth it if I didn't have to ponder the truly awful, things like—

"I think you resist Laura maybe taking over hell because you see it as her destiny, just like yours is to rule the vampire nation and maybe even take care of humanity, too, after some awful disaster in the future blots out the sun." Marc watched me and, when I didn't leap at him and rip off his face and stuff it down his pants, took a breath (he didn't need to breathe but . . . old habits) and added, "Maybe if Laura can refuse her destiny, the thing she's expected to do, maybe you can, too. Maybe this whole big mess in the future . . . maybe it can be somebody else's problem." Then he shut his eyes with a grimace. "Be gentle. I've got no idea how long it'll take me to grow my nose back."

"Maybe it *could* be somebody else's problem," I said in a watery voice, then downed my smoothie in a monster gulp and abruptly sat down. Vampires weren't prone to brain freeze, but at least it stopped me from bursting into tears like a six-foot blond baby. "And don't judge me, okay?"

"I'm not judging you," he soothed. He came around to my side of the table and rested his clammy zombie hands on my shoulders. "I'm just calling into question every moral and legal decision you've made in the last few years."

"That's exactly judging me!" I said, indignant, and Jessica laughed so hard she dribbled smoothie down her chin and onto her hot pink T-shirt.

"You shush," I told her, but she cheerfully disobeyed and kept yukking it up and dripping everywhere. I finally got up and handed her about eighty napkins before she ruined her pants, too.

CHAPTER
THIRTY-FOUR

We'd finished our smoothies and most of the tension was gone when Sinclair decided to ruin everything and bring up bad shit again.

"My own, why do you insist on behaving as if you do not have the skills to rule us?"

"Um . . . because I don't?" Sinclair was usually smarter than this. And nakeder than this. Wait. That wasn't right. I really, really needed to have sex with him soon. This was getting ridiculous. Almost a week! Cripes.

"No, he's right. Your track record's not that bad," Jessica said, probably thinking she was soothing me.

"My track record blows."

"Nuh-uh."

"Yuh-huh."

"You did only set that poor kid's ghost free after how many decades?"

I remembered the kid. God, she'd scared the shit out of me. I hadn't known until then I could see the dead . . . the real dead, ghosts, not just vampires. I'd been terrified of her. And the kid . . . she'd just been sad.

"And then you got rid of a serial killer—"

"Laura did that," I objected. "I was the one cowering in the corner with the last victim. Believe me, we were both trying to figure out where it all went wrong in our lives. Laura's the one who swung into action." And then some. I'd nearly thrown up when I saw what she'd left of him. Oh, sure, a serial killer, he had it coming, right?

Nobody had that coming.

"—and you figured out that evil old librarian had kid-napped Sinclair—"

"Okay, that I will take credit for," I admitted. "I did eventually realize in between my search for the perfect wedding dress who had stolen my king, and after finding a caterer, I got around to killing her eventually."

"For which I was grateful, my queen." He said it with a straight face, but I could sense the smile lurking beneath. I gave him a later-for-you look.

"So one cool thing among dozens of incompetent fuckups."

"And you didn't let the werewolves kill all of us when

Antonia died. The Werewolf Antonia," Jessica added because, stop me if you've heard this, there were *two* hellbound Antonias in my life. "In fact, the WIC kind of liked you. Werewolf in Charge," she added before Marc could ask. "And then you got the devil to let Antonia be alive again!"

Well. Yeah.

"See?"

Maybe.

"Don't forget, pretty much the first thing you did was kill that Nostro creep . . . how bad was that guy? And you killed him and took over."

"It was a little more complicated than that," I said, "and I wasn't alone, Sinclair and Tina—"

"And you totally saved Garrett."

"Well, yeah—"

"And you saved Dickie's life that time when all those witches were gonna—"

"Um, I didn't." Witches? I'd never met a witch in my life, except my stepmother. "Look, guys, I appreciate what you're doing, but all you've proven is that I should seek psychiatric help, not that I should be running the joint. By which I mean the world, eventually."

"And you tried to save the other Fiends after you saved Garrett. It wasn't your fault they—"

"Were disgusted with my lame leadership and turned on me in rightful fury?"

"Well, you found out your sister was the Antichrist," the Antichrist reminded me. "And you took that pretty well."

If memory served, I'd had a giant tantrum when I found out she was two inches taller and ten times more beautiful than I was, but what the heck. They were trying to be nice. It wasn't their fault they were completely totally utterly wrong when they thought I sometimes maybe knew what I was doing.

"I think we should get out of this kitchen," Jessica announced. "Am I the only one who feels like we've been in here half a day?"

"You have to admit, it's pretty interesting."

"Nope. I don't."

Laura shrugged. "Okay, but there's just one other thing I want to get cleared up . . ."

"Aw, shit!" Jessica sat up straight and put a hand on her belly, looking puzzled. "What was that?"

"Gas? You've eaten . . . um . . . everything, I think." Multiple smoothies on top of the chocolate chips on top of the grapes on top of the Peanut Buster Parfait on top of the Filet-O-Fish on top of the Cinnabon *with* extra frosting.

"I don't think it's gas . . ." She rubbed her stomach and frowned.

"It's absolutely gas. You said yourself you're not due until next summer."

"I thought you were due next month," Marc commented.

"It depends on where I am," Jessica explained, like that would make sense to any of us. She must have been getting light-headed from, I dunno, not enough carbs? Too many carbs?

"Owwwww! Guys, I think . . . I think I might be in labor."

"No you're not. You are not! This is not a wacky premise for a Thursday night sitcom. This is a mansion full of the damned and the pregnant, and you are not in labor!"

"Oh, shit, here comes another . . . ahhhhh . . . son of a *bitch*." Marc was getting to his feet. And I was getting into my ninth panic attack of the week. "Betsy, this is labor. These are labor pains. I am in labor, which will eventually result in—aaaahhh, cripes!—a baby."

"Well, stop it! Stop it right now." Once again Jessica was trying to make it all about her. The woman had no shame. "I mean it: quit that."

She sat up so abruptly I flinched. Then she grinned. "Gotcha."

Startled silence, broken by my wheezing, "You bitch." The relief was actually making me light-headed.

"Hey, it worked. For a few seconds you forgot all your problems."

"For a few seconds, I knew terror the likes of which I had never known in life or death, you bitch."

"You're welcome," she said, and I honestly didn't know whether to punch her or hug her. So I just got the heck out of there.

CHAPTER
THIRTY-FIVE

An hour or so later, I'd thought of some great rebuttals for their "you probably wouldn't totally suck at ruling the world, maybe, at least not *too* much" arguments, but before I could run back to track them all down and berate them with my logic, Sinclair came out of the library and basically scooped me up and tossed me over his shoulder, caveman style.

"This might work on other vampire queens," I said to his ass as he steadily climbed the stairs to our bedroom, "but it's leaving this one cold."

"No. It isn't."

"Smug bastard."

"Yes."

"I don't love you," I told his ass. His marvelous, marvelous ass. Jeez, how many friggin' stairs were there, anyway? "Not even a little bit."

"Liars get spanked."

Oooh, really? That could be all sorts of dirty nasty fun. And frankly, we'd been a little short of dirty nasty fun around here lately. It was high time, no, *past* high time to get naked with the vampire king, naked and sweaty and rude, among other—

Sinclair stopped, two stairs from the top. I could tell he was listening, but had no idea for what. At least I knew better than to shrill, "What is it?" the way annoying movie heroines did when the good guys were trying to listen for the bad guys, only the annoying movie heroine's "What is it?" comes at just the wrong time for them to—

There was low growling from far down the hall, growling that was getting steadily louder. Lame. And who'd be growling, for God's sake? Jessica was probably napping by now. Nick/Dick was also napping, unless he'd finished and had gone back to work. Laura didn't growl. I was pretty sure Marc didn't, either. In fact, the only logical candidate for a growl was—

"Oh, shit. The full moon!"

Sinclair sighed and put me down.

"With all the crap going on, I totally forgot about the full—"

And here came Antonia, like she'd been cued by the god of missed sexual opportunities. In her wolf form, she was all black, her lush fur the exact color of her messy hair. Her eyes were glowing pools I tried not to stare into—Antonia was pretty touchy on two feet. On *four*, she was a goddamn hurricane of fur and teeth.

It didn't help that she'd only recently been able to even turn into a wolf during the full moon. See, she'd been born into their Pack, but some Pack members (you can hear the capital *P*, right?) didn't ever Change. Just looked human all the time, though they weren't. And these poor guys, they were treated like dying invalids by the ones who could turn into wolves. You know the drill: *Oh you poor thing, I've gotta go turn into a wolf now, see ya later . . . or never.* Like that.

Anyway, when the librarian had kidnapped Sinclair before our wedding, Antonia had gotten snatched, too. And when I killed the librarian ("You can choke and die on those overdue books, bitch, and fuck your late fees!"), I'd somehow fixed it so Antonia could, for the first time in her life, turn into a wolf.

We were all still adjusting. Case in point: a big-ass ebony-black scary-ass werewolf with about a thousand gleaming teeth was racing down the hall toward us, her growls like tearing velvet, and she probably wouldn't hurt us, probably, but this *was* Antonia, a woman whose idea of a polite greeting was, "Why don't you get the hell out of the way?" A woman the entire Pack had feared *before* she'd ever figured out how to Change. A woman the devil wanted to get rid of because she'd been such a pain in the ass in hell. The *devil*. In *hell*.

Maybe we should just hit the carpet and cower like crying little babies?

Believe me, darling, I'm giving it serious thought. She likely would not hurt us, but . . .

Before we had to indulge in our mutual cowardice, Antonia ran right up to us. Then we saw her legs bunching as she gathered herself, saw her sort of screwing herself into the carpet, and then she launched herself right over us.

We turned in staring unison to see her sail over our heads and fly down most of the steps, hitting the fourth from the bottom, catching herself, and then one more light leap . . . and then she was galloping for the front door, only there was a great big picture window in the—

KKKSSSSSSSSHHHHHHHHHH!

Exit Antonia.

"Aw, son of a—"

More footsteps. And now here came Garrett, racing down the exact path Antonia had just taken, zipping past us with a panted, "Sorry!" Then bounding down the stairs, taking them four and five at a time like a big skinny pale gazelle, bounding through the new hole in the picture window with a final, "She's got issues with claustrophooooooooobia!"

Oh, and he'd been naked. Did I mention that?

I turned to my husband, who was, like me, pretty much frozen in startlement. "So now we've got a bitchy werewolf running around in our sleepy neighborhood, with a naked sometimes-feral vampire hot on her trail."

"Yes."

"We should probably go do something, I dunno, royal and leader-ish."

"Yes," my husband said, with a last mournful glance at my cleavage. Then he sighed, turned, and started down the stairs. "I shall attend to it, my own."

"Don't be dumb, I'll help."

"Please." He turned and held up a hand. "I continually worry for you, now more than ever. Please stay here where things are relatively safe."

"Here? Safe?" I laughed. "C'mon, I'll help. We'll see the funny side of it," I added, trying to cheer him up. "You know, eventually."

He shook his head but smiled at me, and the smile was almost enough to make our sexless trek through the neighborhood something to look forward to.

CHAPTER
THIRTY-SIX

That was how I ended up getting arrested. You know how things seem weird and disconnected at the time the madness is happening, but later, when you can sort of step back and take a good look, you see how they were really linked?

Yeah, *none* of that happened. Sinclair and I (and Tina, and then Nick) went after Antonia and Garrett, and I got arrested, and the whole thing was stupid and a huge pain in my ass, and it didn't help that Sinclair found the whole thing sort of hilarious. The rate we were going, the thought of turning him into the Book of the Dead wasn't so repugnant all the time, how's that for weird and sad?

*　*　*

"And just what the hell is that?"

"A Kimber Custom semi-auto, Majesty," Tina replied, always soooo polite. She did something to the pistol, which was all shiny and steel-ey, and it made an ominously cool ratcheting sound. I was a shotgun girl (goose and duck hunting with my mom when I was a teenager) and a rifle girl (just because it was always so fun to try for a target two hundred yards away, and even more fun to *hit* a target two hundred yards away). Beyond that, I knew poop-all about guns.

It shouldn't, but it always did: I always found it freaky to see tiny delicate looks-like-a-sorority-escapee Tina matter-of-factly reload ammo (Sinclair had set her up with a whole reloading bench in a corner of our vast disgusting basement, and that thing clanged and banged half the night sometimes), tote rifles and shotguns around in gun cases, produce pistols like magicians made doves appear, and clean said pistols in the kitchen. I guess I sometimes expected her to spend time sitting on our porch in hoopskirts and a bonnet, sipping mint juleps.

I'd mentioned that to her once, and her reply had been succinct and respectful: "Mint triggers my gag reflex, my queen." Not a sentence I heard much, even around here.

"Ooooh, pretty!" I mock-gasped as she popped the clip and examined it.

"Yes, well." A small, demure smile was on her face. "You do like shiny things."

"But why do you have that one?"

"Because I always try to buy American." I had no idea if she was kidding or not.

"You think we'll need a gun? We're just going after Antonia to make sure she doesn't eat anybody. And Garrett because he'll scare the neighbors with his nudeness more than a big black slavering wolf will." (Minnesotans had a strong streak of the prude, especially in November.)

"Oh, this is just the gun I had on me, Dread Queen," she assured me.

Oh. How silly of me. Of course. That was just the gun she had on her.

"Shall we split up?" Sinclair asked, his rumble of a voice more than a little comforting against the dark Antonia and Garrett had fled to.

"Sure. We've done almost every other stupid horror movie cliché over the last few years. Why not? Is there a lake where sexy teens were killed, say, ten years ago tonight? Because that'd be the perfect place to split up."

"I love you," the king told me, "but I do not always understand you."

"I know."

"There's no need to split up. Antonia went that way, and of course, Garrett is right behind her. If we get moving, we'll—"

Which was when the cop car pulled into our drive, flashing cherries.

"Oh, shit!" Then I cheered up. "It's just Nick."

"What the hell?" he asked, practically leaping out of the vehicle. He looked more wild-eyed than he had in the kitchen during our showdown, which was alarming. "Jess said something broke the big window on first? And is running around the neighborhood?"

"Yeah, but it's—"

"She texted me 9-1-1! And she only does that when Byerly's is out of chocolate-covered bananas! And they aren't because I was there this afternoon and bought her a bunch more! So she's really freaked, you guys!"

"It's just Antonia," I soothed. Frazzled freaked Nick was making me nervous. "Um, in her incredibly dangerous huge wolf form during the—"

Nick/Dick groaned. "I knew it was the goddamned full moon and I forgot!" He was so distraught and stressed, he didn't notice Tina's and Sinclair's mutual flinch. Instead he slammed his hand down on the hood of his car, and this time I was the flincher. I was used to him being pissy in the old timeline, but not hysterical. Was I destined to screw up his life no matter what timeline we were in? Depressing thought. "All those witnesses we had to interview *again*, and then Jess hasn't been sleeping well so I haven't been sleeping well, and then the thing with the bananas, and with the you from the future, and the devil—"

"We get it. You're swamped."

"We are having a baby!" he reminded us, like any of us could forget The Gut That Walked Like Jessica.

"When? Because there's been some confusion." He just stared, like he had no idea what I could mean. Fine, I'd deal with that issue later. "Look, it's being handled, okay?"

"Handled as in you're talking to me in our driveway while a werewolf who makes Howard Stern seem soft-spoken roams our neighborhood while being chased by her naked vampire lover who was tortured so thoroughly he has no idea how many innocent people he killed before clawing you up and turning you into a vampire queen?"

I stared at said driveway. "Anything sounds bad when you say it like that," I mumbled.

He rubbed his close-cut hair so vigorously it looked like he was trying to knock himself out. Which maybe he was— he did admit to being sleep-deprived. "Are you in charge or not?"

"I am," I said firmly. I was. Right?

"So you're responsible."

Have a care, my love.

I've got this, worrywart.

"I am."

"Fine. Elizabeth Taylor, you are under arrest."

"I'm sorry?" Heh. Crazy night, because it almost sounded like—

"You're under arrest," one of my roommates said, while two more of my roommates stared at each other in total bafflement.

"For what?"

"For sucking at your job," he snapped.

"Well, I'm doing the best I can!"

"Yes! That's the problem."

"Yeah? Tough, you fascist asshat! It's me or it's nobody, so it's me."

Sinclair raised his eyebrows, and I could read the bum like a *Lucifer* graphic novel. Normally his alpha maleness would dictate he put himself in direct opposition to whatever Nick demanded. On the other hand, he was also a big fan of keeping me out of harm's way. The local pokey was wall to wall with lawbreakers (sorry . . . alleged lawbreakers). Our *home*, on the other hand, where we were supposed to relax and feel safe and occasionally have sex, was crawling with werewolves and zombies and the devil and decrepit versions of me and grumpy fat Jessica. If he let Nicky-Dicky haul me away, he could appease a valuable asset (he'd always been a big fan of getting close to a cop) and track down

Antonia without worrying about me—which was how he'd wanted to handle it in the first place. So he was stymied.

"You have the right to remain silent." In a jingly flash, his cuffs were off his hip. I was so astonished I stood still and let him cuff me. And I was having big-time déjà vu: this was prom night all over again, except with much less booze. "If you give up that right—"

"You're *arresting* me?"

"Uh . . ." Tina began. I could read her like a comic, too . . . she was appalled, but couldn't see a way out. Her king wasn't moving an inch. But her queen was about to get hauled to the local hoosegow. She couldn't back us both, so she picked the route that led (probably) to my immediate safety. "Uh, my queen, perhaps until we, ah, secure your—the mansion. I think it's better if the detective is occupied with you, rather than trying to be occupied with, ah, Antonia or Garrett."

"Stop talking," I told her, and she did, looking faintly grateful.

"What's the charge? Sucking at being the queen of the undead?"

"Sure, that's a good one. You have the right to remain silent."

"Fat fucking chance!"

"If you give up that right—"

"I'm going to stab you in the face."

"—anything you say can and probably will be used against you in a court of law."

"A *lot*."

"If you can't afford an attorney—"

"You know I can, butt-munch."

"—one will be provided for you."

"Do you know what I'm going to provide for you, Nick?"

"Do you understand these rights as I have read them to you?"

"I've mentioned the facial wounds I'm planning to inflict, right?"

I could still hardly believe Sinclair was going along with this bullshit. Not being able to have sex with me was just *ruining* the man.

"You had to still be a cop in this altered timeline, didn't you?" I said bitterly. "You couldn't have been an accountant? Or a clown? I should tear your head off your shoulders."

"Never happen," Nick said, managing a smile. A sickly, stressed smile, but it *was* a smile. "You wouldn't hurt me if someone stuck a gun in your ear, Bets."

What could I say? That one statement was why I found out what the backseat of a detective's car looked like from the inside. I was pissed, but I kind of loved that he was betting his life that I wouldn't hurt him.

Which simply wasn't true. I'd hurt him—I *had* hurt

him plenty. But he didn't remember it, because it had never happened to him in this timeline.

Did it not happening mean it didn't happen? I remembered everything, good and bad. I'd hurt Nick . . . except I hadn't. Argh. I hated timeline-based Zen-isms.

Brain tangle or not, stressed and sleep-deprived or not, Nick had said the one thing guaranteed to make me come along meekly to jail.

So off to jail I went, arrested by one of my roommates. A fine argument for kicking everyone out of the mansion except Sinclair. Maybe.

CHAPTER
THIRTY-SEVEN

"Listen, Nick—"

"Jeez. Betsy. My name is Richard, Dick for short, Dickie to Jessica and people I really, really like, so knock yourself out. Do I have to paint it on my forehead?"

"I would actually find that very helpful," I admitted. "I don't have the longest attention span."

"Yes, I've noticed," he managed through teeth that were grinding like . . . like things that grind together. (I should probably be getting more sleep, too.)

"Also I'd like a map for all the rooms in the mansion, because I think at least two bathrooms are missing. Where did they go? Are they lost in time? Are they in hell? Did they never exist because this is the timeline we're supposed to be in? Did they once exist but no longer since whoever built the mansion in this timeline used different blue-prints?"

"I've really got no idea. And I can't believe, with all the stuff you've got on your plate, I can't believe you're worried about bathrooms."

"And were they redone before they vanished into a parallel dimension of extra bathrooms? Or are they still kind of gross? Because that tile, it was just getting sad. Booger Green, what were they thinking? Nick? Are you listening? You should be paying attention to me."

"Can't think why. And it's Dick, okay?"

"Like it matters! I've got more important things to worry about than you changing your name every time I accidentally change the timeline."

He almost stood on the brakes. "What? You—*I'm* not the one changing anything, you're the one—wait, did you say every time? Oh my God, what have you done that you haven't told me about?"

Told *him* about? Hmm. Apparently N/Dick and I were gossip buddies in the new-if-not-necessarily-improved timeline. "Do we have a lot of intimate chats, Dee-Nick?"

"Do not, nope, I mostly get your goings-on from Jess. Pillow talk, you know?"

"Don't do that!"

"What?" He looked around wildly. "You see Antonia? I wouldn't run over her. On purpose, anyway . . . prob'ly . . ."

"No, not that, don't *talk* like that. I don't want to have to picture you and my best friend banging away."

"Her inner thighs are like velvet," he said dreamily.

"Please." I moaned and clutched my bangs amid the clanking of my cuffs—at least he'd cuffed me with my hands in front. "Please don't put that in my head. Please don't put that in my head. Please. Anything. I'll do anything not to think about Jessica's velvety inner thighs. I'll come quietly, I swear."

"Ha! Never in your life. Listen, I'm sorry about what just happened, but—"

"Too late, fascist! Assuming you're velvety right, then Jessica's thighs might be the velvety way to velvety thighs. Right? Oh my God!" I threw my head back and screamed at the car roof. *"You put it in my head!* No one's hurt me worse than you, and I'm telling you that knowing *you* know I have met Satan herself, you velvety inner thigh bastard! Oh, God *damn* it!" What could I do? Kill myself? To what effect? Kill him? Satisfying, but no guarantee. Kill Sinclair? Illogical, but it would be pretty satisfying. And it did have weird logic. If I killed him and skinned him, I wouldn't have to worry about killing and skinning him in a couple of hundred years, right?

Meanwhile, Nick-Dick was laughing so hard he nearly drove into a streetlight. *Oh, sure, Sinclair, I'm loads safer in the long bony arms of the law.* "I'm sorry, I'm sorry!"

"Shut up, Nicki-Ticki-Tavvi."

"Don't call me that. How about you just call me Berry?"

"How about I just call you asshat?"

"Richard?" he asked hopefully.

"You're hauling me off to jail! After making me visualize things I never wanted in my head! Why are we arguing about your name when you're hauling me off to *jail*? Will I even show up in your system, being legally dead and all? Oh, this is gonna be a disaster. A new disaster, I mean. Because we've got plenty of other disasters. If we were a corporation and we had meetings, they'd be called old business. But it's still business."

He waited until my lips had closed for half a second . . . hmm, he was used to arguing with me . . . then jumped back in with, "You're not legally dead. Everyone thought the funeral was a really bad joke pulled by your stepmother."

"That bitch."

He glanced at me in the rearview mirror. "Uh, Betsy . . . she didn't actually do that, remember? That was your cover story. Can you, uh, try to keep the truth and the lie separate? I guess it's a little tricky, what with two timelines in your head."

"You think? Besides, I wouldn't put anything past that pineapple-colored, hair-spray-shellacked bitch."

"It was the story we put out rather than telling the world

you got run over like a gopher and came back as the queen of the undead."

"Great, thanks for the trip down memory lane, and you must really be sleep-deprived because you just missed the exit for the Cop Shop."

"Yeah? That was careless. Or maybe I'm calming down a little and realizing arresting you was a little on the stupid side."

"It *was* stupid."

"Or maybe I just wanted to get you away from the mansion and the crowds of people hanging out there these days, get you where vamps or weres can't overhear us talking, to see if you've got a plan yet. Because what you tell me is gonna help me figure out what I've gotta do, too." He met my gaze in the rearview mirror. "Betsy, I've gotta think about Jessica first. All the time. I'm sorry. That's just how it is. Even if it inconveniences or embarrasses you. Look, I don't know how it was with us—me and Jess—*there*. But that's how it is with us *here*."

"You prick. Don't you dare make me like you for doing this stupid inconvenient illogical weird annoying thing."

He laughed. "Has anybody ever made you do anything?"

"I've got bad news, pal. I don't have a clue what to do, okay? The only thing I've figured out is that I can't half-ass it anymore. I've got to embrace the queen thing. I've got to get as much power as I can, however I can—"

"Uh, Betsy—"

"—so that when the time's right I'm powerful enough to save Sinclair. And myself! And maybe my mom! But not BabyJon because he apparently comes out of all this pretty okay."

"You, uh, don't see the inherent flaw in your . . . uh . . ."

"Awesome plan?"

He blinked rapidly, either because he had a lot of crap in his eye, or didn't want to cry. Or stare. Naw, he just needed another nap. "So your plan to avoid becoming a ruthless dictator with absolute power is to gain as much power as you can at all costs?"

"Well." I had to think about that. "Okay, it sounds bad when you put it like that. So I'm fucked."

"Could be," he agreed.

"Too bad if I am. I can't keep passing the royal buck. I've gotta embrace my role, right?" I absently twisted the small chain holding my handcuffs together while I thought. "So I become ruthless and powerful to help Sinclair, but I destroy Sinclair for some reason when I'm the Queen Bee on top of the frozen world." I twisted faster while my thoughts ran like dazed mice. "Oh, Christ, are things really trashed either way? Is that the big life lesson here? Because—ah, shit."

"What?"

"I owe you a new pair of cuffs." I held up my hands two feet apart, demonstrating the broken chain.

Dickie groaned and banged his head on the steering wheel hard enough to wring a quick *"Hnnk!"* from his horn. "Do you know how much paperwork I have to fill out to get another pair?"

"Sor-*ree,* Detective I'm Gonna Arrest My Landlady."

"Look, I'll release you from my custody. Like you couldn't break out of holding in half a second."

"Wouldn't have to break," I told him with no small amount of smug. "Just mojo the nearest guy with a key. Plan B."

"I don't want to know what Plan A was, do I?"

"Nope."

"Fine, so I'm gonna let you go, but you have to promise not to kill me in my sleep."

"I'm not going to do that."

"Kill me? Or promise?"

I grinned at him in the mirror. "You pick . . . Richard."

"Sexy *and* creepy. The original one-two punch."

"You can't get back on my good side by saying nice things like that. This *isn't* over," I threatened. "By which I mean, it's over." I mean, really. Who had the energy?

"Just please remember to call me Richard from here on out, okay? That's not so much to ask, right?"

"Says the stoolie cop—"

"'Stoolie cop'?"

"—who arrested me without cause! Shut up and get me out of here already."

"I'm glad you hosed the timeline," he said cheerfully. "I like liking you."

"I'm not talking to you."

I didn't mean it, though.

I liked it, too.

CHAPTER
THIRTY-EIGHT

Here's the thing about Minnesota, and it's nothing to do with *the cold (which wasn't that big a deal) or the Minnesota Nice thing (more Midwestern Nice, I'd found). Minnesota was new. That's why I liked it.*

I mean, it was just the coolest thing. The planet was zillions of years old, but Minnesota had only been around for, what? Less than two hundred years! Isn't that something?

I don't think it's a failing in all Minnesotans, just this one: we don't really have a sense of history, of age. Stephen King said Rome was a sprat (or maybe it was Greece?), and at the time I assumed it was the drugs talking. But I get it now. Compared to the planet, Rome (or was it Greece?) was a sprat. But compared to Rome, Minnesota was a preemie.

*   *   *

"Oh Father, please help your wayward child."

I looked up, annoyed. "Dammit, Lena Olin, ever heard of knocking? Don't you have a netherworld to lord it over? And don't pray for me. It creeps me out."

"Is that a blog? Are you . . . are you blogging?" Hmm. Normally I'd be pleased to see the devil look so horrified about any of my antics, but mostly I was annoyed at the interruption.

It wasn't completely asinine. Royalty wrote stuff down, right? Stuff for the ages, right? So I'd try to get in the habit. Because if I wrote about things I liked, maybe I wouldn't write the Book of the Dead, which was full of things I didn't.

I know, I know, but . . . it was the only thing I'd come up with so far. And sitting around doing nothing just wasn't acceptable anymore.

"None of your business, that's what it is. Don't you have some of the damned to bug?"

"Don't *you* have a shoe sale to crash?"

I gasped at the snide insult. "I *never* crash shoe sales! That's like spitting on . . . on . . . on something you would never spit on. Watch your step, Snidely McDevil."

"Yes, I'm quite terrified."

"You get how lame it is that you're sort of hanging around like the creepy aunt who doesn't have any friends her own age, so she likes to hang with your friends, who are too polite to tell the geezer that her wanting to hang around them all the time is not only sad but creepy? Right?"

"You know I'm a fan of free will. My own, too. Why shouldn't I want to 'hang' wherever I like?"

"Because it's so so so lame? And don't make me laugh. Free will! Ha! You're so full of shit."

"To borrow a page from your own book, some people are afraid of me, you know. And wouldn't dare talk to me like that."

Afraid? Why did that tickle something in my brain? Somebody else had mentioned fear and the devil. Too much had happened in too short a time. And also, I wasn't that bright.

So: onward. "You love to yak and yak about free will, while the whole time you're encouraging people to be bad."

"Yes! Free will. I'm not making them do a thing. Not one thing."

"Please! Someone wouldn't have killed someone else if the devil hadn't encouraged it. Then you sit there on your throne of fire and preach—"

"I never 'preach,' and I don't have a throne of fire. You're confusing me with my father."

"—about free will like it's not *your* secret plan to dominate, oh *hell* no, it's God's. It's a cheat, isn't it? Sure, we've all got free will . . . and you're always there trying to talk us out of it. Always. You never stop."

"That's right," she said, startling me with her quick agreement. "I never do." She glanced at my laptop and made a tiny curl of a smile at me. "Really, Betsy. Blogging?"

"Not that I don't love our little chats, but Laura's not here."

"Yes, I know. She's sitting in."

"And Elderly Me isn't . . . what?"

"Hmm?" Lena Olin examined her beautifully polished, pearly nails.

"Laura's what?"

"Sitting. In. She is my . . . how did you put it? 'Temp worker of the damned'?"

"So."

"Yes."

God, I hated when she was smug. And she was smug a lot. I was thoroughly out of my league with her—duh, she was the devil—and I hated every second of it. The few, the very few, times I could one-up her were never enough to make things even close to even.

One of these days, I seethed to myself, *one of these days I'd have so much power that cunning bitch will never be able to—*

Whoa.

Okay, that was not the way to handle this. That was no way to think. Ever.

I yawned. "So you got my little sis to sit in for you, and you're spending your first day off in a zillion—"

"Five billion."

"—years telling me you got my sister to sit in? Really? That's how you wanted to spend your day off? Pathetic, thy name is Lucifer." I forced a chuckle and made myself stare into my laptop like I was still interested in my queen journaling.

"She's got quite the aptitude for it."

"Uh-huh."

"In fact, she reminds me of you."

"Mmmm. There's just one *t* in *pathetic*, right?"

"The other you, I mean. The one who's done something. The one worth talking to."

"She said, talking to me, anyway. Go away, Lena Olin. Go take God out for a late Father's Day brunch. There's an Old Country Buffet around here somewhere."

I could actually feel the room getting warmer around me as she struggled to hold her temper. It made the shock and fear I'd felt about hearing what Laura was doing almost not very bad news.

Because why *was* she hanging around? It was like she wanted something. Wanted something from me . . . *not* Laura. But what?

As bad: Ancient Me lurking in her own past. She wanted something, too, but she'd at least been a little more open. She was waiting for me to do something. Or waiting for me not to do something. Ah yes. So helpful.

It stank. There was no logical reason for them to be just . . . hovering in my life. So something big and bad was coming, was on the way, or worse . . . was here.

"You're kind of a voyeur, aren't you? You like watching us."

"I'm a fan of man," she said, swiping Al Pacino's line from *The Devil's Advocate*.

"You really like to watch. Most of the time I see you, you're not actually doing anything. You're just hanging around until something happens. It's kind of gross," I told her in my most pleasant tone.

"I wouldn't expect you to understand, idiot child."

"And here with the superiority thing again. Yes, you're so far ahead of us poor mortals we can never ever ever understand all your layers of awesomeness." I laughed. "Wow, I could hardly get that out with a straight face."

"I like you more when you don't think so much."

I'll bet you do. Also, no one has ever told me that, ever.

"He thought too much, too, except at the end, when He simply refused to think for Himself." Satan was staring over my shoulder, lost in thought. I'd seen her like this once or twice before, and it never failed to unsettle me, and make me feel a little sorry for her.

Which I *hated.*

"Are you aware you're talking out loud?"

"Stupid boy, oh that stupid, stupid boy," the devil muttered.

"Aww . . . not Jesus again." You know how some people talk to themselves? She talked to Him. The kid she couldn't save. The one thing the devil admitted regretting. Not the whole turning-against-God thing. Not getting half of heaven to turn on Him with her. Not talking all sorts of people through the ages into indulging their worst fears/lusts/rages/murders/hatreds. All that? Just a day at the office.

Him, though. The boy. She felt bad about Him.

I sighed and shifted in my chair so I could face her. "I can't believe I'm saying this to you, but you should ease up on yourself. Free will, right? He had it, too. He knew what was coming. Knew since He was a kid, or at least, that's the way I heard it. And you gave it the old college try, tempting Him . . ."

"*Warning* Him!"

"Okay, okay, don't get your asbestos panties in a twist. You tried to warn or tempt or whatever, and you couldn't, and they—"

"They killed Him. Like some half-dead alley cat . . . you see grimy little kids poking it and prodding it and after three days of that kind of handling the poor thing just gives up. That's what He did for all you unworthy *idiots*. And His reward was . . . nothing." She was actually giving off heat now. Being in the room with her was like standing in front of an oven full of roasting beef. I thought about all the old wood my house was made of and got, um, perturbed.

She was pacing now. The oven was pacing, and the heat waned and grew strong and waned, depending on where she was in the room. "You're all still unworthy. Mankind isn't even potty trained. A six-week-old puppy bitch knows not to shit where she eats. You guys can't figure out what a *puppy* knows."

I leaned back in my chair and looked at her. Either I was getting used to these confrontations, or my fear circuits were burning out. Cool as a cuke, that one, almost always. But I'd seen her angry before. I'd *made* her angry before. I'd even hurt her. But I was never sure if I was working my agenda, or hers.

See, one of the (many many many many) things I hate about the devil is how you can be booking along, minding your own business, thinking that everything you're doing is part of your bigger plan, and you never find out until it's leagues past too late that it was *her* plan you were following. Always hers, all along.

You were ready to pull the cart, but guess who'd been holding the reins the whole time? And never told you about the spurs 'til you felt them digging into your ribs?

"Are you channeling a cowboy or indulging a heretofore-unknown longing to be sidekick to the Lone Ranger?"

I blinked. I'd probably been staring at her with a blank look on my face for five minutes. "What, you read minds now?"

"More desires than minds, and yes. On occasion. It's not much of a trick. As a species, you're not especially complex."

And here she was again. Just hanging around. Nothing was going on. Oh, except Ancient Me had hitched a ride from the future and was *also* hanging around.

Too bad I had no idea what to do about any of it. We were all in a holding pattern, and I couldn't imagine what I could do to blast us out of the waiting game.

Nope. I wasn't a secret genius, or a computer freak. I wasn't a doctor or a cop or a farmer turned philanthropist. I wasn't an old wise vampire and I wasn't a pregnant millionaire. I wasn't a Pack werewolf with all the power and backup that implied, and I wasn't a formerly feral vampire who had survived decades of torture.

I wasn't anything like that. I had been a slightly above average office employee before I died, and a considerably below average vampire queen after I died.

What I knew was barreling into situations with no prep

and no help. What I knew was stomping right through a problem until I somehow stumbled over the—

You have to look to your strengths. You do have some, you know.

Oh.

Oh!

I clicked to save my queen journal, all two paragraphs of it so far. Slapped my laptop closed. Stood. Stretched. "Say, Lucy . . ."

"Do *not* call me that." Her mouth was twisted in a sneer, but she was watching me carefully. Almost . . . nervously?

Satan is afraid of you. Don't you find that at all interesting?

As a matter of fact, I did. Finally.

"Lucy, how about we cut the shit?"

The devil looked into my eyes . . . and she knew that I knew.

CHAPTER
THIRTY-NINE

"Why? Why, Beetlejuice? That's really all I want to know before we do what you want us to do. Why?"

"Beelzeb—"

"Stop it. Why?"

She sniffed. "I can never make you understand."

"No kidding. I've had a head full of how superior you are and how wormlike I am. Fine. But you gotta try, okay, O great and powerful asshat? Before you kill me and I die screaming—which I've been doing for the last six months, anyway—you gotta try. I can't die not knowing. I won't."

She spread her hands, and in one of those weird why-am-I-thinking-this? moments, I saw again how beautiful her hands were. "What do you want to know? I'll do what I can."

"Fine. Thank you." I took an unnecessary breath . . .

funny how some habits were so hard to let go. That was probably a metaphor for something. "First there was nothing and then there was God and He made you guys and that's all there was for a while, just Him and the angels, and then He made us.

"So you were never human and you'd never understand anything about our pathetic stupid lives, right? And even if you *were* ever human, you've been around for five billion years, so any perspective you ever could have had would have gone kaput ages ago, so you'd never understand anything about our pathetic stupid lives, anyway. It's like you're watching a bunch of grasshoppers and they're so outside of your experience it's not even worth trying to be their king, trying to even *explain* you're their king; it's just easier to do your own thing with them and never mind the fallout, right?"

Satan shrugged her elegant shoulders. "Right."

"So why, why, why?" I cried. I realized I was almost crying, and hoped the devil wouldn't notice. "Why even bother? Why the tricks, why the sneaking? Why are you still trying to get people to be their worst, do their worst, all the time? What do you get out of it? It can't still be interesting. It can't do much of anything for you after all this . . . you've seen every bad thing in the human condition. A million years ago you must have known there were never going to be any surprises. It's gotta all be just so . . . *fucking* . . . *boring*. So what's the *point*?"

"Well," the devil began. Then she paused, thinking it over. Finally: "If there was one, I forgot all about it a long time ago."

"No."

"Yes."

"No. It's not that easy. You don't get off that easy." I was pretty sure I was gonna faint. Things were definitely getting swimmy around the edges. Yep. Wait—no. I'd held off rage-and-terror-induced unconsciousness for the nanosecond. "No."

"Yes. That's all. The reason is there is no reason. The reason is you don't know and I don't care. The reason is green. The reason is number twenty-seven. There was no point, is no point, won't be one no matter how much you shrill and whine and bitch. So live with it, or die with it."

Yes.

That was just right.

I took another unnecessary breath. "Laura's watching the shop, huh?"

"Yesss . . ."

"So no one's gonna notice if you go missing for a while, I bet."

"What in the worlds are you—"

I launched myself at the devil.

CHAPTER
FORTY

Here's the thing about the devil: she's really strong. She's really smart. She's really fast.

And she's really old.

And tired.

She was still giving off heat, but it didn't hurt me. Either it wasn't real heat—the stuff in my world that could burn things like mansions and fences and people—or I just didn't give a shit. Or it was something else, something I knew nothing about. Yeah, it was probably the last thing.

We slammed back and forth like a couple of alley cats, spitting and snarling and clawing and punching and kicking. I could hear walls cracking, furniture breaking. A snap that was prob'ly a couple of my fingers. Maybe one of her ribs? Nope, one of mine.

"Good time to start praying," she forced out through gritted teeth.

"Don't need His help to kick your ass all over this mansion."

She seemed to think that over, which was exactly what I hoped she'd do. The devil was a bitch, but she was a smart bitch.

Come on, Lena Olin, you jaded horrible thing, come on! You don't want to do this here. You want to do it on your turf!

ELIZABETH!

Shit! Sinclair, knowing I was up a creek *sans* paddle and coming on the run. The gorgeous idiot could really screw this up for me. Us. Okay, me.

"If you won't . . . pray . . . for you . . . will you pray . . . for me?"

"Never in life," I gritted back. Also: WTF? Don't tell me my nutball seat-of-my-ass hunch was actually *right*. I'd just wanted to do something. I didn't expect to be right.

Also: I should be paying attention. No sooner had that occurred to me than I managed to jerk back before her fist plowed through the wall where my head had just been. Were there any dentists for the undead? If the devil knocked my teeth down my throat, would they grow back, like a shark's?

(The things you wonder when you're trying not to be beaten to death.)

We had to leave. We had to get out of here. My stupid plan wouldn't work here. And then, of course, there was Sinclair to worry about.

ELIZABETH!!!!!!!!!!!!!! I'M COMING KEEP HER THERE KEEP HER THERE WHATEVER YOU DO DO NOT DO NOT DO NOT LET HER TAKE YOU KEEP HER IN THE HOUSE KEEP HER IN THE HOUSE DO NOT LET

"Time to change the venue," she muttered, and the world fell away.

CHAPTER
FORTY-ONE

Yes! We were in hell!

(This was what my life was. I was glad to fall through a hole in the world and plop into hell, where my sister was temping for the devil. Oh, and the devil was trying to goad me into killing her. Unless I'd guessed wrong, in which case the devil was gonna squash me like a grape.)

"Tricky, tricky," she panted, easily dodging my fist. And then my kick. But my other kick landed—ha! A perfect day to wear my pointiest leather boots. Take that, Satan! And that! And—

"Ow!" She was pretty fast for someone at least five billion years old. What had I been thinking?

I remembered my theory. I remembered my utterly

insane idea that this wouldn't be a fair fight . . . and why that was actually good for me. Why it could be the saving of me . . . and him. And maybe even the future.

Because time is a wheel.

"You think . . . He loves you?"

"Really? We're gonna chat about God while we're trying to kill each other?" My ears weren't ringing so much as booming. And it was suddenly almost impossible to see out of my left eye. Was that my blood or hers making everything look pinkish-red? Probably mine.

"It's the last . . . conversation . . . I plan to have . . . with you. So answer."

"Yeah, then. He does. Sure He does."

"And me?"

"Of course . . . He still loves you . . . moron! That was never the issue . . . moron! You big stupid moron!" Normally I didn't have to think of what to call people I was pissed at. Asshat, dumbshit, shitstain, fuckface, jizzbucket, fucktard, dickweed, cockknocker, jizzhole . . . it all usually came tripping off my tongue in a glorious rain of obscenity.

Had to work for the insults now, though. It was hard to think what with all the red stuff in my eyes and the booming in my ears, which I was pretty sure were also bleeding.

I felt her hot little hands close around my neck and start to squeeze. I punched. Punched. Punched—nothing.

Should have found the time to take a martial arts course. Yoga couldn't help me now.

It was tough work, bitching at the devil while being throttled, but I was up for the challenge. "How come . . . older you get . . . dumber y'get?"

"Yes, He does," Satan replied, a thoughtful look on her bloody face. "I suppose He does. He must, you know. It's one of His rules. I think I . . ."

"Gggsssshat!"

"I think I want . . . I'd like . . . to go home."

"Stop it!" Laura, yelling from a galaxy far, far away. "Stop it, don't, you're killing her, *stop killing her*!"

No idea. No idea who she was talking to. Her mom? Her sister? A player to be named later? Wow, look at all the blood coming out of me! Almost as much as a live person. Weird.

"Don't! Don't! What are you doing? Let go!"

It was good that Laura was here. Was almost here. What was keeping her, anyway? I needed her here. My plan wouldn't work without her here. *Oh, Laura, I'm so sorry you're here.*

Lena Olin grinned at me through bloody teeth. Her hair had been yanked from its neat coiffure and she looked kind of Medusa-esque. With luck she'd need a deep-conditioning treatment after she'd beaten me to death. "Uh-oh."

"My thought . . . xxxactly," I gurgled.

"You'll have to do it in front of her."

". . . kkk . . ."

"You'll have to steal her future while she watches."

". . . nnn . . ."

"Him or her, Betsy? Now's when we see."

". . . favor . . ."

"What?" I actually landed a good one—*splat!*—in the middle of her narrow face. Finally, I'd surprised her. Really surprised her. Not the fake stuff she usually showed me. Had been showing me all along. "What, stupid girl?"

". . . want one . . . favor . . . a wish . . . want it . . ."

It was probably all the skull fractures, but her eyes, usually brown, and recently dead black like a night sky without stars, seemed to burn. Eyes on fire, that's what they looked like—and it wasn't quite right. She wasn't human, this was an angel, I was killing an angel and she was killing me and she was a creature I did not understand, could never have understood, asking for an explanation had been a waste of time and had only increased her contempt and her eyes were like nothing I'd ever seen, her eyes her eyes oh God oh please help me now God her terrible terrible eyes . . .

"Yes! One! For what you'll do. Now do it! Your worst, vampire queen, show me your worst and *choose*!"

I almost didn't. Almost couldn't. I had never been so frightened, never. In the end it was my essential stubborn nature

255

(fuck you Lena Olin you're scary but you're gonna die or I'm gonna and I'm fine with dying again because time is a wheel)

that allowed me to reach for nothing

"Stop! Stop! Stop!"

and grasp the Antichrist's hellfire sword

"Don't! Betsy! Motherrrrr! Don't!"

which only Laura or one of her blood could wield

"Let go of me! What are you—let go!"

and shoved it into the devil's heart. Or where the devil's heart would have been, had she ever had one.

Laura's last shriek cut off like someone had thrown a switch. Maybe someone had.

Shocked, Satan looked down at the piece of light sticking out of her chest. I have to admit, I was surprised, too, though I was pretty sure this had been what she wanted, what she had been planning from the minute Laura was born, the minute I'd come back from the dead.

But knowing wasn't the same as doing. Astonished together, we looked at the chunk of Laura's soul, the pieces of her self she made into weapons that could kill angels and vampires, and then at each other. Neither of us knew what to do.

So I shoved the sword in harder. I dunno . . . it just seemed like the thing to do. So I went with it.

"Finally," said Satan, and died.

I wasn't falling for it, though. I mean, probably she was dead.

But because Dr. Taylor didn't raise no fools, I took off her head with the back swing. "I chose," I told her head as it bounced past me. "Happy now?"

CHAPTER
FORTY-TWO

"Betsy, my God!"

Had I ever been so tired? I looked up as my sister finally reached me. It seemed like she had been screaming forever. No more screaming. I'd had my fill of screaming for the day. Night?

I hoped she wasn't going to be difficult about giving me a ride back home. "Just Betsy," I said. I wiped some of the blood from my eyes. "Not your God."

"What are you doing?"

"Taunting your mom's severed head." It had stopped rolling, and I stifled the urge to boot it farther away. My sister wasn't likely to take that well. And it was pretty disturbing that I wanted to do it, even. "There's no way to make that sound not crazy, is there?"

"Why did you—why were you—" The Antichrist burst into tears. "Why? Why?"

"To save him. And me." It sounded simplistic. The truth did, sometimes. It didn't matter what I said, anyway. Laura was never going to forgive me. We were probably going to become really bad enemies over this. At the least, she was gonna blow off Thanksgiving.

Oh. Thanksgiving. Since Satan hadn't killed me, I still had *that* to worry about.

"And you! What did you think you were doing? My mother respected you! My mother—"

"Was right to fear me." Ancient Betsy, looking as close to happy as I'd ever seen her. We stared at each other for a long moment, and then she said, "This. This is what I was waiting for."

"Yeah, no shit." Sure, *now* it was obvious. She couldn't have said, "I kind of need you to kill the devil to save the future"? Was that such a difficult fucking speech? "Thanks for all the help." Actually, judging from the bruises slowly purpling her face, it looked like Laura had fought like a, well, hellcat.

But Sneaky Evil Me didn't have to entirely prevent Laura. Just figure out the right time to follow her to hell—did she ask Laura to take her? Or could she move back and forth on her own after all these centuries of hanging with the devil? Anyway, she only had to slow Laura for a few crucial seconds.

And she had.

"I am really hating your face right now," I told Crooked Wily Me.

"Yours is almost unrecognizable!" she replied with what sounded like sincere admiration. "Satan really made you her bitch before you cut off her head. My condolences, Laura," she added.

"Shut the fuck up!"

"Laura!" we both gasped. Okay, under the circumstances, Laura's response was one hundred percent appropriate. It was just a shock to hear the Antichrist make with the potty mouth.

"You," she said to (aw, nuts) me. "You . . . what you did here . . . it's not just unfathomable. It was stupid."

"Ah," Ancient Me mused. "A day without the Antichrist sitting in judgment on you is a day without sunshine."

"Give her a break, we just decapitated her mom." God, was I really gonna turn into that vicious chilly bitch? Just . . . appalling, really. The idea. The *horror.*

"I didn't know you hated her so much. When I was you, I didn't hate her. That came later."

"It's not that I hated her so much," I explained to myself, "but that I love Sinclair so much."

She smiled. "Yes. You did. You do. I never killed the devil. That's the—"

"Thing you were waiting for, yeah, yeah. And as for

'stupid,' Laura, I'm aware that me killing your mom while Other Me slowed you down is gonna make things awkward for a while."

"For a *while?*" Laura looked like she couldn't decide whether to cry or choke me or rage or kick me or barf. I sympathized, as much as I could.

"I know it seems horrible—"

"Seems?"

"—okay, good point, but this way I won't write the *Book of the Dead* eighty zillion years from now. The devil—" Made me do it, I almost said, recognizing at the last second what a huge cop-out that was. "Satan and Old Yucky Me were allies, right? And through that relationship, you and I were allies in the future. But now that Satan 1.0 isn't around, she won't spend the next bunch of centuries helping me do all sorts of nasty things, like scribbling my blog on Sinclair's skin."

"And you know that, how?"

"Uh . . ." A lucky guess? Instinct? My super secret vampire queen decoder ring? "Old Me didn't do that." Pointing at her mother's severed head. "Ergo, the future will be different than the one you and I fell into. Because I *did* do that." Probably. But this was no time to insinuate in any way that I wasn't 100% confident my impromptu plan would work.

The devil was dead, and that was maybe worth celebrating. Except I knew things, in one respect, weren't gonna change. Not really. The devil was dead, long live the devil.

"You shouldn't have done that."

"What?" My sister's face, her voice. Her mouth was smiling. Her eyes weren't. "Laura?"

"You'll regret it."

Oh, sure. Add it to the list! I had gobs of regrets. Getting drunk at senior prom and barfing all over my science teacher's/dance chaperone's shoes. Falling for a Jimmy Choo knockoff when I was thirteen. Signing up for the Miss Burnsville pageant of my own volition. So long a life, so many regrets.

"You shouldn't have killed my mother."

"Yeah, I was afraid that's where this was going."

"If for no other reason," she said, and her voice was calm, and her hair was bleeding red through the blond and getting redder and redder, so I was getting scareder and scareder, "than because you created a job opening."

"I've gotta come right out and be honest: you're sort of terrifying me right now."

"This isn't over."

By which she probably meant, this isn't over.

"Wait. Laura!"

She'd opened up a portal to somewhere and stepped toward it. She did it without once looking away from me. She did it as easily as I'd have flipped a burger on a grill. And—this is weird—I was actually scareder at this moment than when Satan and I threw down.

"Laura!" Going, going, and now almost . . . "I had to

save the future, dammit! It's not like I killed one of the good guys, right? It wasn't personal! By which I mean it was very, very personal! It's not that I hated your mom so much, it's that I love Sinclair so much! You hear me yelling, right? Because it feels like I've been yelling at you for hours!"

"Save your breath," Ancient Me advised.

"Don't make me put you on the spreadsheet I haven't started and keep forgetting about!" I yelled. "Get over here or—"

"Spreadsheet?" Ancient Me asked.

"—*you're off the Christmas card list!*"

. . . gone.

CHAPTER
FORTY-THREE

"*So, what? Do we try to hail a cab? The Antichrist left in a* huff—with good reason, I'm not saying she didn't have good reason—and are my ears bleeding?"

"Yes."

"What's so fucking funny? Are my eyes bleeding?"

"Yes. You. You're so fucking funny. I can't believe you did it."

"Yeah, that bish—bitch—never knew what hit her. Not Laura. The devil." I should probably hail a hell cab and make it take me to an ER or something.

"She was wrong, though. Laura."

"Nuh?"

"You knew what you were doing when you killed Lucifer Morningstar."

"Corningware." I was gonna vomit. No, wait. I wasn't. Prob'ly. Ow. "Heh."

"Lord, you're just as much an irritant when you're heavily concussed and near death."

"Am not. 'Cuz time's a wheel."

"Ah!" She sounded pleased. "Marc did remember. I thought he might."

"Not really. Fuzzy. Like a dream. He'd say, 'n' then he'd f'rget. Um. What'd I say?"

"Time is a wheel." She stuck out her finger and made a circle. "If you live long enough, Betsy, you eventually catch up to yourself. That's the secret. That's the meaning of life, in case you ever wondered. When you did things I didn't remember doing, I figured it out. All I had to do . . . was live long enough . . . to *un*do."

"I don' geddit."

"Yes, well. Another time, perhaps. Get it?" She actually giggled. "Another *time*? Do you see what I did there?"

"Time's wunna those things, um, those round things guinea pigs run in?" I was going to throw up. No, pass out. No, throw up. No, both. "Ummm . . ."

"And you knew what you were doing the entire time. You *knew* you were creating a job opening. Betsy? Stay awake, dammit. Don't you understand how much I want to talk to you about this? You're being really quite selfish. Think of my needs for once. So, elaborate: you knew who'd have to step in. The only person who could."

"Nuh? Meh. Uh?" Hey, Ancient Me was getting small and wee! Ancient Me was Wee Me! Good-bye, Wee Me! Good-bye! Good

(bye)

CHAPTER
FORTY-FOUR

I woke up with the taste of blood in my mouth, which even a few years ago would have been horrifying. And I felt loads better. I could think again! More or less.

"Welcome back." Ancient Me was peering down at me, and I was sucking on her—

—her—

"Aw, man!" I scrambled away from her and lunged to my feet. She looked resigned, examined her cut wrist, then stood and put pressure on the wound she'd doubtless inflicted on herself when the world went bye-bye for me. "What would you call that?"

"An act of kindness and generosity?"

"Is it cannibalism, or more like, you know, masturbation?" Had I ever been so horrified yet fascinated to hear an answer? Ugh. There was something wrong with me. "And now that I feel better, time is a fucking *wheel*? So *bogus*!"

"Bogus. Does it bother you that you, a woman in your thirties—"

"In my thirty! I'm a woman in my thirty. I'm still just thirty. Thirty forever." Not depressing at all.

"—has the vocabulary and syntax of a teenager?"

"Nope. Not once. And that's enough out of you; now *I've* got questions. You probably have answers. So start talking."

"Don't be tiresome," Ancient Me yawned.

"Time is a wheel? Really?"

"Oh. He finally remembered. I've been waiting." She had the nerve to sound disapproving. She had the gall to make that last sound like *Marc* was the one to do something that let *her* down.

"He always remembered, he's just had kind of a hard time lately *what with dying and all, you heartless twat*!"

"Everyone does it sooner or later," Bitchy Me shrugged. "And dying isn't the end of the world. It's not even that interesting."

"You know what this means, right? This wheel crap, this you-wrote-the-Book bullshit? That we're not the vampire queen, among other things."

"What?" Got her . . . she actually sounded startled. Uneasy, even.

"Dumbass! They're not prophesies, the Book of the Dead doesn't tell our future. They're memories. *Your* memories. Writing down something that happened to you isn't a prophecy, don't you get it? It's a blog, and with all the lameness that entails."

"I wrote about things that happened to you." No, she didn't like my analogy one bit. Damn, what a rush. Even if I was wrong, it was almost worth it just to rattle that chilly bitch. "We both did what we could as best we could, whatever way we could. And I will tell you one more truth, infant: when I leave here, I don't know what I'm going back to."

"Yeah?"

"Yes."

"Why'd you help me?" I asked, deeply suspicious.

"Which time?"

"The time when I woke up with your blood in my mouth. And if I didn't make it clear before, yerrrggh."

"I wanted to finish our conversation."

"Why?"

"I was curious."

"Why?"

"Will it be worth it, do you think?"

I didn't say anything. Just looked at her. I didn't owe her

shit. In fact, I was sort of hoping that when she left hell, she'd cease to exist. I also hoped when she left hell, I'd never see her again. Was that so much to ask? To not ever see myself again? I'd changed the timeline again . . . hers, this time. What was she going back to? And why did I still care?

Finally, when it was clear she was ancient and crotchety enough to outwait a dead frog, I gave her what she thought she wanted to hear.

"Yeah, Me Who Should Cease Pretty Soon. It was worth it to save Sinclair and me—"

"Us."

"—and Marc and the future. I sacrificed my sister's happiness and freedom for my husband's life."

"Uh-huh. And tell me, how long have you been working on this plan? Or was there no actual plan? Did you have another lightning flash of pure dumb luck and decide on the spur of the moment to act and then found to your amazement that half-assing it actually worked?"

"I'll have you know I painstakingly and with considerable foresight—"

"Pulled it right out of your ass."

"Well, yes. And I decided to do it when the devil was bitching about my queen blog. Is that what you wanted?"

"No."

"Then here comes the part you'll like: I'm not sorry. And I know I should be."

Choose, she'd said. *Show me your worst and choose!*

And I had. Sinclair, of course. I'd sworn to save him. And then I did.

"I never promised to save the Antichrist," I told my other self. "Not in this timeline, or any other. I think I'm more like Garrett these days than anyone else. He's sneakier in this timeline. He tricked me into pulling Antonia out of hell; he wouldn't have done that in the old timeline. And there are things—there's stuff I wouldn't have done, once upon a time, that I can do now."

"So?"

"So. In the end, I just did what I'd always set out to do. And succeeded in spite of myself."

"That," she said. "That's what I wanted. The thing you did. And then the thing you didn't do."

"Well, *great*. Can you get me home? Or do I have to hang out in hell and hope Laura doesn't make me cool my heels here for a few decades?"

"Oh, I can get you home. *You* can get you home, probably. But that's a topic for another century. You've transcended the feeble limitations of your own mind long enough for one day."

"Thanks."

"That wasn't a—never mind."

"If you're so smug, do you know about the wish?"

"Of course I do."

"What is it?"

"You doubt me?"

"What *is* it?"

"Why don't you tell me?"

"You don't, Decrepit Me!" I nearly shrieked my relief. "You don't know about the wish! Ha! I think things really are changed! I think we really pulled it off!"

"Why are you screaming? I'm standing three feet in front of you."

"You don't know," I whispered. "So blow."

She frowned, but her curiosity was too much for her. "What wish? What do you mean?"

Yes! One! For what you'll do! The devil's last gift . . . or curse. Because maybe there wasn't going to be an HEA for the king and I. This wasn't a fairy tale. In which case the thing I wanted more than anything would ultimately doom us both.

Yuck. Those kinds of boo-hoo thoughts weren't like me. Ancient Me was harshing my buzz.

"If you could wish for any one thing, what would you ask for? Second chances? To never be a vampire? To not write the Book?"

"All those," she decided, thinking. "And none of those."

"Yeah, okay, thanks, Yoda. Me? The world's full of things I want." Have Christian Louboutin's parents meet and breed in this timeline. Have the Ant leave me alone forever. Produce my father because it's weird that I haven't seen him since he died. Let Jessica love me even after she has a baby to love more. Find out what the dealio is with her weird pregnancy. Keep a closer eye on Garrett. Wish my mother's marriage had never imploded. Wish that Aztek had never run me over . . . no. Even after everything, that was something I'd never wish for. I had to die to figure out what to live for, why is it like that sometimes?

"But this is getting boring," I decided. "And if I'm bored, you've got to be damn near petrified."

"Damn near," she agreed.

"So send me home. Then we don't have to look at each other anymore and maybe not even think of each other anymore."

"Infant."

"Crone."

"Ingrate."

"Psycho."

She was getting smaller. Or I was. No, she was. Wait. What was happening, exactly? This wasn't like traveling through portals with Laura. That was startling, even jarring. This was more like the world was fading away and making everything teeny before it

"Dupe!"

disappeared.

CHAPTER
FORTY-FIVE

"Aw, dammit! That bitch got the last word!"

I sat up, shivering, then realized why I was cold all over. That heartless ice-bitch twat had dumped me in the snow in my own front yard . . . practically the same path I'd walked when I left to bury Giselle and this whole weird thing started. (Note to self: get the dead cat away from Marc and properly inter the thing.)

Okay, I was cold, but I was home, and whole, even! And the devil was dead, and Sinclair was safe. Probably. Ooh, but he was gonna be pissed. I'd have to figure out how to spin this.

It's not so much that I manipulated the devil into bringing me to hell so I could kill her while keeping you out of danger, sweetie, it's more like we were playing a life-or-death session of Truth or

Dare. Naw, he'd never buy it. *I had no idea when I practically forced her to leave our bedroom and bring me to hell that things would get even more violent! Honest!* Nope. Um . . .

I squinted at the mansion . . . the sun was starting to set behind it, so it had to be around 4:30 in the afternoon. How long had I been in hell? And why hadn't any of my eighteen roomies noticed I'd been tossed ass over teakettle on the front lawn? Where *was*—

"Betsy! Hey!" Marc the Zombie had thrown open the front door. "Jeez, where've you been? We've been looking all over, we've all been freaking ou—"

Then he was shoved aside and went sprawling almost all the way to the edge of the porch, and Sinclair was galloping down the porch steps, suit jacket flapping as he raced to me.

"Oh, Elizabeth." My normally graceful husband slipped and skidded to his knees, then seized my hand in a grip that made it go instantly numb. I could feel the little bones in my hand grinding together and gritted my teeth; from the expression on his face, he had no idea he was hurting me. "Oh, my dearest queen."

"What? I'm fine. Are you okay? I'm okay. Would you believe it was all sort of my plan? Sort of? Don't be mad, okay?"

"How did you do it? How?"

Okay, he was being lovier and dovier than usual. "What

are you doing? Are you sick? Is there a huge pain in your left arm radiating to your black, black heart?"

His shoulders were shaking. *He* was shaking . . . trembling all over. Could vampires suddenly develop epilepsy? Was he cracking up from extreme horniness since we hadn't had sex in almost a week?

"Yeesh, it's not like we'll never have sex again, it's only been a few days. Get ahold of yourself. Man up."

"How did you ever do it?" He was still on his knees as I climbed out of the snow and to my feet, looking up at me and not letting go of my other hand. "And how will I ever be able to show the depths of my joy and love and admiration?"

"Try Hallmark. Will you get up? You're ruining those slacks." This was all very alarming. I didn't like it at all. What the hell was wrong? Things should be fine, what was wrong?

His dark gaze was boring into me, his eyes suddenly enormous in his pale face. His hands shook and he was staring up at me from his knees in a way that both touched and frightened me. "Please, Sink Lair, you're scaring the shit out of me. I'm kind of missing my way-too-arrogant annoying husband who I occasionally feel like kicking in the balls. Please get up."

"I loved you before you did this. I would have thought it an impossibility to love you more."

"Eric, you're—"

"Shut up, darling."

I shut up.

"I would have died for you before this," he told me while kneeling on our lawn. "Now I *want* to die for you, and would right now, just so I could show even the smallest measure of my gratitude. And you, my love, my own, you don't think you did anything spectacular. You never think you've done anything spectacular." He laughed, a deep rolling laugh that didn't go at all with the on-his-knees all-hail-the-queen thing. "It's one of the few things you are truly stupid about."

"Well, thanks tons, jerk. Can I list a few of the things you're truly stupid about? Thing number one: not knowing that crouching in snow will wreck your suit. Thing number two: the way you sneak into the kitchen and hog the last of the strawberries for an emergency four a.m. smoothie and think I don't hear your furtive rustling. Thing number—wait."

I finally caught on, and couldn't believe it had taken me all these seconds to put it together. (Don't judge. I had a lot on my mind. Also, I'd nearly been beaten to death an hour ago. Or a day ago.) The sun was *setting*, not set. It was late afternoon. It was *not* full dark.

In other words, the sun was *shining* on my favorite vampire! Even better, he wasn't bursting into flames. My husband hadn't been able to truly see and feel sunshine for decades; he had said good-bye to the big blazing ball of gas for good when he let Tina kill him. Before I loved him, he had allowed himself to be burned alive for love of me. And he had always indicated to me that he felt it was a fair trade.

No. *This* was a fair trade.

"The wish! It worked!" Damn! She'd pulled it off. I was impressed. And terrified. God, she'd had so much power, what would I have done if she hadn't wanted to finally die? "Okay. I can explain. The thing is, Satan owed me a favor, and this is what I came up with." Good-bye forever, Christian Louboutin Volpi Leather Knotted Peep-Toes. Sinclair must never know what I had to give up. Some things were too terrible to tell. "Okay, but wait . . . how did you know you could run out here in the snow and the sun? Did you— aw, man." I shook my head. My husband disliked being on fire. But he disliked worrying about me even more. It wasn't the first time he'd charged, heedless, into sunshine to save me. To think he needed to charge into sunlight to save me. "Say it with me, Sinclair: *don't* go into the light. Do not. Except now you can. Okay, but that doesn't mean those times you did and got fricasseed were a good idea." Wait. Fricasseed was when chunks of meat were cut up and cooked in gravy. (Thank you, Food Network!) "Roasted. It doesn't mean those times you got roasted were a good idea, is what I meant." Like Jim Gaffigan, the Food Network was now my porn. My wonderful fricassee-filled porn. In life I had never once been sexually aroused watching Ina Garten whip up turkey lasagna.

With an effort, I tried to focus on the here and now. Sinclair wasn't on fire. That was huge! And all I had to do was *not* wish for Louboutin's parents to conceive him. All I had to do was say so long to his Rodarte shoes, his peep-toe pumps, his signature red soles . . . oh, Christian . . . forgive me . . .

But still and all: more than fair. A bargain, I figured.

"A favor? From the devil?" He sobered instantly. "And what will it cost, my queen?"

I smiled at him. I was ankle-deep in snow, and only a couple of inches away from yellow snow (stupid roaming neighborhood dogs who don't respect my territory!). My sister was either going to kill me or . . . no, she was probably going to try to kill me. My good friend was a zombie. My best friend was growing another person to love. The devil was dead; long live the devil.

All those things . . . and I couldn't stop grinning like a chimp. That was something else I was truly stupid about, I figured . . . I tended to ignore the big problems in favor of individual victories.

"Oh, Elizabeth." He was shaking his head, and a small breeze kicked up and ruffled his dark hair, and some of it fell into his eyes. I reached out to straighten it, when he grasped my wrist and planted a kiss in the middle of my palm. "What did you give up to bring this about? What might you still have to do to repay?"

I shrugged, still smiling. "This is the part where you ask me if I give a tin shit."

"Elizabeth. Tell me truly: What have you done?"

"Exactly what I had to. Every step of the way."

Sinclair narrowed his eyes at me. No, wait, he was squinting in the late sunshine. No . . . he was definitely narrowing his eyes at me. "That wouldn't be another quote from that awful *Sin City* movie, would it?"

"Frank Miller is a living god! It isn't awful!" I tried to calm myself. We were never going to see eye to eye on the purely awesome graphic novels of Frank "Living God" Miller. "Okay, well, I killed the devil. But it's okay; she was pretty sick of still being alive and always in charge of hell. Oh, and Decrepit Me helped by keeping Laura out of it until it was too late. Also, Laura's mega-pissed at me now. That could be a problem for us later."

Sinclair shook his head, not in denial, I knew, but because it was a lot to take in. "I do not—all right, beloved, you can take me through it—and that explains what happened to the *Book of the Dead.*"

"Oh, man." It had started talking? It had started walking? It had applied for several credit cards in my name to wreck my credit rating? The horror. "Tell me."

"Nothing bad," he was quick to assure, "only mysterious. I went to the library to look at it. I was willing to risk a little insanity if it meant I could help you—"

I restrained myself from punching him in the nose. "Are you insane, Sink Lair? Oh. Wait . . ."

"It was gone," he finished, which startled me into shutting up. "I assumed your sister . . . except if you have slain the devil . . . which I will insist you elaborate on some time later . . ."

"Right, Satan's dead now." I was figuring this out even as I said it. My vague plan formed in the eleventh hour in a panicked moment of extreme stress was sounding more and more . . . what? Why couldn't I put my finger on the right word? What was the opposite of *disaster*? "So she won't ever help Ancient Me in a hundred little ways over the next few hundred years. So the BoD won't ever be. Right? That's probably right." Although . . .

Laura would be the new and improved Satan. I was pretty sure God wasn't going to like that job slot staying open, and she was the only person on the planet qualified to take over. But no matter how pissed the Antichrist was, I couldn't see her grabbing Sinclair, keeping him in hell for decades and ultimately skinning him so I could write my frigging memoirs on him. "But why do you remember it? Right? That's right, isn't it . . . that you shouldn't remember there even was the BoD because the timeline changed again." Ow. Thinking this hard made my frontal lobe throb.

"Future Elizabeth's timeline changed," he pointed out. "We are in our present, remember. It makes sense that we would remember something that no longer exists."

"You hear yourself, right? 'It makes sense'? 'No longer exists'?"

He tilted his head to the side in acknowledgment. "A good point. As much as any of this insanity makes sense, I should say. But your older self, she will return—has returned?—to an entirely different future, I suspect. I imagine that is why she lingered here at all."

"I don't want to talk about that withered skank. And also, I don't get it," I admitted. "Not any of it." Hate time travel. *Hate* it. "But the BoD being gone, that's the best news I've heard in days." Now if only America would cancel Thanksgiving, my life would be perfect. As perfect a life without Louboutin shoes could be.

"Then I heard you in the yard and—and—" Bemused, he shook his head. "I just ran for the door. I did not consider the fact that it was still daylight."

"Awww. That was so stupid. Sweet! I meant to say 'sweet'."

He arched an eyebrow at me as the corners of his mouth turned up in a wry smile. "Yes, perhaps. It would not be the first time I acted before thought where you were involved, and as long as you are running around in the universe, it will not be the last."

"Don't blame me for your poor impulse control."

"I was worried you had done something more destructive than usual. And then I . . ." He tilted his head back to look at the sky. He spread his arms like a dark angel in a slick black suit. ". . . and then I did not burn. And here you were. And Lucifer is dead by your hand." He smiled at me, which warmed me (good thing, too; we were having this long *long* conversation in a snow bank), but his face had an expression I was beginning to see more and more. A big helping of pride, mixed with astonishment and a dash of fear. Bake in the fires of hell until done. "I am relieved you are safe. And astonished that you have done all this and lived to walk away from it."

"Is this the part where you talk a long time about how awesome I am?"

"No. This is the part where we make love in a snow-bank."

Yeesh . . . one of those things that sounded good on paper but was hideous in actual execution (like communism). I couldn't get frostbite or slowly freeze to death (like poor Kurt Russell in *The Thing*), but I could get cold(er) and my clothes could get clammy and damp and my hair could get a ton of (yellow) snow in it and I could wreck my boots, my awesome leather pointy boots that had gouged chunks of flesh out of Satan's shins before she let me kill her.

"Can't we just make a couple of snow angels and then find a hot tub to bang in and call it a day?"

"Your powers of persuasion are as potent as ever," he replied, straight-faced, and then let loose with another one of those long deep laughs I loved loved loved. "I shall accede to your demands."

"Have I told you, you've really got a way with the syrupy love talk. My knees went weak the moment you said 'accede to your demands.' You had me at 'accede'! 'Accede to your demands,' cripes, what are you, a strike negotiator?"

From experience he knew to ignore my shrill bitching, and hugged me hard enough to make my ribs groan (no, wait—that was me groaning), while he lifted me a good half foot off the snow. "My love. My love. My love." His mouth covered mine, his teeth gently nibbled at my lower lip, and then I wasn't cold anymore. If anything, it felt like I was coming down with a fever. A *sex* fever!

Note to me: never say "sex fever" out loud, because it will sound even lamer than it did in my head just now.

"Er . . . what was that? I didn't quite catch that one."

"Never mind."

"Oh, Elizabeth. I love you and I'm frightened for you and awed by you and I cannot believe you let a tactical advantage like that go by, that you squandered a favor, a *wish*, as if the devil were a genie you conjured, wasted it on—"

"Unless you want to spend the day finding a divorce lawyer, never finish that sentence. Sink Lair, get it through your head already: I'd do anything for you. I'd squander anything for you. And again with the seductive wordplay: squander."

"Darling?"

"Don't set me down unless you move me half a foot to my right! I don't want to go in the yellow snow."

"Darling, shut the fuck up and kiss me back."

So I did. I knew I shouldn't reward his ordering me around by giving him kisses and probably a blowjob (*if* we went inside . . . there are some things a girl shouldn't do on her front lawn), but I did, anyway.

It's not my fault! When I wasn't squashing the urge to kick him in the shins, I thought he was irresistible. Sometimes I wanted to kick him *and* I found him irresistible; how was that for a mixed signal?

It was amazing to me; it had always been amazing that he thought *I* was, too. I prayed I never got so jaded that I could shrug off the depth of his feeling, the astonishing scope of his fierce devotion.

It seemed to me that if I ever started taking the love of

a king for granted, it would be like losing my grip on basic humanity. If I couldn't be surprised and touched and over-whelmed by love, what was the point of any of this?

He scooped me up in his arms and tramped through the snow toward our front door. "What? No snow angels? Right to the hot-tub banging, huh?"

"Oh, there are angels, all right," he replied soberly. "And I am fortunate to be married to one."

"Oh, boy! Comments like that will not get you laid, they will get you laughed at. Except for today, when they get you both. Let that be a lesson to you."

That made him laugh again, and that got me laughing, and then he was staggering through the snow and I was clinging to his neck and we didn't see the porch railing until he'd run into it hard enough to rattle my teeth and send us both sprawling like a couple of bowling pins.

We were still rolling around on the porch and roaring and holding our stomachs when Jessica opened the door and stared down at us. From our vantage, all we could see was the curving bulge of her enormous stomach and then, far, far above the curve, her small face, creased with sur-prise. (Marc, I assume, had figured I was fine and limped back inside. Mental note: Apologize on Sinclair's behalf. Explain everything. Beg pregnant/zombie friends for for-giveness. Rinse. Repeat.) She didn't say a thing for a few seconds, which we found even more hilarious.

"Hi, guys. Marc's sulking with a huge bump on his forehead and says you can both get frostbite on your 'nethers' for all he cares. So . . . do you want me to let you back in when you're finished?"

CHAPTER
FORTY-SIX

No we did not. Which is to say, we were stumbling and staggering through the house (Jessica had left the door wide open for us, proving again that we had either too much security or not enough, and never any sort of happy medium) while our mouths and hands were busy.

Awesomely busy. Thoroughly busy. Big-time all-the-time busy . . . we were kissing each other hard enough to leave bruises (theoretically) and tugging at each other's clothes (literally). My outfit suddenly seemed to be made of buckles and rubber—stuff really hard to get out of, and Sinclair's suit was proving just as intractable.

I stumbled and he tried to catch me and went over himself. We might have had more luck if we stopped kissing long enough to take in our surroundings, and clothing, but nothing doing. So we both went down in front of the sweeping staircase that led (eventually) to our bedroom.

(my love my love my Elizabeth my own)

I rolled to my side while Sinclair yanked at my sweater. A button went flying (I was wearing a sexy old-lady wool cardigan, complete with *faux* pearl buttons and a Kleenex tucked up the sleeve . . . okay, I'm kidding about the Kleenex) but the rest of the wool was resisting him. Stupid Merino wool! What'd I ever do to those sheep that their wool should resist me now, at the moment I was most horny?

(my love my love I love my love I love you my Elizabeth)

His Caraceni suit jacket was cooperating, or so I assumed when I heard the purring *"ri-i-i-p!"* of a seam getting yanked. Now I only had the super-sturdy pants to tear through, the tie to shred, and the Egyptian cotton shirt to tear into strips. The stairs were going to look like they were awash in crepe party streamers. Streamers made of Egyptian cotton. Dammit! Why'd Sinclair have to be rich? Why couldn't he just shop at Wal-Mart with most of the rest of us, where any clothing he bought would rip *itself* to shreds after the first trip through the wash?

As we tore at each other's clothing with our mouths sealed together in the fiery sharp kisses of vampires

(my love my love dammit what is this she's wearing?)

our frustration only mounted. Frustration with the high-quality clothing we'd stupidly worn. And okay, sexual frustration, too. It had been days! Almost a whole week! I thought of the movie *Zoolander*, when the models find out the heroine hasn't had sex in years and are horrified: "How do you live? How do you live?" Now that I think of it, there are many wise messages hidden in *Zoolander*, and if we as a society could only see the genius hiding beneath Ben Stiller's ridiculous hair, we—ow!

"Friction burn," I yelped.

"I am so—nnnf!—sorry—unff—beloved!" He was now wrestling with the tank top which I wore beneath the long sleeved shirt beneath the cardigan he'd gotten through.

Of all the days to layer! Chalk it up to a hazard of living in Minnesota.

By now we'd sort of lurched to our feet and had made it up a few more of the many many many many stairs, and I felt a flash of pain zip through my mouth as he broke the skin in his urgency.

"Ow!"

"—so sorry—darling—nnf—"

I bit him back, lightly, which was a tactical if yummy error, if his increased urgency was any indication. We both fell to the carpet again, but I finally had his pants open. There is no sexier sound than the clink of a man's belt hitting the floor, even if his wife then falls on the buckle and spends a few seconds yelping and grabbing her knee. We really should separate, stand, and then carefully sprint to our bedroom, where most of the breakable furniture was already broken and thus there were less things to hurt ourselves on. Or hurt ourselves with.

I forgot all about the plan once I had my hand on my husband's dick. Yep, that plan went right out the . . . the thing that plans go out when . . . when I can't think of them . . . was there ever a plan? A plan for what?

I'm confused. And also very horny.

(Oh oh oh oh oh oh oh oh oh oh oh oh do not do not stop oh oh)

Thank goodness Sinclair wasn't confused. He'd keep us on the straight and narrow. If there had been a plan, he'd know what it was. But he didn't need to remember because he wasn't confused. In fact, he seemed more single-minded than

(oh your your your fingers are are you have the face of an angel and the touch of a sorceress you you more do more harder harder oh oh)

usual.

"Seriously? You guys? Right there on the stairs, huh?" Someone was talking at us. I had no idea who. I didn't remember anyone else except Sinclair. Did Sinclair and I live alone? Had we ever done anything or known anyone before each other? Cannot remember. There's nothing before his mouth and his hands and his great big—

"Hey! You realize you're leaving a trail of what appears to be cotton, Merino wool, and cashmere?" Someone else we didn't know was talking at us. This was weird because the only other person in my world was my love, my own, my king, Sinclair. Probably I was just hearing voices. Probably it was only psychosis. Probably we didn't have roommates. "You know that saying, 'get a room'? Well, *get a room!*"

We'd stumbled to our feet, made it up a few more stairs, and then Sinclair tripped on his shoelaces

(shoes first! Dammit! I never think of that)

(nor I, my love)

and down we went again. But now there were a mere seven thousand steps between us and our bedroom. He fell almost full-length on top of me, which would have sent air whooshing out of my lungs if I'd had any. As it was, I could feel my ribs flexing and creaking from the impact. But I never once let go of his dick. Because when Betsy Taylor starts something, she by-God finishes it!

"Aaaggghh, Elizabeth!"

"Sorry."

But victory would be ours because at last—at last—my panties were exposed and I was tugging them aside and the whole never-letting-go thing

(heh, that reminds me of Titanic *when Rose is all "I'll never let go, Jack, I'll never let go" and then SHE LETS GO!)*

(darling please stop nattering in my head before I take you right here on these stairs)

(oh no you don't! I'm taking YOU right here on these stairs)

(I surrender you win have your way with me I shall offer no resistance)

(now what was I—oh, yeah, since I never let go of your dick I still have your dick and will now ruthlessly)

(yes)

(guide your dick)

(yesyesyes)

(into me. So let that be a lesson unto you, Sink Lair, we should never let the possible end of the world and/or the hideous deaths or awful transformations of everyone we love interfere with our frequent marital nooky because it's just not a good—)

"Elizabeth," he panted, pulling my bra free with a quick yank

(yow, friction! friction burn!)

"Please stop saying those things in my head. I would really like to have an orgasm now, so shush."

Well, he wasn't alone. And I was trying to oblige him. But my foot was now caught between the banister and the wall, and my head was at a weird forty-five degree angle because of how my neck was resting on the step, and he still had his tie on although his shirt was in shreds, and I was pretty sure one of his buttons had fallen into my bra and when my bra went flying so did the button but I had no idea where, and someone was still

"Dick, don't! Use the side door, the side door! Do not go in there if you value your sanity!"

yelling from somewhere.

We thrashed and wriggled like a couple of bass yanked

from the Mississippi and tossed on a dock. Horny bass. On a deck that was carpeted and looked a lot like six thousand stairs. Then Sinclair once again got to his feet, hauled me up with a yank on my elbow, kicked the part of the banister just below where my ankle had gotten lodged, freed said ankle, then slung me unceremoniously over his shoulder in some sort of undead fireman's carry, and staggered up the rest of the eight thousand stairs.

"Oh thank heavens," someone said at us. "They're . . . I think it's safe. They're going to their room. We can all have the courage to start our lives over and work past this domestic trauma."

I had to sort of clutch Sinclair's back to keep from jouncing off his shoulder and tumbling back down the stairs, so I dug in

(ouch! Beloved, you have the curved talons of a tree sloth)

and wondered: had I ever felt so happy, so horny, so relieved, so delighted, so insulted, and so loved like this before, ever, in either my old life or the new?

Not even close. And speaking of close—ah! The melodious sound of Sinclair kicking our bedroom door open drove all other thoughts out of my head. He nearly tripped on the sizable piece of wood that had detached at his kick, then tossed me on our bed and turned back to make sure the board was moved and the door as shut as it could be. Unfortunately, it was a brand-new mattress (we went through them pretty often), and still chock full of sproinginess. In his lusty haste, Sinclair had tossed me pretty hard. If we'd tried to re-create it a hundred times we couldn't: the new mattress spit me back out, ejected me like it was a damned launching pad, and I hit the carpet.

(—*the hell?*)

What was it with inanimate objects keeping me from banging the vampire king today?

Sinclair turned back from the door, surprised to see me on the carpet, but too horny to care, or speculate about physics, or discuss attempts to re-create what just happened, or wonder why every inanimate object in our house was determined to keep us apart.

"My own."

"Yes. Mine, too."

He fell on me. Or I fell on him. We didn't know. And we sure didn't care.

EPILOGUE 1.0

"You're really moving out?"

"Yup."

"I still can't believe it."

"I couldn't believe all the shrill bitching about a piece of glass. But you bitched."

"Three-thousand-dollar piece of glass," I muttered. "And you knocked over Mrs. Hemze's Christmas tree during your rampage."

"I went back and fixed it the next day."

"And Mr. Peterberg's."

"Fixed that one, too."

"And the Katzes'."

"Crybabies."

I had mixed feelings about Antonia and Garrett

leaving . . . me, who got off on complaining about the open-door policy for roomies. But I hated to see the two of them head off into the world that had treated them badly, with no one to lean on but themselves. What was kind of cool (but I would flambé my summer sandals before admitting it to Antonia) was that the solitude was the point, for them.

They hadn't made that much of a mess of the neighborhood . . . frankly, people who put up their Christmas lawn stuff before Thanksgiving deserved whatever happened. But we found out later they'd been talking about moving out for a while, even before the full moon madness hit . . . they just weren't sure how to ask me about leaving.

Ask me. Like I was their boss or their . . . their . . . well. I wasn't, was the point. They never had to ask. They just had to tell.

So there was that.

But on the other hand, Garrett was weird and Antonia was bitchily blunt. So it was harder to stay sad . . . assuming I even *was* sad. Like I said, it was hard to know how to feel about this latest development. It had been a weird few days. Even by our standards.

"Can you wipe that sappy expression off your jowls, Betsy?"

My point! Right there in a nutshell. "Antonia, you bitch, I do not have—"

"If you cry, I'm punching you in the forehead."

"See if I ever bring you back from hell again," I sulked.

She cupped her elbows in both hands and shook her head; all that dark hair flew around like it was being sucked into a wind tunnel. I never saw the wench so much as glance at a hairbrush, but she never got tangles. Yet another mysterious werewolf power, no doubt.

"At least tell me what you use for a conditioner before you leave," I begged.

She made an irritated noise that sounded like a cross between a sigh and a snort. "I knew you wouldn't really get why we're taking a vacation from our lives."

"Because if you don't burn through your Pack vacation time by the end of the fiscal year, you lose all the hours you stockpiled since you were a fuzzy cub who peed on the furniture every ten minutes?"

"Stick to what you know, shoe girl," she retorted. "I'm saying this again. For the last time, so pay attention, bimbo queen: I died. I went to hell. And then you asked the devil to give me a second chance. And the devil—the *devil*, mind you—was so anxious to stay on your good side that she agreed."

"Just what I've always wanted: my very own personal recapper."

She ignored me, the ruthless tart. "You secured my freedom and put yourself in jeopardy to do it. Believe me, it pains me to be this nice to you. I haven't had any coffee yet, and these gaggingly sweet words are sticking in my throat like gristle."

"Well, I *am* pretty great . . ." Egads. Garrett would be trapped in a truck with caffeineless Antonia for *how* long? He'd probably go feral all over again.

"So here we are: a fresh start! Something most people don't ever get, and we *both* got one. Thanks to you. And you didn't know us very well." She could never not look amazed when she told this part of the story. It sort of cracked me up. "So what to do with it, right? Because when you think about it, d'you realize how many people die and then get to come back?"

"Uh . . ." This week? This month? Last year? Twenty years from now? Forty? A hundred?

Antonia nodded. "Right. Dumb question."

"Not for most people," Garrett said. He had just finished taping a cardboard box absolutely bulging with skeins of yarn. It was the sixth box. That guy was gonna knit the whole world a hat/scarf combo. I guess everybody needed goals. Garrett's was to master yarn bombing, whatever the heck that was (I prayed it didn't involve a yarn shop and an incendiary device). "But we're not most, so . . ." He shrugged and started taping another box. We were using the kitchen as a packing station . . . the high counters, large room (big as a restaurant kitchen at least), and acres of counter space made it ideal. It was also making me really want a blueberry smoothie.

Smoothie cravings aside, I understood Garrett's disinterest in their destination: he had no idea where they were going, and he didn't give a tin shit. He was going with Antonia. That was what mattered; it was the *only* thing that had ever mattered. Anything beyond that was whipped cream on the sundae of his life. Or, I dunno, the bobble in the sweater of life.

Aw, jeez, it was too late . . . they'd already corrupted me with their weird knitting rituals and jargon.

"Uh . . . the other thing . . ." To my surprise, Antonia looked almost . . . embarrassed? No way. This was the girl who on a whim had stripped on our lawn last spring and hosed herself down while waving to the occasional passing school bus.

(Werewolves are weird.)

So scratch embarrassment. But then what . . .

"I like you a lot, Betsy."

That was kind of a relief. Honestly, sometimes it was hard to tell with her.

"And after what you did for me and mine, my life is yours. Only right now, I'd like my life to be somewhere else for a while. You get that, right?"

"Miraculously, yes," I said dryly. "Next time just break out the hand puppets. It'll be quicker."

She didn't so much as quirk her lips in a sarcastic smile. Hung on to the poker face instead. I don't know why I expected anything else. "But if I stayed, I'd be obligated to keep the Pack abreast of your doings. I live with *you*, I help *you*, and you help me back because we all take care of each other, but at the end of the day I'm still me and you're still you. *That's* what I liked best about this place. About our . . . um, our home."

I nodded, hoping I had a semi-intelligent look on my face. Luckily Antonia took pity on me (maybe she was coming down with something) and elaborated: "I'm still Pack, and you're still not. It's a lifetime of conditioned behavior I'm not up to trying to break right now."

"But Michael, the leader guy—"

"Pack leader, imbecile, must I carve it on your forearm?"

"He knows you're alive. Again."

She nodded as Garrett began trundling box after box of yarn, needles, and patterns to the Come-N'-Go rental truck out front (their disturbing logo: "We'll Help You Come N' Go!"). Don't judge; they were way cheaper than U-Haul, even if their pink and white trucks reminded me of a bottle of Pepto-Bismol. "Yes. And he's the *only* one, for now. He won't even tell his wife. I got his word on that, and where Michael's concerned, that's always going to be good enough. The others will find out, in time. Maybe."

"He's letting you leave us, then?" I was a little surprised Michael hadn't called her home. Or insisted she stay. But I wasn't surprised she didn't want to go. We found her annoying; her Pack was afraid of her. "Just like that?"

"Sure. He knows I want to see a little more of the planet besides New England and Minnesota before I die and go to hell again."

"Hell *again?*"

She puffed her hair out of her eyes, exasperated at the glacier slowness of my thought process. "Of course, dumb shit. Where else would I end up? Except . . ." She smiled then, an expression of dazzling warmth, and I was reminded that when I wasn't controlling the urge to staple her lips shut, she could be pretty great. "Except I want to hit the trail for a couple of years first. D'you know Garrett's never been tubing? Or fishing? Or free climbing or tie shopping? He's never made cookies or been to a zoo? He's never been to a baseball game or ridden a roller coaster. He's never been to a casino, or on an airplane. Which reminds me . . ." She hollered for Garrett, but she was still standing in front of me, so my ears nearly fell off. "I got the tickets!"

"Ow."

"Crybaby."

"Tickets?"

"To the California Wool and Fiber Festival," she said in her typical try-to-keep-up-dummy tone.

And what to say to that? A simple farewell to a couple of roommates had once again taken a bizarre turn. I considered various bitchy replies but in the end settled for, "I didn't know there even was such a thing."

"That's because you're a drooling moron, Betsy." She flashed her dazzling smile at me, taking every bit of the sting from her words. All her words in the last few minutes, come to think of it. "Now pay attention. I know it's going to be hard, what with you being unable to learn or adapt to any situation at any time under any circumstance, ever, but watch me." She pointed to her eyes. Uh . . . weird. "Listening?"

"Yeah, and staring into your eyes, which, now that I noticed them, seem weirdly far apart. Have you always had the hammerhead shark thing going, or am I only now noticing?"

I thought I'd get a snotty retort, but she nodded. "That's exactly what I'm talking about. I've lived here how long and you've only now noticed I've got wide-set eyes."

"Like a shark!"

"Shut up. Pay attention. You've *got* to pay attention, Betsy. Only Michael knows I'm alive, but for form's sake, he's got to send another Pack member out here. It'll be ostensibly to form and maintain friendly relations between his awesomely buff Pack members and your sneaky pale leeches. So watch for a new werewolf in the neighborhood. Or her. Because they'll be showing up soon."

"That's why he's letting you leave," I said, suddenly getting it. "He can't send a sub without the Pack finding out you're alive, so he's letting you vamoose . . . you get rewarded for returning from the dead, he gets to send fresh eyes and ears out here to watch us."

"Yes."

"Sneaky bastard."

"Yes. And if he heard you say that—"

"Well, jeez, don't tell him."

"—he'd be flattered," she finished. "I think that's everything."

"Really?" *That would be great. I feel like I've been listening to her for a month and a half.* "Okay, well, let me go get—"

"Good-bye."

"No you don't!" She turned back, and arched her brows in surprise. "You gotta let the others say good-bye."

"Why?"

Argh. The weird thing was, she was honestly puzzled. She wanted to go, we all knew she was going, she would be back, the end. Why draw it out? For what purpose?

(Werewolves are weird.)

She scowled at me. "You're not going in for a hug, are you? Are you going to cry? You'd better not cry."

"Don't worry; you've killed the thing inside me that thought this was going to be a tender farewell."

"Oh. Good. Besides, we're not saying good-bye forever.

We'll head on back after a few months. Maybe a year. Okay, two years . . . anyway . . . you're not crying, are you?"

"Only from the stress of *not* kicking you until you've got bruises the size of softballs."

"Ha! Okay. Good. You only ever have to call. We'll come on the run. Don't lose that number—I keep that cell on me most of the time. I know you can't help being kind of stupid sometimes, but make a real effort not to lose that number."

Wow. For Antonia, this was downright warm and fuzzy. Still, it was hard to keep swallowing my irritation. Did vampires get peptic ulcers? "Yeah, thanks, and . . . say! Don't you think it's time you climbed into your car and drove and drove and drove away from here?"

"Past time." She started to swing the door shut, then paused and glanced at me once more. "Um . . . Betsy . . . there's one more thing . . ."

I braced myself, or tried, for what had to be coming: I hate your breath, I think you're dumb, pay attention, mind your own business, don't you dare cry, drop dead, stop obsessing over what to put on your feet, don't call after ten p.m., don't call at all, you can't pull off pigtails, you can't pull off plaid walking shorts, shut up, go away, get the hell out of here, can't you see we're having sex . . .

"I'm so happy I know you. Nothing in my life was as good as the time I spent here with you guys. Hell itself wasn't even so bad compared with how the Pack used to . . . well." She shrugged, and her smile trembled. "I'd . . . I'd do anything you asked, is what I wanted to say. Just . . . whatever you need, you only ever have to . . ." She shrugged again, embarrassed to be saying it, but unwilling to leave it out. "I'd do anything for you."

Before I could recover (My heart! Cut down in the prime of life from a shock-induced heart attack! Woe, the humanity), she was out the door and screeching, "Garrett! We can't bring another dozen boxes of yarn; we didn't rent a big enough truck! You're gonna have to choose, weirdo!"

I cried. Sure I did; it was all part of my sinister plan. I told her I wouldn't, then willfully went ahead and bawled for ten minutes after that stupid pink and white truck pulled out of our driveway.

That oughta show her.

EPILOGUE 2.0

Infant Me was gone. Infant Laura was gone. My (live!) husband also. I was still here, but not for much longer: it was time for me to be gone, too.

But I wanted to savor this feeling, I wanted to savor the emotion I was enduring for the first time in centuries: I was afraid.

Time to go back, and yet I lingered. I wasn't worried about the 'port . . . centuries studying at Lucifer's knee, and then Laura's, so to speak, had left me almost as skilled as she was. Would be.

But when I went back to my time, what in the world/ worlds would I find?

I had not killed the Lady of Lies, my sister's mother. But she was dead by my hand.

Jessica had not lived to have children, and I, of course, had killed Nick for what he had done to her, and never mind that it had been a senseless accident. But he had done nothing to her here, and she would have children, a miracle I could still hardly believe. Interesting that in a life filled with vampires and weres and Undersea Folk, portents and spells and magic, that a rather ordinary occurrence, a normal, nonparanormal pregnancy, seemed wondrous to me. Although on reflection there did seem something odd about her gestation. A problem for the other me, another time.

I *had* killed my husband. Except he wasn't dead. And though I had no certainty Sinclair wouldn't die years from now, without the BoD warning him, we would not have fallen out. It wasn't the coming ice age that would wipe the globe of human locusts, but humanity's overreaction to it. Globally speaking, few worried about the steadily dropping temps until the first of the catastrophic crop losses began. Bad growing season followed worse growing season and only when millions had starved to death (in Texas and Maine and Kentucky and Florida and Wyoming), only then did humanity act. Or over-react. They meant to *carpe* the *diem,* not *morte* the *diem,* but guess what?

Sinclair reacted to my plan with horror. But how else to save the remains of a starving nation than fix it so those millions didn't need to eat? Or pee or bleed? And when the newly dead rose, who best to lead them? The ones who had led for centuries, of course. It wasn't megalomania, no matter what my husband declared. It was logic.

Sinclair disagreed. A lot. And so he died. Except maybe this time . . .

Somehow Infant Me had changed things. I had no idea how. I barely knew why: she saw the end, not why it had to be so. It was the reaction of a child: fix it, Mommy! And like a child who didn't understand what was impossible, perhaps she—*we*—had.

Time to go back. Time to go home. What was waiting for me? *Who* was waiting for me? I felt a bit like that movie character from ages back—Sarah Connor. For the first time in a long time, I hadn't read ahead. I didn't have the dubious comfort of foreknowledge. The instruction book hadn't been lost, or even destroyed: now there had never been a Book of the Dead.

I was afraid.

I was happy.

And beyond everything, beyond all the miracles, I dared to dare to hope: was it possible I was returning to a world where, once, Christian Louboutin had designed the most glorious shoes in the history of footgear? Could God be that good?

Time to find out. I was going home.

EPILOGUE 3.0

I had to lie to get out of the house, of course. I told Sinclair I wanted to hit the Blue Wednesday pre-Thanksgiving sales at the Mall of America. Anyone who has ever shopped at any time in America, ever, knows there's no such thing as Blue Wednesday, just Black Friday. But the vampire king was too busy setting up lawn chairs on the south side of the yard so he could sunbathe in thirty-degree temps to care where I flitted off to. When I left he had the lawn chairs arranged to his satisfaction, and was sorting through the half dozen pairs of sunglasses he'd dashed out to get after our snow/stairs/sex shenanigans.

Delk still wasn't home from his book tour (that was a fish to fry for another day, and fry I would . . . just not this week), but his dog sitter was. I cheated a bit and mojo'd her into selling, but I was paying what the dogs were worth and then some, and Delk would never miss two pups out of a thousand. Or however many blobs o' fur were lurking on the Delk puppy farm. From the way they liked to swarm my ankles, there were at least a hundred of the things.

I gave her a check and left contact info for Delk in case he wanted to talk, and she gave me leashes attached to small black dogs. I tucked each one under an arm like fuzzy wiggly footballs and took them to the car, picking my way through gravel and snow while Fur and Burr squirmed and yapped in my grasp.

"It must be Betsy Makes Tons of Sacrifices week," I muttered at the two blobs of black fur. "This is so nuts. They'll be in my house. My *house*. There'll be no escape." As I pulled out of the driveway and headed home, Burr relieved herself in the backseat, and I knew I'd been right to take Sinclair's Mustang. Not only could he fully care for dogs again, but he could wash his car in the driveway at high noon if he wanted. As Fur begin nibbling on the leather piping, I figured he'd want to get on that pretty quickly.

"That'll learn him to leave me to fend for myself on the porch while a thousand of your fuzzy brethren are chasing me in my own yard while I'm trying to bury the dead cat my zombie friend is cutting up so he doesn't rot," I told Fur and Burr, who took a few seconds from their peeing/

chewing to look at me with their big dark eyes and yap in shrill response.

Aw. Okay. They *were* kind of cute. In a slobbery incontinent way. But it wasn't about me; Fur and Burr were about cold cruel vengeance. My wrath would go forth into the world as black lab puppies! Beware, beware, the heck-bound puppies come for *thee*!

You'd think the king of the vampires, of all people, would catch on: you don't mess with the vampire queen.